BILL BAILEY'S LOT

OTHER BOOKS BY CATHERINE COOKSON

NOVELS

Kate Hannigan
The Fifteen Streets
Colour Blind
Maggie Rowan
Rooney
The Menagerie
Slinky Jane
Fanny McBride
The Garment
Fenwick Houses
The Blind Miller
Hannah Massey
The Long Corridor
The Unbaited Trap
Katie Mulholland
The Round Tower
The Nice Bloke
The Glass Virgin
The Invitation
The Dwelling Place
Feathers in the Fire
Pure as the Lily
The Mallen Streak
The Mallen Girl
The Mallen Litter
The Invisible Cord
The Gambling Man
The Tide of Life
The Girl
The Man who Cried
The Cinder Path
Tilly Trotter
Tilly Trotter Wed
Tilly Trotter Widowed
The Whip
Hamilton
The Black Velvet Gown
Goodbye Hamilton
A Dinner of Herbs
Harold
The Moth
Bill Bailey
The Parson's Daughter

THE MARY ANN STORIES

A Grand Man
The Lord and Mary Ann
The Devil and Mary Ann
Love and Mary Ann
Life and Mary Ann
Marriage and Mary Ann
Mary Ann's Angels
Mary Ann and Bill

FOR CHILDREN

Matty Doolin
Joe and the Gladiator
The Nipper
Blue Baccy
Our John Willie
Mrs Flannagan's Trumpet
Go Tell It To Mrs Golightly
Lanky Jones
Nancy Nutall and the Mongrel

AUTOBIOGRAPHY

Our Kate
Catherine Cookson Country

BY CATHERINE COOKSON AS CATHERINE MARCHANT

House of Men
The Fen Tiger
Heritage of Folly
Miss Martha Mary Crawford
The Slow Awakening
The Iron Façade

CATHERINE
COOKSON

BILL BAILEY'S LOT

GUILD PUBLISHING LONDON

This edition published 1987 by
Book Club Associates
by arrangement with
Bantam Press
a division of Transworld Publishers Ltd

Printed in Great Britain by
Biddles Ltd, Guildford and King's Lynn

To all the nice women who loved Bill Bailey
and haven't come across him yet:
Don't give up hope;
He's kicking around looking for just someone like you.
Oh, he won't mind really what you look like;
It's your Paw-son-al-ity that'll get him.
Just keep in mind what his mother used to say:
One way to a man's heart is through the oven door.

1

'Get up those stairs.'

'Mam! Mam!'

'Don't "mam" me. Get up with you.'

'It . . . it was only a little swear, Mam, it wasn't a big one.'

'Yes, it was a little one, but one of the worst little ones.'

'*Oh! Mam.* Don't smack me. *You're hurting my legs.*'

'That's nothing to what you're going to get. Get in that room there!'

Fiona Bailey pushed her eight-year-old son into his bedroom, and when he jumped on to the side of the bed and sat on his hands, she said, 'Get your things off.'

'I . . . I haven't had my . . . t . . . tea, Mam.'

'And you're not going to get any tea; you're going to bed.'

'Oh! Mam, Mam, I'll not say it again.'

'No; I can assure you you won't say it again.' She now grabbed her son by the shoulder and, twisting him around, she pulled off his coat, dragged his pullover over his head, then said, 'So do you want me to take your trousers off or are you going to?'

'Oh, Mam.' The tears now were washing Willie's face. 'I'll . . . I'll never say it again. I . . . I promise. It was only once.'

'It wasn't once. Don't lie. I heard you at least three times using the same word.'

'Well, it was because he used it at me. He . . . he said he wanted to come and see our house and . . . and he wanted to see inside. And I . . . I knew you wouldn't like him to come in.'

'Why wouldn't I like him to come in?'

Willie's head now swung from side to side as he tried to explain.

'Well, 'cos . . . 'cos he's from Bog's End and . . . and he's the one I made you laugh about when . . . when our school won and . . . and the nun woman ran him off the field 'cos he was tearing into everybody.'

'Get your trousers off.'

'Oh, Mam. Are you going to tan me?'

'No. I'm not going to tan you.'

Fiona now stood stiffly, watching her son divest himself quickly of his trousers and his pants and then struggle into his pyjamas. This done, she said, 'Get into bed.'

'Mam . . . I'm hungry. I . . . I didn't eat much of the school dinner. I didn't like it.'

'That's your fault. Get into bed.'

Fiona now saw the look that she knew only too well come over her son's face: his nostrils twitched, his lips came tightly together. And when he said in a small voice, 'I'll tell Mr B . . . Dad when he comes in. He'll give me my tea,' her own face stretched and her hand began to rise; but he saw the warning sign too late, for as he was about to scramble into bed, her hand caught him none too gently across the buttocks, which brought a yell from him: 'Now I will! I'll tell him. And . . . and he won't hit me for saying a four-letter word.'

'Won't he just! He'll wipe the floor with you if he hears just one whisper of a four-letter word.'

The tears were sniffed loudly. He rubbed the back of his hand across the bottom of his nose as he cried, 'There's lots of four-letter words, like like and love, and I don't like you and I

don't love you, and I'm going to make myself die now and you'll be sorry.'

As she straightened the cover on the bed Fiona said, in a much cooler voice now, 'I don't think I will because I just do not want anything to do with boys who use filthy words.' She walked towards the door where she turned and, pointing a stiff finger towards him, said, 'And don't you dare get out of that bed until I tell you.'

On the landing she stood and drew in a long slow breath. It was odd, she thought, how her four children, including Mamie her adopted daughter of five, would all revert to the name of Mr Bill when they wanted him to champion them. While he was their lodger they had all called him Mr Bill. It was only since the Christmas before last, months after she and Bill had been married, that they had given him the title of Dad. And now, over a year later, she could still picture his delight and the emotion their acceptance of him as their father had evoked.

She was passing the landing window when she caught sight of her husband. He was standing on the drive and there, right in the middle of the daffodil border stood the awful boy who had caused all the trouble. . . .

Unaware of 'the trouble caused by the awful boy', Bill looked at him and demanded, 'What were you going to do with that brick?'

'Nowt.'

'Standing opposite a window, swinging a brick in your hand and you were goin' to do nowt with it? You were goin' to throw it through the window, weren't you?'

'Aye, I was. And I will an' all.'

'Well, you try it on, laddie, and I can tell you this for nowt, you'll beat that brick to that window.'

'Oh, aye? Well, you'd better not lay a finger on me, mister, else me da'll wallop you. He's a big fella, six foot three he is.'

'Oh, aye? So he's a big fella, six foot three; but you're not a very big fella are you, and you're ruining the daffodils. Come out of that!' And as his voice rose his hand went out and

grabbed the diminutive figure and before the boy knew what was happening to him he left the ground and landed on the drive at Bill's feet. And still with his hold on the boy's shoulder, Bill said, 'What's your name? Come on; you've had enough jaw up till now. What's your name? If you don't tell me I'll yank you along to the police station.'

'I've done nowt.'

'Haven't you? You're trespassing and you were about to throw a brick through my window. That's enough to put you along the line for some time.'

'Sammy Love.'

'*Sammy Love?* That's a gentle name for the likes of you. Well, Sammy Love, what you doin' here in my garden?'

'Settin' Willie home. Are you his da?'

'Whose da?'

'Willie's?'

'Yes. Yes, you can say I'm his dad.'

'Well –' The boy attempted now to shrug himself free from Bill's hold, saying, 'Leave loose of me shoulder, mister; you'll crumple me jacket, then I'll get me brains knocked out when I get home if it's messed up. An' yer hands are mucky.'

Bill slowly released his hold on the boy's jacket, then looked him up and down, remarking to himself that he was decently put on. But his rig-out certainly didn't match his attitude or his tongue, both would have been more fitted to those of a ragamuffin.

'Well, go on, tell me, what are you doing here? All right. You set Willie home, but why the brick business?'

'Well –' The small figure kicked at a broken daffodil lying on the path, one of the victims of his boots, before turning and looking at Bill and saying, 'He wouldn't take me into his house. I just wanted to see like, what it was, I mean, inside. He said his mam wouldn't like me to go in. So I told him what I thought about his mam.'

'You did?'

'Aye, I did. And we had an up an' downer and she came out

and she went on and she lost her hair yellin' at me and him, an' she yanked him inside. She's a starchy bitch.'

'Careful! Careful!'

'Well, she is. As me da says, our old girl's not much good but there's worse, and she's worse.'

Bill curbed the urge to take his hand and swipe the little beggar back into the middle of the daffodil border that he had only recently left. But then he saw something that stopped him: the boy's chin started to knobble; his lips were drawn in between his teeth, his eyelids were blinking rapidly. And then he turned, not only his head, but his whole body away and kicked at the offending daffodil once more. 'Have you any brothers or sisters?' Bill asked quietly.

'No, none.'

'What . . . what does your father do?'

'Nowt. He's on the dole.'

'Does your mother go out to work?'

The face came round to him, the look in the eyes almost fierce now as the boy said, 'Not any more. She did off. She's always doin' off.' Another kick at the daffodil and a mutter now as he ended, 'But she comes back. She always comes back. Me da says, wait long enough an' she'll come back. An' she always does, she always comes back.'

He was nodding his head now as if reassuring himself. But when Bill's hand came swiftly out to catch at his, he tugged away from him, saying, 'I've done nowt. I didn't throw it. I'm not goin' to any polis station.'

'Shut up! Who's talkin' about polis stations? You wanted to come inside, didn't you, and see what it was like? Well, come on.'

The boy swayed back on his heel and looked up at Bill and said, 'Eeh! no. She'll pepper me if I go in there. She told me I hadn't to come back here any more, else what she would do.'

'What did you do to make her say that? Did you hit Willie?'

'No, no, I didn't. It was the language I suppose. That's what she said, using bad language.'

'Did you use bad language?'

'No, I only said, f . . .'

Bill turned his head sharply away; his eyes closed for a moment. But when he again looked at the boy and spoke his voice was low and it conveyed horror to his small companion as he said slowly, 'No wonder she nearly lost her hair. That's a very, very bad word. And her son, I mean our son, never uses words like that.'

'Well, he did. He shouted it back at me, he yelled it. That's what brought her out.'

Bill's shoulders heaved with the breath he drew in. Aye, yes; it would bring her out if Willie came out with that particular four-letter word. Oh my! But anyway, he had asked the youngster in and in he must come, and for more reasons than one.

'Well, let's go and face the music,' he said.

The boy said nothing more but kept pace with Bill at a run as he strode up the drive, round the side of the house and into the kitchen.

Fiona turned from the stove, her mouth in a slight gape, but the mouths of Mark, Katie, and Mamie were wide open. Mr Bill, or Dad, as he was, had brought in that boy who was the cause of Willie being walloped. He was the one that used language; they had all heard the language, and both Mark and Katie had been warned that if they ever said such a word what would happen to them. As for Mamie, she wasn't sure of what she had heard; and she wasn't very interested in words in any case. But she was interested in Willie. She loved Willie, and she had just stopped crying because he had been sent to bed. And Mama B, as she called Fiona, had warned her that she'd be sent to bed too if she didn't stop her howling. So they all gaped at the boy whom their dad was holding by the hand.

'Hello, hello, Mrs B.' Bill looked towards Fiona, and what she said, and with emphasis and meaning, was, '*Bill!*'

'Yes, Mrs B?'

'*Bill!*'

'Yes? I heard you.' He looked down at the culprit, saying, 'That's my name . . . Bill.'

The boy made no reply. He did not even look at him; his eyes were fixed on the tall young woman who was staring at him.

'You're lucky, you know' – Bill now nodded towards Fiona – 'he intended to put a brick through your window. Didn't you?' Again he looked down at the boy. And now the boy, glancing sideways at him, gave him what could be called a deprecating look and kept his silence.

'Anyway, all he wanted was to see inside your house, Mrs B, 'cos it's such a nice house. He asked Willie if he would bring him in but apparently Willie said he didn't think you would like him to. That isn't true, is it? You'd like him to see your house, wouldn't you, Mrs B?'

Fiona turned towards the stove. Her shoulders were slightly hunched and Bill, allowing his gaze to drop to Mark, conveyed by his look a need for co-operation. And in answer Mark gave him a little grin.

Bill was now divesting himself of his coat, but as he did so he looked towards the boy again, saying, 'Sit down,' and indicated the chair by a motion of his head.

'Don't wanna.'

For the second time in their short acquaintance Samuel Love was picked up by the collar, and when his bottom hit the hard kitchen chair with a resounding smack he lay back against the rails and gasped. Then Bill's attention sprang on Katie, saying, 'And don't you dare move away along that table.'

Her face now puckering itself into primness, Katie said, 'I wasn't moving along. Anyway, I've finished my tea; I was just going to get up.'

'Well, you can leave your departure for a little longer. Sit where you are; he hasn't got fleas. Well, he doesn't look as if he has . . . Have you got fleas?'

'No, I 'aven't got fleas.' The voice was indignant, and to it was now added, 'I get a bath every Friday. Me da sees to it, he

stays in . . . Fleas!' The word held indignation. 'And I 'aven't no dickies in me head neither, or nits.'

Bill turned away; his Adam's apple was jerking quickly in his neck. He made his way towards the sink where Fiona was standing and, pressing his shoulder to hers, he looked down into the soapy water as he muttered, 'Go easy on him, love, he puts me in mind of somebody you know, but I'll tell you more about him later.'

But when she showed no sign of complying with his mood, he played on the mother instinct. Taking his finger and whirling it around the suds, he muttered. 'He's from Bog's End. Apparently his mother goes off and leaves him. The fact that Willie has a mother and lives in a nice house has drawn him like a magnet. Besides, it would seem our Willie has cottoned on to him an' all. So come on, lass, give him some tea.'

'*What!*' The word was hissed. 'If you had heard him, *the language.*'

'Oh aye, I know all about it. But down that quarter it's just like God bless you.'

'Oh, be quiet!'

'Dad.' Mark's head was pushed between them and they both looked at him as he whispered, 'I . . . I think he's crying.'

They turned and looked at the small figure sitting on the kitchen chair, head bowed, and as Bill took a step towards him the head came up and the voice bawled at him, 'I ain't cryin'. I never cry. It's just me nose runs.'

'By! lad, you've got hearin' as good as mine and I've got a pair of cuddy's lugs on me. No, of course you're not cryin', but if your nose runs use your hanky.'

It was evident within the next few minutes that the boy didn't possess a handkerchief, and it was Katie who, slipping from her chair and going to the wall at the side of the fireplace, pulled a paper square from a roll; then, turning to the visitor, she stood a good arm's length from him as she offered it to him.

There was a moment's hesitation before it was taken; then there followed the sound of sniffles and a long blow.

'Do you drink tea?'

'Aye.'

'What have you in the name of eats, Mrs B?'

Bill looked towards Fiona, and she, going to the fridge, took out a small plate on which there were a number of sandwiches covered with cling film, and on the sight of them Mamie piped up, 'That's Willie's tea, Mama B!'

'There'll be plenty more for Willie.'

Taking the cover off the plate, Fiona now placed it in front of the boy and forced herself to say, 'Do . . . do you like egg sandwiches?'

He stared up into her face. This was the wife who had yelled at him, told him to get away and never to come back near her house nor her son. 'Go back where you belong,' she had yelled, 'you dirty-mouthed little urchin!' He remembered all her words, and here she was asking him if he liked egg sandwiches. His mind presented him with two answers. One was to say, 'No!' and throw the plate of sandwiches into her face; the other was to say, 'Ta, yes.' He decided to choose the latter, but just because he liked the fella that had brought him in. He had a big mouth but he seemed all right.

'Ta, yes.'

'Well, eat them up.'

He took up one of the sandwiches and bit at it almost delicately because he was under surveillance from three pairs of eyes, not counting the bloke and his missis. Then of a sudden everything changed; the big bloke was yelling again: 'Come on you three, scram! Upstairs with you and get on with your homework. And I don't want to hear anything from you until I've had my tea.'

'I don't see why we can't have our tea in the dining-room an' all.'

His hand outstretched, he made a dive for Katie's bottom, but she was out of the door, giggling now, and with Mark following, pushing Mamie before him.

Bill hadn't asked where Willie was, but he knew where he'd be after that fracas. And so, slipping out of the door, he pulled Mark

to a halt, saying under his breath, 'Tell Willie I'll be up shortly.'

'O.K.' Then, under his breath, Mark said, 'He looks a rip,' and jerked his head back towards the kitchen. 'There's a lot of them about, Mark, more's the pity,' Bill answered.

Back in the kitchen, he noticed immediately that the sandwiches had gone from that plate on which there was now a piece of fruit loaf, and although he purposely took no notice of the boy, nevertheless, he noted the swiftness with which this, too, vanished.

When presently Fiona placed a bowl of red jelly in front of him, the boy looked up at her for a moment but didn't speak; nor did he touch the spoon that was stuck in the jelly until she went into the pantry and the fella followed her. Only then, the kitchen to himself, did he pick up the spoon. But he didn't use it straightaway to ladle up the jelly but looked at the handle. It was like one of those his granny had in a box: she always brought back a spoon from a day trip. On one it said, 'A present from South Shields', on another 'A present from Scarborough', and she had one 'A present from The Isle of Man'. She'd had to go to Liverpool and get a boat to go there, and all that week his ma kept saying she was praying for storms and shipwrecks. He hadn't understood what she meant at first 'cos the sun was shining all the time, until his da called his ma a vindictive bugger and reminded her that his mother was a good swimmer although she was sixty, which was dead old.

This spoon hadn't any writing on it; well, not writing that he could read, but it had things like two crossed swords and some letters in between them.

He gobbled up the jelly. It was nice. This was a nice house. A nice kitchen, warm and bright, theirs was poky. His ma used to be always on about the poky kitchen, but then she was always on about every part of the house. When she kept on about it his da used to sing, 'I never Promised You A Rose Garden'. His da could be funny.

'Have you finished?'

It was the fella again. He jerked in the chair as if coming out

of a dream. His hand came out of his pocket and was laid flat on the table, the fingers spread.

Bill said, 'Well, your one aim was to see inside the house, wasn't it? Don't you want to look round now?' and held out his hand, and the boy slid from the chair. He didn't take the proffered hand though, but looked at Fiona standing next to Bill. But his question was put to Bill: 'She let me?'

'Well, if you're not sure you'd better ask her.'

He didn't, but stared at Fiona until she forced herself to say, 'Well, if you want to see the rest of the house you'd better come along, hadn't you?' and she moved towards the door, leaving Bill to indicate with a jerk of his hand the boy should follow her.

In the hall, Bill, spreading an arm wide, said, 'The Baronial Hall, sir. It isn't as big as some I've seen but it's nicer than most.'

Sammy did not look around the hall as one might have expected, but down at his feet and the carpet over which he was walking. But when they entered the sitting-room his head came up and, after gazing from one thing to another, his disappointment was evident in his voice as he said, 'You ain't got no telly?'

'Oh yes, we have, sir; it's behind those closed doors there.' Bill pointed to a cabinet in the corner near the fireplace.

'Coloured?'

'Yes, of course it's coloured.'

He did not ask for proof of this but turned his gaze on the window and the long pink velvet curtains topped by a French pelmet.

Fiona was walking towards the door again, and once more Bill piloted the boy after her and into the dining-room.

Here, it was evident the boy was immediately impressed, for his gaze travelled swiftly from the silver on the sideboard to the china cabinet, then to the long table running down the middle of the room with its accompanying eight chairs, his gaze coming to rest on the far end of it, which was set for a meal.

Turning to Fiona and his head bobbing, he said, 'We're gonna have a big house someday, we are.'

For the first time Fiona looked fully at the boy and her voice was soft as she said, 'Yes, I'm sure you shall.'

'And a gardin.'

'Yes, and a garden too. Yes, a garden.'

She turned abruptly from him now and hurried from the room, and as she made for the stairs she pointed along the passageway, saying in an off-hand manner, 'There's a room along there; it's my husband's study. It isn't very interesting.'

'What do you mean, it isn't very interesting? It's the best room in the house. . . . Go on. Up you go!' Bill pushed the boy towards the stairs. And when they reached the landing Fiona, still leading the way, did not turn round as she stated, 'We won't do an inspection of the bedrooms; I think you might just like to see the playroom.'

When she pushed the playroom door open, Mamie wriggled her plump body down from the old couch and ran towards her, while Katie and Mark, sitting one at each end of the work table, both looked at their mother in not a little amazement. But she stared hard back at them, defying them to make any comment on her apparently altered attitude.

'There now, what do you think of this? It's the busiest room in the house.' Bill looked down on Sammy; but Sammy didn't look at him nor speak, he was once again gazing from one object to the other in the room, taking it all in yet not believing what he saw: the big doll's house in the corner, the battered rocking-horse, the train set taking up part of the floor under the sloping roof in the far corner of the room, the long bookshelves holding two rows of books, the bottom row seeming in order, the top row all topsy-turvy; and then, hanging from a peg in the wall near the window, what he took to be a great long puppet of a Chinaman.

'You going to stay with us?'

Sammy turned and looked into the round bright face of Mamie and he repeated, 'Stay with you? No, no; I'm goin' home. I'm late as it is.' He now turned quickly about and, looking up at Bill, he said, 'He skelps the hunger off me, me

da, if I'm not in.' Then, walking past Bill and Fiona, he turned a half circle and made for the door, only to find he was looking into a cupboard.

When there was a burst of laughter from Katie, Mark, and Mamie, he turned on them, crying, 'Think you're clever don't ya, think you're clever buggers. Me da's right, yer all a lot of nowts up here, a lot of nowts.'

Before Bill could bawl a reprimand Mark rose swiftly from the table and, moving towards the boy, he said, 'We didn't mean anything. I mean, we do that, daft things like that, and we live here. We are always doing daft things, aren't we . . . Dad?' he turned to Bill, and Bill said, 'You're tellin' me. I had no notion at all what a daft lot you were when I took you over. If I'd had an inkling of it I'd have run a mile.' He now nodded towards Sammy. 'I haven't been here all that long, you know. I'm their stepfather, but you've got a real dad, so you say.'

Sammy was definitely nonplussed at this change of front: the big-mouthed fella said he wasn't their father but their stepfather. Stepfathers were terrible; his ma always said that. You don't know you're born, she would say; you should have had a stepfather like me. He thinks too much of you, she used to say; and that was after his da had belted him. He couldn't understand his ma, he couldn't, but he wished she'd come home. He wanted to get out, away from this swanky house and these people. He turned from Mark and made for the right door this time, and Bill, signalling to Fiona to stay where she was but beckoning Mark to follow him, escorted his visitor downstairs.

Sammy made straight for the front door which he found difficult to open, and as Bill unlocked the door he said to the boy, 'By the way, where do you live?'

'Rosedale House in River Estate, flat fourteen.'

Rosedale House, River Estate. Bill pursed his lips as he looked down on Sammy. That estate was deep in Bog's End, a good distance from here. 'That's some way,' he said. 'Have you got money for your bus?'

'I can walk; I've got legs.'

'You're so sharp you'll be cuttin' yourself one of these days, lad.' Bill was yelling again. 'I can see you've got legs, and any more answers like that, and in that tone, you won't be standing on them but sitting on your backside. You understand me?'

From the look on Sammy's face he understood, but said nothing. And when Bill put his hand in his pocket and brought out a ten-pence piece and offered it to the boy, Sammy just stared at it; but then he jerked backwards when Mark grabbed the coin from Bill's hand and, thrusting it at him, said, 'Look, take it. Come on.'

Sammy took it, thrust it into his pocket, then turned away without further words and walked towards the gate, Mark at his side now.

Outside the gate Mark was somewhat surprised when Sammy, looking up at him, said, 'Will she keep him in bed all night?'

'Who? Willie?'

'Aye, who else?'

'No, no, he won't be kept in bed, not all the evening anyway.'

'Will she give him his tea?'

Mark stopped himself from smiling. This kid was really funny: bossy, cheeky, as coarse and common as they come, yet he was enquiring if Willie was going to get something to eat. And so he said quietly, 'Yes, he'll get his tea. Mam never remains angry long; she'll have forgotten about it by tomorrow. Willie an' all. He'll likely greet you like a –' He had been about to say, brother, but that would be stretching things too far, and so he substituted, 'Buddy.'

'You a Yankee?'

'*Yankee? American?* No; what makes you think that?'

'Then why do you say buddy? Only Yankees say buddy on the films.'

'Oh, I think it's a very common word . . . . name.'

'No, it isn't.'

'All right. All right.' Mark's voice was loud now. 'We won't go into it. Go on, get yourself away.'

'I don't need tellin' twice.'

Sammy got away, but in a slow defiant manner: his hands thrust in his pockets, he strode down the street. But he had not passed Mrs Quinn's gate when he turned and yelled, 'I don't like your house anyroad,' before breaking into a gallop.

Bill was still standing at the front door when Mark came running up the drive; and laughing, he called, 'I heard that. He had to have the last word.'

As Bill closed the door Mark said, 'He's a type right enough,' and Bill answered, 'Yes. Yes, Mark, he's a type, but he's got guts if nothing else. And I would say he's got little else.'

They both turned now as the kitchen door opened and Fiona came into the hall carrying a tray, and as she passed them and made for the stairs she remarked to no one in particular, 'If you're wise you'll make no comment. You may begin your tea, Mr Bailey, it's all ready. And you, Mark, finish your homework.'

They both stood and watched while she mounted the stairs. Another time Bill would have taken the tray from her or told Mark to do so. What he did, however, as she disappeared from view was to push Mark in the shoulder, and Mark pushed him back. Then they both hurried from the hall, along the corridor and into Bill's study in order that their laughter shouldn't penetrate up the stairs.

When Fiona entered her son's bedroom and saw the round, tear-stained face just visible above the bedclothes, she had the desire to run to him and gather him into her arms. But she put the feeling aside, walked slowly to the bed, laid the tray on the foot of it, then said calmly, 'Sit up and have your tea.'

Willie did not obey her, but, his face crumpling, he whimpered, 'Oh! Mam, Mam, I'm sorry. I . . . I didn't mean it, what I said, I didn't, I didn't.'

The urge overcoming her outward demeanour, she pulled the clothes back from him and drew him upwards, and when his arms went about her neck she hugged him to her, saying, 'There, there; it's all over.'

'I'm sorry, Mam. I do love you. I didn't mean it, I didn't.'

'I know you didn't, dear. I know you didn't. Come on now.'

She pressed him from her and as he dried his face she said, 'Do you know that your sparring partner has been here?'

He nodded and gulped, then said, 'Mark . . . Mark told me Dad brought him in. Did you . . . wallop him?'

She pressed herself back from him, saying, 'Wallop Sammy Love? I'm not big enough; nobody's big enough to wallop Sammy Love.'

'Oh, Mam.' He tossed his head from side to side, sniffed again, then said, 'He . . . he was all right until tonight. He . . . he used to wait for me at the school gate, I . . . I told you, because he gets out sooner than us. But he's only ever walked with me a little way. It was the first time he came right home, and . . . and then I knew you wouldn't want him to . . . to come in.'

She lifted up his chin by placing her finger beneath it, and, looking into his eyes, she said, 'Did you want him to come in?'

And shamefacedly now, he muttered, 'Yes . . . well, yes, I did because he seems –' He shook his head at this stage as Fiona urged, 'Seems what?'

'I . . . I don't know, Mam, sort of' – his head was still shaking – 'I don't know, Mam.'

'Do you know that he nearly threw a brick through the window? Mister . . . your dad just caught him in time.' It was odd, she thought, how she, like the children, would at times revert to Mr Bill, harking back to the days when he had been Mr Bill the lodger. What had life been like before he had become her lodger? Oh, what was the matter with her? This was no time for reminiscing about how Bill's arrival on her horizon had changed her life.

She rose abruptly from the bed now and, lifting the tray, she said, 'Come on, eat this up and then you may go into the playroom for half an hour. By the way' – she pointed down to the tray – 'that's part of tomorrow's tea; he ate your egg sandwiches.'

'He didn't!'

'Oh yes, he did. And your cake and your jelly.'

Then putting her hands out quickly, she held her son's face tightly between them for a moment before hurrying from the room.

Bill was already in the dining-room and had started on his meal, but at the sight of her he rose from the table while still chewing on a mouthful of food and, pulling another chair from under the table, he said, 'I just had to start; I could eat a horse between two mats.'

'Didn't you have any lunch?'

'No; I hadn't time. I've had a rough day.'

Taking his seat again, he put his elbow on the table and rested his head on his hand for a moment, saying, 'I was like a bear with a sore skull when I came in that gate tonight.

'I was fuming inwardly against the big boys who can scale down their margins until it's impossible to try and compete. And then I met Mr Samuel Love and he took me back to a part of my childhood and I saw meself in him, gob, brick an' all, because although I had decent folks I was a hell-raiser. And that little chap's a hell-raiser because he hasn't got decent folk, I should imagine by what he came out with.'

'Never mind about Mr Samuel Love.' She put her hand out towards him. 'You don't think you stand a chance to get the estate?'

'Not a pigmy's stand.'

'But Sir Charles Kingdom?'

'Yes, there is Sir Charles Kingdom, or there would be, but he's out of the picture for a time; he's in hospital having an operation; old man's water trouble.'

'Well, he's the big noise in all this; it's his land they are going to build on, or it was before he sold it; he should have the main say. Are the same members on the finance board as before?'

'Yes, there's Ramshaw, Riddle, and Pilby. Of the old lot there's only Brown missing. But they are all naturally hard-headed business men, and it seems even if Sir Charles were there the score would be three to one. But there must be more; in fact, someone said there were ten; and I'm not surprised, for

there's a great deal of money at stake. By yes, I'd say there is.'

'But it was Sir Charles himself who told you to put your estimate in, wasn't it?'

'Yes, he did. But even so I couldn't see him letting sentiment stand in his way when it means a thousand or so off each house. And there's a hundred and ten of those, besides the two rows of town houses, one at each end, and the six shops, and the children's play centre. It takes a lot to cover sixty acres. There's been nothing like it around here for a long, long time; each house having its own quarter acre of garden and the designs all different. God!' He thumped his head with the palm of his hand for a moment. 'How me and McGilroy have worked on those plans for months. It means as much to him as it does to me.'

'Who are the firms that are in for it?'

'Oh' – he tossed his head back – 'I understand there's even a London one trying. I do know there's one from Carlisle and another from Doncaster. Anyway, what kept me busy part of the day was I had to talk to our fellas. You know, when these two houses are finished that'll be the finish of us around here because there's not another thing going. And when Barney McGuire put it to me that I should lower my estimate and this would give me a better chance, I had to hold me temper and say, aye it would, and yes, I'd do it if they would all agree to me cuttin' their wages, say by a third. Oh, the moans and groans. But you know what? After they shambled out they put their heads together and came back to me and said they'd all be willing to take a cut, twenty per cent they said. I was touched. I . . . I was,' – he nodded towards her now – 'because most of the time they're wantin' a twenty per cent rise. They're no better or no worse than the rest of 'em. But they were willin' to stand by me to a man. Anyway –' He smiled weakly at her, took another bite of food, then said, 'It's a nice bacon pie. Any more taties?'

'Yes, plenty.'

She helped him to some potatoes and peas; then she said quietly, 'You're not to worry about us, Bill. Do you hear? Those

three went to the local junior before you came on the scene; they can go back there and then to the Comprehensive; it's not going to hurt them in the long run.'

'Like hell! they will.'

'Bill, listen to me.' She gripped his hand. 'Before you came on the scene as the lodger' – she pulled a face at him now – 'I was really up against it. We were living then from hand to mouth but we were surviving. That's why –' she now pursed her lips as she ended, 'I had to lower our status in advertising a bedroom, full board, and suffer my mother's indignation and wrath at my letting the side down.'

He laughed and squeezed her hand. 'Have you heard from her today?'

'No; but the phone could ring any time now.'

'It's a form of torture, isn't it, she's putting us through? Ever since Katie blew my gaff.'

'Well, you shouldn't have pretended that you are what you're not. You took the mickey out of her and she'll never forget it.'

Bill sat back in the chair and laughed. 'Eeh! but I did enjoy meself that day,' he said; 'and not just from the knowledge that I could do it . . . to pretend to be what I was not. It was her own fault: she shouldn't have got into that fix and asked our lot to move her on Christmas Eve. I can see her face now when I went in, talking like the County lot with marbles in their mouths. And the lads playin' up around me, touching their forelocks, jumping to my word. Eeh! I did enjoy that. And do you remember when she came in unexpectedly at New Year, I was forced to go into me act again? And Katie had to come out with "Who you imitating, Mr Bill? You do sound funny. Doesn't he, Mam? Anyway, Gran knows how you really talk." Trust Katie.'

'Well, as I said, you shouldn't have taken on the part. And you know, I've had to suffer for it every day since. Before, I wouldn't perhaps hear from her for a week or more.'

'But she says she saw through my game. She didn't, you know, I had her really gulled. She wasn't sure whether I had been taking elocution lessons or you had been instructing me.

Anyway, enough of her. And by God! I've had enough of her. You'll never realise what I suffer because of you; you know, when she looks down her nose at me I want to spit in her eye. Last time she came in I wondered if I threw her on the couch and half raped her if that would satisfy her, because, you know, that's what she wants; it's a man.'

'Oh! Bill.' There was a shocked note in Fiona's voice now. 'How can you say such a thing? She doesn't. She's not. . . .'

'She does, and she is. I know her type; I ran the gauntlet of them while in digs. They might be in their fifties but they're not past it. Oh no; you believe me.'

Fiona sighed; then reaching over, she took his empty plate and asked, 'Apple crumble or fruit salad?'

'Why can't I have both?' He grinned at her, then said, 'Apple crumble.'

Left alone, Bill let out a long slow breath and looked about the room as if seeing it for the first time. He should feel he was in heaven: this good solid home, a wife like Fiona, and four good kids ready made. But here he was, amid all this, worried to death and really scared. Aye, at bottom he was really scared because when these two houses were finished there was just nothing in this town, unless he could pull off this gigantic deal. And if he was honest he knew there was little hope. He hadn't told Fiona the whole of it. There were fifteen firms at least in for the job. Besides the London, Doncaster and Carlisle ones, there were the two leading ones that had been building in the North for years, and sixty-acre plots were just their cup of tea. Ah well, he could always go on the dole.

'Dole be damned!' He had spoken aloud. And now he pushed his chair back and marched towards the door, only to run into Fiona, but before she could say anything he said, 'Love, I'll have it in the study.'

'But Bill, you'll be there all evening, in any case.'

'I know, but I've been thinkin' about something, something I could alter on the plans. It's been in the back of me mind all day. Look, give it here.' He took the tray from her. 'I'll do a

couple of hours; and after I've had a bath we'll have a natter. Then you'll go to bed.'

And now holding the tray in one hand, he stuck the index finger of the other hand into her chest, saying, 'And tonight you go to bed, and you sleep.'

'How can I sleep when you're not in bed at one o'clock in the morning?'

'Well, you'll have to get used to that. But of course, there'll be nights when I come to bed earlier when I want me rights. You've got to be of some use to me.'

'Oh! Bill. Stop joking.'

'I'm not joking, it's a fact and you know it. Go on. By the way, get Katie downstairs to give you a hand with those dishes.'

'You go about your business, Mr Bailey, and I'll go about mine.'

When Fiona reached the kitchen she didn't immediately start with the washing up, she stood at the kitchen window looking down the back garden and into the long slow twilight. It would break him if he didn't get that job. Not only was he worried about the family but also about his men who had worked with him for years; they were part of his family too. They had been his only family until she had come onto the horizon. And oh, every day she was thankful she had. Yet she often had to smile when she thought back to her first impression of him, the thick-set, middle-aged, brash, loud-mouthed egotist. That's how she had seen him. But now she knew; in fact he hadn't lived in the house long before she knew that behind that putting-off façade was a deep sensitivity that, in a way, he was ashamed of and did his best to hide.

She wanted him to succeed, to get to the very top in this building business. Yet if he didn't, she knew it wouldn't matter to her, not really; as long as she had him and the children, they would scrape along. But it *would matter* to him. His pride would be dashed because he wanted to be more than just a bread-winner, a meals provider. As he himself often said, men or women like him who had pulled themselves up by their boot laces never wanted to tie the laces at the top.

There was a tap on the kitchen door and she turned and greeted her neighbour, Nell Paget: 'Hello, Nell. Oh, that face of yours. How many this time?'

'Four.'

'Why didn't you have them all out at one go and get a set in?'

'I want to keep my front ones.'

'Sit down. Have a cup of tea.'

'No thanks; I've just had one.'

'Anything wrong?'

Fiona asked this because her friend always made a point of never popping in once Bill was in the house, because she believed in giving couples their privacy. The dirty deal that had been dealt her hadn't embittered her towards the needs of others. Her husband, after thirteen years of marriage, had left her. He had deprived her of the wanted child yet had got another girl pregnant. But it had been Nell's need of a job in the first place that had drawn them together. And so she had baby-sat for her; then later taken over the running of the house when, just after Christmas, she herself had had the operation for what she had imagined was cancer, but which thankfully turned out to be merely adhesions in the colon. Nell was very dear to her. She said again, 'Anything wrong?'

Nell shook her head and held her swollen jaw for a moment before she answered, 'That's what's brought me across. Mother's just said there were some ructions in the garden earlier on. She would have come across, but as you know she's full of cold. And you never get Dad interfering. Mind your own business is his motto.'

She tried to smile.

Fiona now laughed, saying, 'Oh, yes, there were ructions. Our dear Willie was escorted home by a little tyke from Bog's End who apparently wanted to see inside the house. And when Willie told him that I might object' – she pulled a face now – 'there was a battle of words, four-letter ones.'

'Oh! Four-letter ones?'

'Yes. It's a wonder you didn't hear them, they were yelling

them. And of course I did my own share of yelling, but my words were a bit longer. I dragged Willie in and smacked him all the way to bed.'

'Poor Willie.'

'Poor Willie, indeed! And then the other one was aiming to throw a brick through the window when Bill caught him. Anyway, you know Bill and his reactions. Well, he brought him in and it was entertainment from then on; but not my kind, at least not at first, for I certainly didn't take to Mr Samuel Love.

'Yes, that's his name, Sammy for short. But as Bill, in his usual way, pointed out, there were two sides to every question, especially so to little boys whose mothers . . . go off at times.'

'Oh, another one of them?'

'Yes, that's what Bill said, there's many of them. Anyway, forget about us; you want to get yourself inside and into bed.'

'Yes, that's where I'm going.' She rose to her feet, then turned to Fiona and said, 'Heard any more about the big deal?'

'Yes, but the news isn't very good. Too many in for it, I understand. But you know Mr William Bailey; if he goes down it will be fighting.'

'Oh yes, in all ways. You know, Fiona, I've never come across anyone in me life with such a loud voice. He's just got to say "hell" and it's like a blast.'

'Go on!'

She followed Nell to the door, saying now, 'You stay in bed in the morning. I'll pop across once I get them off to school.'

'Oh, I'll be all right by then. See you."

Fiona returned to the sink and the dishes. Life was strange. One time you were on your own with three children to see to, no one to back you up, but a mother to point out that everything you did was wrong; the next minute you had a fellow like Bill and a friend like Nell, not forgetting an adopted daughter called Mamie, and she was the result of Bill's hidden sensitivity. Life was good. If only Bill could manage to pull off that deal it would be more than good, it would be marvellous.

2

It was half-past eight by the time Bill finished his bath, but before going downstairs again he went into the bedroom which Katie shared with Mamie. The latter was already in bed and was sitting up talking to Edward Muggins her Teddy Bear. There was no doubt about the bear's name, it was written across the chest of his sweater. And after Bill had kissed Mamie good-night he then had to shake hands with Mr Muggins and tell him that he must go to sleep and stop talking and keeping Mamie awake. Next he put his head round the door of the playroom, and when three eager faces were turned towards him, he said quickly, 'Not tonight. Not tonight, comrades.'

Katie, getting to her feet and coming towards the door, said, 'You can spare five minutes.'

'No, not even five minutes because I know what your five minutes is: I'd be roped into something. Keep your distance, woman. Good-night, Mark. Good-night, Willie. And good-night to you too, Katie.'

They all answered, 'Good-night, Dad.' Then Katie, having the last word, said, 'Be careful how you go,' and at this they all laughed.

Fiona was in the sitting-room. He went to the back of the

couch and bending over it he rubbed his face in her hair, then said, 'I'll give you another hour then get yourself upstairs.'

'Do you want a drink before you start?'

'Not one of yours, thank you, Mrs B.'

He now walked to the drinks cabinet in the corner of the room and, opening it, he poured himself out a measure of whisky, and drank it raw. He then came round to the front of the couch and, looking down on her, he said, 'Why don't you put the telly on?'

'I prefer to read.'

'Have it your own way.' Then, dropping on to his hunkers, he caught hold of her hand, saying, 'I'm sorry I've been stuck next door so often of late, but it's got to be done if. . . .'

'Oh, Bill, you don't have to apologise to me. You should know that by now. And who do you think's keeping you next door with your nose to the grindstone until all hours? We are, I and my lot.'

'*Our lot*, Mrs Bailey.'

'Sorry, our lot. But it's true: if it wasn't for us you wouldn't give two hoots about getting that contract.'

'Oh yes, I would. Let me tell you, I was an ambitious man before I set eyes on you. You forget, from tea-boy to little tycoon. Little, I admit, but nevertheless a tycoon. Because I'm very proud of that last job of mine, every house has been sold and could have been twice over. The finance company made a nice little pile out of that; and *I'm* not grumbling, I didn't do too bad either. So don't ever suggest, Mrs B, I lacked ambition before I entered your portals and met your mother.' He threw his head back now. 'I often think of that day. She was after my blood, wasn't she?'

'Oh no, she wasn't.'

'Oh yes, she was, until I told her I had been divorced four times and that my intake of whisky was that of a whale. But the last bit that did it was when I suggested she get off her legs because she was such a poor old soul.'

'You were a terrible man then.'

'You never thought I was a terrible man, did you, not from the first.'

'Oh yes, I did. Don't kid yourself. I not only regretted your entry into these portals, as you say, on that first day but for a number of days afterwards.'

'But when I left, you came running after me, didn't you?'

When he found himself overbalancing and thrust onto the hearthrug, he lay there laughing for a moment; then jumping up with the agility of a twenty-year-old instead of a man on the road to fifty, he punched her gently on the jaw, saying, 'A sandwich and a cup of your rotten coffee in about an hour's time,' to which her answer was, 'If you're lucky.'

He was on his way towards the door, and he turned and said, 'I'd better be.' Then just as he opened the door the sound of the front door bell ringing brought him to a stop. Turning his head swiftly, he said, 'I bet that's your mother.'

'No, no.' Fiona had risen quickly to her feet. 'She wouldn't come out in the dark, at least not on her own.'

He pulled the cord of his dressing-gown tight, saying, 'I can't go and open it like this, but I'll be behind the door just in case; you never know these days.'

A moment later when Fiona opened the front door she was amazed to see that the unwelcome visitor of earlier in the evening had returned, only now he was accompanied by an extremely tall and bulky man. And it was the man who spoke, saying in a deep Irish voice, 'You Mrs Bailey, ma'am?'

'Yes, I'm Mrs Bailey.'

'Well, you know all about this 'un. You've had him here the night, I understand?'

'Yes, he was here.'

'Well, he has somethin' to tell you and somethin' to give you.'

It was at this point that Bill stepped from behind the door and looked at the visitor, and the visitor looked at him and said immediately, 'Hello there, Mr Bailey.'

Bill screwed up his eyes and peered at the man. 'I . . . I know your face. You're . . . m'm. . . .'

'Davey Love. I worked for you for a bit about two years gone.'

'Oh aye, yes. Well, come in, don't stand there.' He pressed Fiona aside, pulled the door wide and allowed the very big fellow and the very small boy to enter the hall. Then after closing the door, he said, 'You had better come into the sitting-room.'

'Thanks, I will. . . . After you, missis.' Mr Love's arm went out in a courtly gesture that caused Fiona's features to twist into what could have been taken as a smile or an expression of surprise.

In the sitting-room they all stood looking at each other for a moment until Bill, pointing to a chair, said, 'Well, sit yourself down.' And when the big fellow had seated himself he and Fiona sat on the couch. That left Samuel Love standing to one side of his father, but with his eyes directed towards the carpet, until a very ungentle nudge from his father's elbow that nearly knocked him sideways brought his head up. And now he was glaring up at his parent who was saying to him; 'Well, tell them why you're here. That's what we've come for, isn't it? Well . . . in part. But you get yer say over first. Go on, don't stand there like a stook, go over and tell her what you did, how you repaid her kindness after her stuffin' yer kite with the other lad's sandwiches and his cake an' jelly. You did enough braggin' about that, an' if it hadn't been for yer granny I wouldn't have known how you repaid these good people. Go on, tell 'em.'

The boy now took two steps towards Fiona, then, putting his hand in his pocket, he drew out a spoon and thrust it towards her, saying, 'I pinched it off ya.'

Fiona took the spoon and looked at it. It was one of a set that someone had given her for a wedding present at her first marriage. They were silver-plated, but she had never liked them and the children had used them from they were babies.

'His granny had a few but not as good as that 'un. Presents from here, there, and every bloody where, day tripper things you know. And this 'un here thought he would add to her

collection. I'm ashamed of him, bloody well ashamed of him. He's standing now 'cos he won't be able to sit down for a week: he'll be lying on his face the night. I'll bet you a shillin' he won't repay anybody's good tea pinchin' their cutlery after this. . . . Well! What have you got to say to the lady?'

Sammy cast his father a glance that should have shrivelled him; but the man was too big, and so he looked back towards Fiona and said, 'Sorry. . . .'

'You're sorry who? Begod! I'll knock some manners into you afore I'm much older.'

Again there was the glance; then, 'I'm sorry, missis.'

The boy's gaze was now jerked towards the fella who bawled even worse than his da because he was making a funny noise in his throat as if he was choking. He had his head bent and a very white handkerchief held to his nose. And when his wife said to him, 'Mr Bailey!' he lifted his head and replied, 'Yes, Mrs Bailey?'

Bill wiped his eyes; then in a voice he had to control, he said to Davey Love, 'If I remember rightly you were with us only a short time.'

'Aye, that's right.'

'And if I also remember rightly you're the only man who's ever been on my books that left with two days' pay owing him and never came back for it.'

Mr Love laughed now as he said, 'Aye, that's right an' all. But when I had time to come back you had finished that job and started another 'un. So, I said, to hell! Pardon me, missis; it just slips out, you know. But as I said, what odds.'

'Did you get another job?'

The head went back again, and now there was something in the laugh that was not quite bitter but which you couldn't say was jolly, and the man said, 'Sort of. Ah well, you might as well know, I went along the line.'

'You did?' Bill nodded. 'Along the line?'

'Aye, along the line. Well, you might as well know. You might have seen it in the papers at the time but didn't link me

with it. Of course, me name's not that unusual, but you see, his mother had walked out on me again.' He thumbed towards the boy. 'She'd gone off with her latest fancy man. Oh! missis' – he flapped a hand towards Fiona – 'don't look so troubled, he knows all about it.' He again thumbed towards his son. 'He's been brought up on it. She's like the swallows, she does a flit every year but she usually comes back, mostly on her own. This time though, she landed in the town with him. Well, if she comes back on her own we have it out an' that's that. But I ask you, for a fella of my size an' appeal to be passed over for a little runt! Five foot five he was an' she's all five foot nine or ten if she's an inch. That's why I took her at first 'cos she was near me size. Anyway, the sight of her latest choice was too much for me; I wiped the floor with him, an' a couple of walls an' all.' He grinned widely now. 'He had his quarters in hospital for two months after that an' mine was in Durham for nine.'

Bill could hold it no longer. His body was already shaking before the sound erupted; and then almost to his joy he saw that Fiona was in a similar state. When the man joined in, their laughter mingled, and it didn't die away until Fiona, noticing that the boy was not laughing, held her hand out to him; and he took it, and when she brought him to her knee she said in a voice that she aimed to control, 'It's all right, I understand: you wanted it for your grandmother. Well, there you are, you give it back to her.' She picked up the spoon from where it had been lying on the side of the couch and added, 'And I think I have another one somewhere; I'll look it out for you.'

'What d'you say?'

The boy turned his head sharply and looked at his father and, addressing him now as one adult to another, he said, 'I know what to say, but let me have me breath.' Then directing his gaze on Fiona once more, he said, 'Thanks, missis. Ta.'

'Well, that's over. But not quite.' The big man had both Fiona's and Bill's attention again. 'But mind' – he wagged his finger towards Bill – 'I would have brought him along in any case. Oh aye. That's one thing I won't stand for in him, is light

fingers. As far as I know that's the first time; and it'll be the last, 'cos the next time it'll not be the belt across his backside, I'll string him up. Begod! I will.'

When Fiona closed her eyes for a moment Mr Love put in more moderately, 'Well, that's what you call stretchin' it a bit, missis, but you get me meanin'.'

She was unable to answer him but she inclined her head towards him. And he, looking at Bill now, said, 'When you've done a stretch, whatever for, your name's mud. But believe me that was the first time I'd been up, an' that'll be the last. It was an object lesson with a big "O" for me. Begod! it was. I hope I'm never tempted to bash anybody again. But if I am I'll do it in the dark with a stockin' over me head 'cos they won't get me into Durham again, not in that van anyway. So, what I'm inferrin' like is, jobs have been few an' far atween, sort of. And I'm a man who likes to work, to use me hands, and I give worth for worth, no shirkin' when I'm on the job. So, what I'm asking' you for is, can you take me on 'cos I hear you're startin' on two new houses shortly?'

Bill looked at the big fella. It was his intention to set on two extra men on Monday because of the time limit set on this last piece of work he had in hand which, if not met, would mean loss of money on the contract. Considering what he had just heard, and such was this man's need and the appeal of his raw child, he made his decision.

In the brusque business-like manner he usually adopted when dealing with new starters, he said, 'You're lucky. I was thinking about setting two on on Monday. If you show up then we'll see what we can do.' He could have added jokingly, 'If you don't reach Durham again in the meantime.' But he resisted the temptation, because Durham must have been an experience in this man's life that would be best forgotten. But perhaps not best forgotten, perhaps the thought of it would keep him out of trouble in the future.

Davey Love stood up now and his whole attitude seemed to change: the tone of his thick Irish voice had dropped several

levels when he said, 'That's real kind of you, sir. I won't forget it, and you won't regret it. No, begod! I'll see you don't.'

Bill, too, got to his feet, saying, 'Would you like a drink?'

'Aye; thank you very much, I would that.'

'Whisky? Gin? Beer?'

'A beer would be welcome, sir; you get more in a beer.' He turned a laughing face on Fiona now, and she smiled back at him. Then looking at the boy again, she said, 'And would you like a drink of milk or orange juice?' And he glanced towards his father as if for permission, and when it was given with a nod he said, 'Got any coke?'

The bawl was as loud as Bill's: 'Milk or orange juice! the lady said. Take your choice an' be thankful, you ignorant scut.'

Again that look was levelled at the big man; then Sammy said, 'Orange juice.'

'What else? God an' His Holy Mother! won't you ever learn?'

There was an actual sound of a sigh before the boy said, 'Please.'

Fiona had to hurry from the room, and when she reached the kitchen she stood with her back to the door for a moment, her hand tight across her mouth. She had never thought that this evening would end in laughter, not after the fracas she had had with that small piece of humanity back there, and then knowing of the worry that Bill was experiencing.

Quickly now she poured out a glass of orange juice and put a large piece of cake onto a plate, then both onto a tray. And she was crossing the hall when there was a hiss from the top of the stairs; and there they were, the three of them, and it was Mark who whispered, 'There's company?' And she whispered back, 'Yes. Tell you about it later.'

'What's that for?' Katie was pointing downstairs; and Fiona, stretching her head forward, whispered back to her daughter, 'It's for the guest. He only takes orange juice.'

'Mam!' It was a loud whisper.

'Yes, Willie?'

'Hurry up and come up and tell us.'

'I will. Go on now and get ready for bed, you two.'

'Mam.'

'Yes, Katie, what is it?' Her voice showed her impatience now.

'Can we . . .?'

'No, you . . . can . . . not! Now you, and you Mark, do as I say, get ready for bed. If you don't I won't tell you a thing that's happened.' She moved away amid the muttered grunts.

In the sitting-room she put the tray on a small table and, beckoning Sammy to a seat near it, she said, 'There you are.'

'Ta!' said young Master Love with deliberate emphasis now, and his father, shaking his head, said, 'My! My! You won't forget this night, will you, laddie? There'll be no livin' with you after this. You'll not only want to move from the flats, you'll want yer meals brought to you on a tray.' He now turned and made a face towards Bill, and Bill smiled, and Fiona smiled.

Five minutes later when Mr Love had finished his beer and Sammy Love had got through his orange juice and his piece of cake, the big man said to his son, 'Go and stand in the hallway; I'll be there in a minute.'

The boy rose from the chair, looked from one to the other of the three adults, then slowly walked out, closing the door behind him.

Davey Love now turned to Bill, explaining: 'I yammer on about things and his ma and the situation atween us in front of him 'cos he knows all about it; he's heard it since he was on the bottle. But there's some things it's better him not to know, 'cos kids talk. It's like this: I've a piece of news that might be of some use to you. You see I get around. Well, you do down at Bog's End. It's a particular pub I go to and you hear things. I sometimes give a hand behind the bar. I'm not s'posed to serve, you see, being on the dole.' He stretched his upper lip over his lower one and his face took on a comic, grotesque look. But he continued straightaway, saying, 'One or two things have happened to your lads lately, haven't they?'

'You mean, Mark and Willie?'

He turned to Fiona, laughing and saying, 'No, I wasn't meanin' the kids, missis, I was after meanin' the boss's men on the job.'

And at this Bill said, 'Aye, yes, one or two things have been happenin' to them. It started when they were clearing the site for the new houses.'

'One had his car pinched?'

'Yes, he had.'

'Well, I can tell you where it is.'

'You can? That's interestin'. But how do you come to know that? Did you have a hand in it?'

'Now! Mr Bailey. No, I've told you, haven't I, nothin's gona get me to Durham again.' There was indignation in the tone.

'Sorry. But . . . well, go on.'

After a moment's hesitation Mr Love went on: 'There's two fellas have come to live round our way. I don't know where, but I recognised one right away. He was one of the residents like when I was on holiday in Durham. Well, Kit Bradley, he's the man who runs the pub, and atween you an' me, I think he runs with the hare and hunts with the hounds, as the sayin' goes, 'cos to see him chattin' to a smilin' bobby you'd think they were brothers at times. Anyway, these fellas were in the pub and they put it to him on the side if he would be interested like in a car that was goin' cheap. They had bought it, they said, from a fella who was a brickie and who said he needed spare cash; they said his boss was soon goin' out of business.

'Now them words was the link up for me: his boss was goin' out of business. It didn't hit me at the time but it did after, if you get what I mean. Anyway, one said it had always narked him that brickies could go to work in their cars. The world had turned upside down, he said. I got all this from Kit, you understand?'

Bill made a small motion with his head signifying that yes, he was following Mr Love. 'Anyway, Kit went round to the spare plot aside Gallagher's junk yard where the car was parked. He said it wasn't what he was wantin' but he'd pass the word round. I asked him if he was gona tell the cops, and he said,

no, let 'em find out for themselves. That's what I mean, you know, about running with the hare and huntin' with the hounds. He's a deep 'un is Kit. But anyway, news gets round, an' I heard about this fella who was hoppin' mad an' had been to Gallagher's junk yard lookin' for his car 'cos apparently it was an eight-year-old banger but he had looked after it like a baby. I never saw the bloke meself, but somebody happened to say he was one of Bailey the builder's fellas. Well, as you know, this all happened a couple of weeks ago an' I suppose I could have let on then, but I said to meself, Love, mind your own business. And anyway, anythin' to do with the cops brings me out in spots. An' I'm not kiddin' about that! I have a rash that comes out in me sometimes and I'm covered from head to foot with it. St Vitus dance has nothin' on me when that hits me, I can tell you. Well, there it is.' He spread his fingers wide.

'Do you think the car will still be there?'

'Well, they were in it up till yesterday. It's a bit changed: they've painted it a different colour and the number plates are sure to be changed. It was a kind of grey but now it's a blue. They're barefaced buggers those two, an' I don't think they'd be clean fighters. It would be the knife, or chains. So, I'd tell your bloke if he goes after his car not to go alone.'

'Well, if I've got anything to do with it' – Bill's tone was grim – 'he'll be accompanied by the police.'

'Well, that's up to you. But as I said, one good turn deserves another. Or did I?' He grinned now at Fiona, and she was forced to smile at him.

Bill too smiled now as he said, 'Well, thank you very much anyway. It's been an eventful evening. Our *antique silver* has been returned, then . . . given away again' – he glanced towards Fiona – 'Tommy Turnbull has the chance of getting his car back, an' you've got the chance of a few week's work. I hope it may be longer, but at the moment I can't promise anything.'

'You're in for the job of makin' that big estate some way out, I hear, on Sir Charles Kingdom's land. Is that right?'

'You get about.'

'Oh aye.' Davey Love grinned widely now. 'The Job Centre has more information than Pickford's tourist's office. . . . Ah well, I'll have to be goin'.' He buttoned up his coat; then with an elaborate bow towards Fiona, he said, 'It's been a pleasure, ma'am, a pleasure. An' you can always look back on this night as the night that you had a visit from an honest burglar.' And he thumbed towards the hall, then added, 'But it took a very red backside to make him come clean. As I said to him, there's honour among thieves an' as I've always said to him, don't do as I do, do as I say. At least I used to afore I took that holiday, you know. Anyway, I mustn't keep you good folks any longer.'

In the hall they stopped and looked at the small figure sitting on the second step of the stairs, and it was apparent he had been in some sort of whispered conversation with the three heads at the top of the stairs.

Mr Love looked upwards, a wide grin on his face, and he called loudly, 'Good-night, kids,' and he was answered almost simultaneously by the three voices, saying, 'Good-night, Mr Love.'

Fiona's eyes were wide, her face straight. That was how they used to address Bill, calling, Good-night, Mr Bill. She was about to issue a stern order to her offspring when Mr Love, looking at her, said, 'You've got somethin' to be proud of there, missis.' Then turning to Bill, he added, 'And already made, I understand. He told me.' The jerk of his head was towards his son who was now standing near him. 'He gave me the whole run-down on the family. Never misses a trick, that 'un. Well, come on you.' He placed his hand between the small boy's shoulders and pushed him none too gently towards the front door which Bill had opened.

'Be seein' you, Mr Bailey.'

'Yes, Davey, be seein' you. Good-night.'

'Good-night to you. And it's been a good night all round, it's been a good night. Indeed it has that.'

Bill and Fiona stood watching the tall and the small figure walking side by side towards the gate, and not until they had disappeared into the darkness did Bill close the door. Then, striding towards the stairs, he bawled up to the faces still there,

'Good-night, Mr Love,' mimicking them. 'You've changed your allegiance have you? Good-night, Mr Love. It used to be, Good-night, Mr Bill, didn't it?'

'Well, you're not Mr Bill any more, are you?' This was from Katie. 'You're Dad now.'

'She's right.' Mark was nodding.

But Willie, and in a small voice, said, 'He asked if he could come back again, Mam, Sammy, and I said yes. Is that all right?'

Fiona did not take her eyes from her small son although she knew that Bill was looking at her intently, and her answer was non-committal. 'We'll see,' she said. 'We'll see. Now get yourselves to bed this minute.'

'Good-night, Mam.' 'Good-night, Mam.' 'Good-night, Mam.' The voices followed one after the other; then steps could be heard crossing the landing and now, like the descending notes on a scale, there followed 'Good-night, *Mister* Dad,' from Mark, 'Good-night, *Mister* Dad,' from Katie, and 'Good-night, *Mister* Dad,' from Willie, and a quick scampering of feet. Laughing, Bill put his arm around Fiona's shoulders and, leading her back into the sitting-room, he pulled her down to the couch and, holding her tightly, he kissed her, then said, 'Well, it's certainly been an evening. What d'you say?'

'Yes, it's certainly been an evening, Mr B. And wouldn't it be a shame,' she added, her head now to one side, 'to waste it by spending the rest of it in the study.'

He stared at her, his eyes twinkling as he said, 'You know what, Fiona Bailey? You're a brazen woman, and before you were a brazen woman you must have been a brazen girl called Fiona Vidler. All this refined veneer of yours is just mush; you're sex mad. I could say I've got a headache but I won't.' With a jump he got to his feet and pulled her upwards. 'Come on; I'll give you half an hour, then I'll return to the job.'

'Not if I know it,' she said.

'Aw, lass.' He pulled her to him and kissed her again hard on the lips before almost running her from the room.

3

Mark had taken the bus to school in Newcastle, and Fiona had dropped Katie and Willie and Mamie off at their respective schools. Then having done quite a bit of shopping, she was now lifting two laden bags from the boot of the car in the garage when she heard the phone ring; and it had rung six times more before she managed to open the front door, drop the two bags, and pick up the receiver.

'Fiona?'

Fiona drew in a deep breath. 'Yes, Mother,' she said.

'You've taken your time to answer. Where on earth have you been?'

'I've been out shopping, Mother; and before that I took the children to school.'

'I thought that person next door took the children to school?'

'Only sometimes, Mother.'

Fiona pulled a chair forward and sat down; this was going to be a long session.

'I'm not feeling very well. The lights flickered last night, then went out just as I happened to be coming downstairs and I got a shock and I slipped off the two bottom stairs and twisted my ankle.'

'I'm sorry. Can you walk?'

'Only just. But . . . but it isn't only that. I phoned for the electrician. I got his private number; he lives above the shop in the High Street. And when I asked if Mr Green could come round at once and find out what was wrong his wife laughed at me. She's the one that serves in the shop, a common piece if ever there was one. And you know what she said?'

Fiona didn't say, 'No, Mother,' she just waited, and Mrs Vidler went on, 'Her husband was at the club and when I asked if she could get in touch with him she said, "You're asking something, aren't you?" Those were her very words. And she said that if the whole High Street was plunged into darkness he wouldn't leave the club at that time. And it was only nine o'clock, you know.'

'Well, he'll likely come today, Mother.'

'He won't. I was on to him immediately the shop opened and he said he would be round as soon as he could. How soon was that, I asked. Sometime tomorrow, he said; he was full up with work . . . so. . . .'

Fiona stared at the mouthpiece waiting for her mother to go on; when she didn't she repeated, 'Well, so? What d'you mean by that? You don't think I can come round and fiddle with electricity, do you, Mother?'

'No, I don't. But . . . but that . . . your . . . well, your Mr Bailey, he has men who do all kinds of things on his job, he could send one of them, couldn't he?'

'He could, Mother' – Fiona's voice was sharp now – 'but he wouldn't, or he won't. He did you a big service moving your things and what was the result? You insulted him just because he had altered his voice. . . .'

'Altered his voice indeed! He pretended to be what he wasn't, he ridiculed me.'

'You always said he was a big-mouthed individual. Well, he just wanted to show that there was another side to him.'

'Yes, and one that he couldn't possibly keep up.'

'Oh yes, he could, Mother, if he wanted to. Anyway, I don't

know how you have the nerve to expect him to send one of his men round there. There are other electricians in the town you could contact; surely one of them would come straight out?'

'Yes, I suppose they would, but do you know what they want for coming out? I've already contacted two and the first one said there'd be an eight pound call-out charge; and the other one was apparently a self-employed man, asked if I could pay on the spot, sort of cash on delivery. I put the phone down. So you can't say I haven't tried.'

'Well, Mother, you'll have to try again because I'm not asking Bill to send one of his men round.'

There was silence on the line for a moment; then Mrs Vidler's voice, changing from a plaintive whine almost to an undignified yell, said, 'Of all the most ungrateful women in this world, you are one. You would let me sit alone here in the dark, a woman entirely alone while you are sitting comfortably in the light, surrounded by your children, my grandchildren whom I never see, and your servant friend next door, not forgetting your loud-mouthed husband. But there'll come a day when you'll regret your treatment of me. Oh yes, there will.'

When the phone was banged down Fiona sat back in the chair and, puffing out her cheeks, she let a long lingering breath slowly deflate them before placing her own phone down.

Her children, her servant friend . . . poor Nell, and her loud-mouthed husband. Her mind did not say poor Bill. Why did she always feel so terrible after her mother had been on the phone?

Slowly, she rose from the chair, took off her coat, then picked up the bags of groceries and went towards the kitchen, saying to herself again, 'Four children, a servant friend, and a loud-mouthed husband.'

Her mother was right there. She was very lucky. Oh! she was, very lucky.

The groceries put away, she made herself a cup of coffee, and as she sat sipping it she told herself that she would go next door to see how Nell was. She had phoned her early on and told her

to stay put for the morning, that she could manage and that there wasn't anything to do really. Now that Mamie was at school she had more time to do things because Mamie was a child that demanded a lot of attention. There was a need in her for love brought on by the loss of her parents and her brother.

So she worked it out, as she sipped at her coffee: after she had been in to see Nell she would tidy the children's rooms and get down to some cooking. The freezer needed packing up again.

But having arranged all this in her mind, she still sat on. Then of a sudden she sprang up saying, 'Damn!' It was a loud damn. And now she walked to the kitchen window and looked down the back garden, and the sight of the daffodils there reminded her that she must straighten that patch in the front garden where the young visitor had trampled the flowers down. What she actually did next was: she walked smartly from the kitchen, across the hall, and picked up the phone again.

She had to wait some minutes before a voice answered and when it said, 'Bailey Building Company. What can I do for you?' she said, 'Oh, is that you, Bert? I recognised your voice.'

'Oh. Hello, Mrs Bailey. D'you want the boss?'

'Yes, please.'

'I'll get him in a minute; he's on the job. I just happened to be passing the hut.'

It seemed a long wait, but it was only two minutes; then Bill's voice hit her, saying, 'What's the matter? What's wrong?'

'Nothing's the matter, nothing's wrong, at least not here, not with me or any of ours. But something's wrong with . . . Mrs Vidler.'

'Oh my God! What's happened there? Is she dead?'

'No, she's not dead, Bill Bailey.'

'That's a pity; I could do with a break the day.'

'Listen.'

'I'm listening.'

She then went on to tell him what had transpired on the

phone a short while ago, and before she had finished his voice came loud and clear, 'No way, Mrs B. No way.'

'All right. All right. Anyway I told her that it was an imposition. I said she had a nerve, but she said you had ridiculed her. And you know you had. Now you can't get over that; you know you had.'

'Well, you should be able to stand a bit of ridicule when you get a job done for nowt. Well not quite nowt: she gave the fellas five pounds each. But instead of fifteen pounds she would have had to pay fifty, if not more for that double journey. Oh, aye, she would at that, especially with the firm she picked. So no, no way.'

'All right. All right.'

'Then why did you get on the phone and tell me?'

She paused before she said, 'Well, to tell the truth I'm lonely: Nell's off colour, her face is in an awful state; our four offspring are at school; my husband doesn't come home to lunch; I have a long day ahead of me and no one to talk to. So I thought it would be nice just to have a word.'

'You're a liar, you know that, and you're not going to soften me up.'

'Bill' – her voice had changed – 'I have no intention of softening you up; I'm just putting it to you straight because she said something to me and it keeps going round in my head. And I'll tell you exactly her words. She said, there she was on her own, but what had I got? My children . . . her grandchildren, a servant friend – that's what she called Nell ; and a loud-mouthed husband. Yes, a loud-mouthed husband. Well, taking them singly or lumped together, I thought to myself, I'm very lucky. She is alone, and no matter how bitchy she is, she happens to be my mother and at times I feel responsible for her.'

'Then all I can say to that is, you're a bloody fool.'

'All right, I'm a bloody fool, but that's how I'm made. And. . . .'

'Don't say it.'

'Don't say what?'

'That if you weren't a bloody fool you wouldn't have taken me on.'

She hesitated for some seconds before she said, 'Bill, I wouldn't ever say that even in joke.'

His voice sounded flat now as he said, 'All right, all right. Leave it, will you? Leave it.'

'Bill.'

'Aye?'

Again there was a slight pause before she said softly, 'I love you very, very much.'

There was a longer pause before he said, 'Doing seventy, I can get home within five minutes.'

She pushed her head back and laughed, saying, 'You've got the mind of a frustrated monk.'

'Well, I'm not the only one because I can see you climbing the convent walls any day.'

'*Bill!*'

'Goodbye, love.'

'Bye, my dear.'

Having replaced the receiver she stood looking down at it. Would he do anything? She didn't know.

A short while later she went next door and was surprised to see Mrs Paget in the kitchen in her dressing-gown.

'Why are you up?' she said. 'You still look full of cold.'

'Oh, it's only the sniffles now, I'm much better. But Nell's in bed. I came down to make a drink.'

'Well, you go on back and I'll see to the drink.'

'No, my dear, no. I'll tell you what you can do though, you can go up and have a talk with her. She's . . . she's in a bad way this morning.'

'Do you think she should have the doctor?'

'No, no; no doctor can cure what's wrong with her at the moment. She'll likely tell you herself.'

When she entered Nell's room she saw that Nell was lying in the middle of the bed, her head almost buried under the clothes, and it wasn't until she touched her shoulder and said, 'You

feeling awful?' that Nell bounced round in the bed, saying, 'Oh! Oh, it's you, Fiona; I thought it was Mam. Yes. Yes, I'm feeling like nothing on earth this morning.'

'Your face aching?'

'Not . . . not as much as I'm aching in here.' She pointed to her chest. Then, pulling herself up onto the pillow, she said, 'Sit down.' And at this Fiona sat down on the end of the bed, saying now, 'What is it, What's happened?'

'Well, nothing I couldn't have expected after what's already happened, but when I heard it had, it hit me hard just the same. I suppose because I was feeling pretty low anyway. But I got a letter from a so-called friend this morning. It would have to come this morning, wouldn't it?' She made an effort to smile. 'Harry's woman has had another baby. It was a girl, born last Saturday. You know, Fiona' – she leant forward now – 'although I knew what was coming with the first one and that's why he left me – perhaps he might have left me in any case, but that made him put a spurt on – when I read that letter I was overcome by the most frightful feeling. You know, if he had been near me, I . . . I –' She moved her head slowly and closed her eyes and swallowed deeply before she went on, 'I could really have killed him. For a second I longed just to have a knife in my hand to stab the air and pretend he was there. All those years humbling myself, making myself a doormat just so that he would soften up and give me a child. That's all I wanted. I could have forgiven him anything, his selfishness, his laziness – he was lazy – he had such an imagination he should have been writing books – but I could have forgotten all that and looked upon him as the best man in the world if he had only given me the chance to have a child. I mightn't have been able to carry one, or have one, but . . . but no, he always saw to it that there were no slip-ups. When I accepted the idea that he couldn't stand children, as he said, and there was no possible hope for me ever being satisfied in that way, I still had to put up with being a wife to him. God!' She turned her head on the pillow now and looked away from Fiona. 'The indignities that one has to suffer,

the degradation. I thought I'd hit rock bottom when after all that I heard he'd got another woman pregnant before leaving me; but this latest news makes it even worse. To give her a second one in scarcely more time than nature allows; that really is adding insult to injury.'

When Fiona pulled her gently into her arms, Nell laid her head on her shoulder, and with tears in her voice she said, 'What I would have done all these months if it hadn't been for you and that horde next door and the big fella, but mostly you, God alone knows. Mam and Dad are good people and they haven't a good word for him, but he was their son, so I couldn't let go in front of them, they were suffering enough. But to know that you were there. . . .'

'Nell, listen to me.' Fiona pressed Nell from her, and now she was wagging her finger into her face: 'Bert Ormesby is a good man, he's an attractive man and a sober fellow, as you know. He's got a nice house, everything all ready, and the main thing is, he's more than sweet on you. But he's shy inside; as Bill says, he's had no dealings with women; but it's evident that he wants dealings with you. But from what I can gather you've kept him at arm's length. And I can understand it. But you've got your divorce, you're free, and there's still time enough for you to have a baby.'

'What! heading for forty?'

'Don't be silly. It's happening every day.'

'Not with the first one.'

'Yes; with the first one. They do wonders now, Caesareans, and all kinds of things. Anyway, first things first; let him know that he's free to speak. You know something? I'm sick of him coming next door to make excuses to see Bill about this and that which could be done at work, and the look on his face when he finds you've just gone.'

Nell lay back now on the pillows and, wiping her face gently with her handkerchief, she said, 'I'll think about it.'

'Don't think too long. And what's more, don't lie there crying your eyes about him. Because I'll tell you something: that young mother will get her eyes opened before long.'

'Oh, I hope so. I'm being vindictive, I know, but I do, I hope she sees what she's taken on when she has practically three babies on her hands. You know, he would never do a thing in this house, wouldn't lift his hand to dry a cup. That was his mother's fault, I suppose. No, no; it wasn't, he was born lazy. And there's his father just the opposite, always frantically doing something.'

'Well, anyway' – Fiona rose from the bed – 'get yourself up, that is if your face is not paining too much. Come the weekend, go to the hairdresser and get your hair styled; it's like a dog's tail at the back. It's lovely hair but it will look better if it's trimmed. And put a bit of make-up on. You never wear make-up.'

'Yes, Mrs B. You know, in a way, you're as bossy as Bill. The only thing is, your voice is not quite so loud; but that'll come I suppose.'

Fiona flapped her hand towards Nell, then said, 'I'm off to do some baking. That freezer was packed this time last week with pies, cakes and what-not, and now it's almost bare. Oh, I've got something to tell you, but not now because you can't laugh properly with a face like that. You know, I told you last night about our first visitor; he was Mr Samuel Love. Well, we had him return with his father later. The little devil had pinched a spoon, you know, the one with the coat of arms on the top.'

'Never!'

'Yes. But I'll tell you all about it later. Now come on, get up out of that.'

'Yes, ma'am; and I'll be in shortly.'

'You needn't bother being in shortly, except for a drink; there's nothing to do and, as your mother-in-law says, dust eats no bread.'

'I've just made the coffee,' said Mrs Paget as Fiona went into the kitchen, and Fiona answered, 'I won't stay, dear. Anyway, Nell's getting up.'

'She is?'

'Yes; she feels better.'

'Oh, thanks Fiona. You always do her good.' Then her head

drooping, she said, 'Have you ever thought, Fiona, that you might one day dislike one of your sons?'

'No. No, I couldn't think that way.'

'Well, it's possible. Oh yes, it's possible. And at this moment my feeling for my son goes deeper than dislike. He had one of the best girls in the world. She had one fault, only one, she didn't stand up to him; and she could have because she's not without spunk, but she kept hoping that if she gave him his own way he'd give her what she wanted, the only thing she wished for in the world.'

'There's still time, Mrs Paget; she could get her wish yet.'

'You mean . . . Mr Ormesby?'

'Yes, I mean Mr Ormesby. It all depends on her; I'm sure he's willing.'

'Oh then, please God, something will come of it. She deserves a little happiness. And I understand from what she says he's a churchman?'

'Yes, he is.'

'There's not many about these days. More's the pity. You're sure you won't stay and have a cup?'

'No thanks, dear. I'm going to get down to some baking. I'll be seeing you.'

'Yes, yes.'

As she walked up her own garden Fiona wondered yet again how a nice couple like those two could have such a stinker of a son. . . .

After tidying up she eventually got round to her baking, and by three o'clock she had cleared away and was about to get ready to go and fetch Mamie when there was a knock on the back door. And when she opened it she was surprised to see the man who had been the topic of conversation between Nell and her earlier on.

'Oh, hello, Bert.'

'Hello, Mrs Bailey.'

The tall rather gangling fellow moved from one foot to the other, then quickly explained his presence by saying, 'I just

called round to see if Nell was . . . well, all right, after her teeth, you know. I . . . I was just quite near at Mrs Vidler's seeing to her electric . . . her electric light, you know.'

'Oh, you've been to my mother's?'

'Yes. Yes; the boss said the old lady was without light and . . . and, as I said to myself, it's not so far away' – he made a motion with his hand indicating the short distance – 'and knowing what Nell had been going . . . through with her toothache. . . .'

'Come in a minute, Bert.'

'Oh, well, Mrs Bailey, the boss'll be expecting me. But all right, just a minute.'

Two long strides brought him just within the door, and Fiona said, 'I was just about to get ready to go and pick Mamie up from school.'

'Oh aye; she's at school now. They do grow, don't they?'

Fiona made no comment on this, but said, 'Nell hasn't been across today; she hasn't been feeling at all well. . . .'

'It's those teeth of hers, they do play her up.'

'Bert, it isn't her teeth at the moment that's making her feel . . . well, off colour.'

'No?' He stared at her and waited, but Fiona did not go on straightaway to explain what was making Nell unwell, for she was questioning herself if she would be doing the right thing in playing Cupid. But she felt that if one or other wasn't given a push the situation could meander on, then fizzle out. As it was now, the situation lay between a shy man and a woman who was afraid to be hurt again.

'Of course, you know, Bert, that Nell is divorced?'

'Oh yes. Aye, I know she's divorced. And I think the fella must have been blind or daft.'

'He was neither blind nor daft, Bert, but he was cruel. Perhaps what you don't know is that he left Nell because he had got . . . well, the girl into trouble, as the term is.'

'Aye; well, it's generally the way.'

'But not in this case, Bert. You see Nell had always wanted

children and her husband was adamant that there would be no children of the marriage. He couldn't stand children; he didn't like children et cetera. So, for thirteen years Nell lived in frustration. But imagine what she felt like when she knew why he had left her. And then this morning she got a letter from, as she says, some kind friend who told her that another child was born on Saturday and that it was a girl. She had always wanted a girl. I'm . . . I'm telling you this, Bert, because . . . well, Nell never would. And I think you are fond of her, aren't you?'

She watched him wet his lips, then gulp in his throat before he said, 'Yes; yes, I'm fond of her. I've never been fond of anybody before. I mean, I've never felt about anybody like I have her. For one thing . . . well, I can talk to her; I don't feel all at sixes and sevens. And thank you, thank you, Mrs Bailey, for puttin' me in the picture. I'm a stupid individual, you know, thick.' He dabbed his forehead with his finger, and at this Fiona smiled and said, 'You're neither stupid nor thick, Bert; you're a very caring man, and Nell needs someone to care for her in a special way. We all love her, but that isn't enough.'

'D'you think she'd have me?'

'Why don't you ask her? Why not call in tonight and see how she is?'

He turned from her now and pulled open the door; then he paused on the step for a moment before turning and looking at her again. He said quietly, 'Thanks, ma'am.'

'Bert. Call me Mrs B, will you?'

She watched his face go into a wide grin and he said, 'Willingly, Mrs B, willingly. And again, thanks.'

She watched him bring his bicycle from the wall and hitch himself down to the back garden gate which made him look like an overgrown schoolboy from behind.

She had picked the two girls up from their separate schools. She'd had to wait fifteen minutes for Katie. There had been a rehearsal for the chorus of the concert the school was putting

on, and now Katie was sitting in the passenger seat describing with some elation to her mother that she had also been chosen to do a walking on part. She had four lines to say, then toss her head and walk off; and she was about to deliver the lines yet once again, and with actions, when she turned her head and exclaimed, 'There's Willie! And Sammy's with him.'

Fiona pulled up sharply, and, her head out of the window, she called to the two meandering backs, 'Willie!'

At this Willie came running back towards the car. Sammy's approach was a little slower, but neverthless he was at the window when Fiona, addressing her son, said, 'Well, get in.'

'OK,' said Willie now, and, turning to Sammy, he pushed him towards the rear door of the car, saying, 'Well, get in.'

Fiona was forced to return the glance that her daughter was casting on her now while Mamie was greeting Willie in her usual enthusiastic way: 'Willie, I've made a box to put my beads in,' to which Willie's retort was, 'Move along.'

'Hello, boy.' Mamie was now addressing the newcomer; but Master Sammy Love gave her no reply.

'Sammy's dad says he can stay to tea, Mam.'

Fiona said nothing. She started up the car, but she did so with a jerk. And when her son's voice came at her on a high laugh, saying, 'You'll be all right, Mam, once you've passed your test,' she exclaimed loudly, 'Willie!' and the tone seemed to be sufficiently meaningful to silence the back-seat passengers, at least, for the moment.

'Don't forget, Mam, that Mark's going to tea straight from school with Roland Featherstone.'

'I haven't forgotten, Katie.'

'Well, I just thought you might have.'

'Mam' – Willie's head was on Fiona's shoulder – 'Sammy says his dad says he can come to tea whenever he likes.'

Fiona allowed a number of seconds to pass before she said, 'Oh, did he?'

Then before Willie could confirm his statement Sammy's

voice came loud and strident, 'But that's only if you asked me, missis; and I hadn't to ask, I had to wait.'

Katie's giggle was audible, and Fiona muttered at her, 'That's enough!' Then, in a clear voice she said, 'Well, Sammy, you may come to tea now and again, let's say . . . er, once a week.'

'Fair enough. Ta. I know where I am now.'

'Which night, Mam?' There was a disappointed note in Willie's voice.

'We'll make it a Friday, the day after tomorrow. Will that suit you, Sammy?' There was a note of sarcasm in her tone, and Sammy answered, 'Aye, I suppose so . . . ta.'

Because she was endeavouring to negotiate a corner, Fiona could not put her hand out and slap Katie who had swung round on her seat and, addressing Sammy, had said, 'When can Willie go to your house for tea?'

And she was slightly taken aback when the answer came, 'Any day, except a Thursday like. 'Tisn't posh like your place, but he can come.'

Katie could find nothing to say to this; but when her mother pointedly said quietly to her, 'I'll have a talk with you when we get home,' she gave a grunt and slid further down into the seat.

Fiona had just got them settled round the table and all munching away, Willie doing the most talking, when the phone rang.

It was her mother's voice that greeted her, saying, as usual, 'Fiona?'

'Yes, Mother.'

There was a pause before Mrs Vidler's voice came again, prim-sounding and definitely reluctant with thanks. 'Well, he sent a man round and I must say that his men could teach others quite a lot in civility. He was a very nice and well-spoken man. I'll remember to send for him if I ever have any need in that way again.'

'He works for my husband, Mother. You seem to forget that.'

'Oh no, I don't forget that. I asked him what they were working on now and he said they were building two houses.

And when I asked him what they were doing after he said that it was all up in the air. And I could have told him that for I get around, and from what I hear there are twenty firms in for Sir Charles Kingdom's estate. Whoever gets that will be made; it's bound to go to an experienced builder, I mean a well-established firm. So, have you thought, Fiona, what you would do then?'

Fiona stared hard into the mouthpiece before she said, 'Go on the dole, Mother; and we'll live as we did before Bill came on the scene, three years from hand to mouth when you didn't offer a crumb to help me. But, there'll be one difference now, Mother, I'll be happy, we'll be happy. We'll all be happy. And lastly, Mother, I want to tell you, you are the most un . . .' – her voice rose now – 'the most ungrateful creature I've ever come across in my life.'

The phone was quite used to being banged down; nevertheless, she kept her hand on it, once it was on the stand, as if she had hurt it and regretted her action. But her mother . . . that woman! simply got her goat. Was there another mother on earth like her, so ungrateful and so determined to infiltrate any unhappiness she could into her life? It was jealousy, pure and simple jealousy. But how could a mother be so jealous of a daughter? There must be other mothers like her. If she only knew them, it would be a help because at times she felt there couldn't be anyone quite as vicious as the woman who had borne her. Yet there were times when she had heard people actually say to her, 'Oh, your mother is such a nice person. She has such a gentle manner.' Gentle manner indeed! She now marched up the stairs and into her bedroom where she flopped down into a chair and pressed her hands between her knees, as she had often done as a child when things had got the better of her; and she was amazed to hear herself praying aloud: 'Oh, dear God, let Bill get that contract. If it's only to show her. Please! Please! And it's so important to Bill. It's the most important thing in his life.'

She got up abruptly and, as if she were replying to the Deity, she said, but with no plea in her voice now, 'No, it isn't; we are the most important. But he wants it for us.'

And again she was marching out of the room. She had reached the stairhead when Willie's face appeared at the bottom, saying, 'We're all finished, Mam. We've put the dishes in the sink. Can we go up to the playroom? I mean, can I take Sammy up?'

'Yes, yes.' She nodded at him, and he scrambled away. But she had just reached the bottom of the stairs when the phone rang again. She delayed for some seconds her lifting of it; and then she held it as if it were hot: if it was her mother again she would scream at her, she would.

'Fiona?'

'Oh. Yes, Bill.' The words came out on a sigh.

'What's the matter?'

'Oh, I've just had Mother on the phone.'

'Well, what's the matter with her? She should be very pleased; her electricity's all right.'

'Yes, I know that, dear; but you know Mother.'

'Yes, I know Mother. But listen, dear, I won't be home straightaway; I've got to go to the hospital.'

'Hospital? Have you . . . what's the matter?'

'Nothing with me. But you know Barney McGuire?'

'Yes, I know Barney.'

'Well, apparently he was mugged last night. I've just heard of it. I've been out with the architect all afternoon, going round that land again, seeing where we could cut corners. And I've just got in and Barney's wife phoned this afternoon. She apparently got worried last night when he didn't come back from the club. And they found him in a back alley badly knocked up. So I'm going along now. But you know, Fiona. . . .'

'Yes? Yes, Bill?'

'There's something fishy going on here. First Tommy's car, then Jack Mowbray's shed was broken into, his bike stolen and most of his tools.'

'When was this?'

'Oh, one day last week. These things are always happening, and I thought it was an isolated case. But now Barney. I don't

like it. Anyway, I'll tell you more when I get back. You all right?'

'Yes, yes, I'm all right, dear; but I hope Barney's going to be all right.'

'So do I. Anyway I'll know more when I see him. Ta-ra, love.'

'Ta . . . bye-bye.'

She was turning from the phone when Willie's guest, who had started to mount the stairs, turned round and looked at her and said, 'Ta, missis. It was a nice tea.'

She was forced to smile, saying, 'I'm glad you enjoyed it, Sammy. By the way, are you sure your father knows you are staying?'

'Well, I said I might be able to, but I'll tell him it's just Friday nights after this, eh?'

'Yes, yes.' She moved her head twice.

'It's a good job you didn't say the morrow night 'cos I go to confession on a Thursday night straight after school.'

'Oh, you . . . you do . . . go to confession?'

'Aye.'

Willie, now two stairs ahead of him, turned round, leant on the bannister, then said, 'He tells all his sins to a priest. If he doesn't the nuns whack him.'

She walked towards the foot of the stairs now and, looking at Sammy, she said, 'But how do the nuns know whether you've told all your sins to the priest?'

'Oh, they can tell, missis, they can see through you. If they know you've missed anything out they wallop you on the ear.'

'The nuns wallop you?'

'Oh, aye. Me da went for one of them. He said what he'd do to her if she walloped me again. Well, I mean, on the ear! She could . . . well, do it on the backside, but not on the ear. Me da's dead against bein' walloped on the ear, you see, 'cos his da was deaf. He's dead now, his da. but his da was deaf 'cos of bein' walloped on the ear. So me da told the nun what he would do if she walloped me on the ear again. And so she hasn't done it, but instead she nearly shakes the bloody life out of you.'

Fiona glanced quickly to the side to see if Katie or Mamie were in sight. They weren't. Then, wetting her lips a number of times, she stepped up a stair and, putting her hand out, she gently touched Sammy on the shoulder, saying, 'Now, Sammy; you know what I think about swear-words.'

He stared up into her face, and his small bottom jaw moved from side to side before he said, 'But I thought it was only the little ones, the four-letter 'uns.'

'Yes, it was the four-letter 'uns, I mean, ones. They are vile words. But there are other words, too, like the one you've just said, and that's swearing. There's a difference, I know; but . . . but it's not nice to swear.'

He studied her for a moment; then his head slightly to the side, he said, 'Everybody does it.'

'No, my dear, everybody doesn't do it, except perhaps when they are very annoyed.'

'Your man bawls, his da' – he thumbed towards Willie now – 'or step-da, or what, he swears. Willie says he does.'

She looked at her son, and he, nodding at her, said, 'He does, Mam, at times, Mr Bill, I mean Dad, he swears.'

'Only when he is very, very annoyed. Oh' – she shooed them now as if they were two chickens – 'get upstairs. Go on with you.' And they both turned and ran from her. But at the top her son turned and called, 'Mam!' And impatiently she asked, 'What now?' And the reply made her turn quickly away, for Willie, nudging Sammy with his elbow, had said, 'Sammy says you wouldn't be half bad if you let your face fall a bit more.'

She was in the sitting-room before she seemed to draw breath. She wouldn't be half bad if she let her face fall a bit more. Really! What were things coming to. She'd have to do something about this, and with the thought she moved towards the door. But then stopped. No, she wouldn't. She was thinking now like her mother. Better to let her children know that there was another life being lived by other children, then they would appreciate their home more. And on the other hand, Sammy might learn from them. 'Huh!' and it was an audible reaction;

she couldn't imagine either Sammy or his father learning from anyone but each other.

Accompanied by Mamie, Katie now entered the room, Katie saying, 'Mam, I've washed the tea things and dried them, and Mamie helped.' And Mamie chimed in, 'And I didn't break nothin', Mammy B.'

'That was a clever girl. Now away with you both upstairs.'

'Mam, I'm sorry about that bit in the car when I acted snobby; because at tea time he was all right: he didn't take anything unless Willie pushed it towards him or I offered it; and then he said thanks, well not thanks, just ta, but it all means the same. He's awful, Mam, but you can't help sort of liking him after a time. Did he really say four-letter words?'

'I know a lot of four-letter words. At school today I wrote them on the board for the teacher: Cats, dogs, bears.'

'Bears have five letters, silly. Come on with you.'

As Katie pushed Mamie before her out of the room, Fiona looked after them and mused on how that child had fallen into place in this household. It was as if she had been born of herself. And in a way she was a very lucky child, discounting the fact that she had lost her parents and family, because she would grow up to be a comfortably rich young lady. The compensation for the loss of her parents had been a considerable sum and it was growing with the interest. Whereas, Katie, what would Katie grow up to be? An independent spirit. Yes, for richer or poorer Katie would make her own choice, and she would see that she was allowed to do so.

4

Bill sat looking across his desk at two of his workmen, Dave McRae and Alec Finlay. Dave was a tiler and Alec a bricklayer; but both could turn their hands to anything on the job. Bill was fond of them and appreciated their work. And now, looking at Dave, he said with some concern, 'You feeling all right though?'

'Oh aye, boss, I'm feeling all right, except inside where I'm bloody mad. As the others are sayin', there's something fishy goin' on. First, there was Tommy's car swiped. I know he's got it back, but they didn't get the blokes. Then Jack's shed broken into and his bike and tools taken. Now me being set on; but by God they got as much as they sent if not more: my boot caught the smaller one where he'll feel it for days, I'm tellin' you. But what would have happened to me? Likely landed up where Barney did, in hospital, if it hadn't been for those two blokes happening to come along at the time, which made the bastards scarper. Anyway, Alec, he's got something to tell you. He didn't think much of it, did you, Alec, at the time? But it might give us a lead. Fire away, Alec.'

Because of a slight stammer Alec Finlay always had to be prompted into speech, but now he said quite naturally, 'Brown, boss . . . you know, I saw him at the gate one day last week. I

was just on le . . . le . . . leavin'. You and Harry Newton were away on t . . . t'other site and I was havin' wo . . . wo . . . words with the w . . . w . . . watchman and I noticed a car had pulled up at t'other side of the road. It was no po . . . posh do but when the driver saw me, he started up. But I cr . . . cr . . . crossed the road before he g . . . g . . . got go . . . go . . . goin'. And when I thought I rec . . . rec . . . recognised him I looked back and yes, 'twas him . . . Brown. He had snooped around the estate often enough so I co . . . co . . . couldn't mistake him. He must have been si . . . si . . . sittin' lookin' in on the gr . . . gr . . . ground, 'co . . . 'co . . . 'cos we were just g . . . g . . . gettin' the foundations goin' then.'

Bill rose to his feet. 'Brown.' He nodded from one to the other. 'Yes, yes, Brown; that could be the answer. But I understood he was in London.'

'He was divorced a short time ago, I heard,' Dave nodded at him now. 'Aye and somethin' else has come to mind. It was rumoured he was back with his piece again, the one he had afore he left.'

'Any idea where they live?'

Dave shook his head. 'Not a clue, boss. All I knew about him was the gossip.'

Bill put his hand on a heavy paperweight on the desk and pushed it around in a circle and watching the movement for some minutes before he said, 'I'd like to bet we've got the answer to what's been going on here, because these attacks and the pinching are certainly no coincidence. It's never happened before to any of you, has it?' Without waiting for an answer he went on, as he pointed to Dave, 'Go round the fellas and ask if anybody knows where Brown's hanging out now.'

'That's an idea.' Dave nodded. 'Somebody's sure to know something, a bit anyway. And by God, if it's proved that he's put these fellas up to dirty work, he'll land up with more than one black eye and a split lip, I can tell you, even if I go along the line for it.'

The two men were making for the hut door when Bill stopped

them, saying, 'You said you had an idea that one was much taller than the other?'

'Aye; that's what I got and from the feel of it an' all. I didn't get a look at their faces 'cos they were between the lights. I saw them comin' towards me, and they walked past me. Next minute I knew they were on me.'

'That sounds exactly what happened to Barney, same technique, yet Davey Love said those two fellas had scarpered after the car business. When the police got round there they had left their lodgings. He said he had heard they had crossed the river. Look, send Love in will you?'

'Will do.'

When the two men went out Bill sat down again and once more he fingered the paperweight, pushing it round in circles that gradually merged into one.

Brown. Of course. Who else? for in a way he had ruined Brown's career the night his son had smashed up the showhouse on the Brampton Hill estate. That night Brown's wife had treated the man like a dog, in this very room and in front of him as she had made a bargain with him that if he did not call the police to deal with their son she and Brown would remove their home and business interests from Fellburn down to London, and, too, their son would be sent to school in what appeared to be the wilds of Scotland. And after this she had approached him again, saying she was going to divorce her husband, and then practically throwing herself at him with the bait that he could then run her businesses, of which she had a number. That was if, and it was a capital IF, and he had told her in his own inimitable fashion what he thought of her, and ending up with the words that he wouldn't touch her with a barge-pole. Even now he could recall the look she gave him as she went out to her car, which then, once started, shot out of the yard as if driven by a rocket.

Yes, yes; this was Brown's doing; for without any doubt he had been the cause of the man's ruin; his visible ruin at least, for he had learned that Brown had been in effect nothing more than a paid hand in the businesses, but all the time playing the

big fellow, talking big money that he had nothing to do with at all.

When he had asked her if the businesses were in her name, she had said, yes they were, and if her husband made a fuss when they broke up he would get less than what she would have offered him in redundancy pay.

Both had been mean, vindictive types. But now Brown must be out to get his own back. It couldn't be his own men: he had eleven good men on this job, and they had nearly all been with him for years now. And he had made them feel that they were part of the company because at the end of the year they got their rake-off of the profits. He had made it known to them when he was given the last big job, for he saw it then as good policy to let the men know they had a finger in the pie. But it looked as if Brown was out to disable his team in one way or another. Well, he would see about that. By God! he would.

When a tap came on the door he called, 'Come in.' And when Davey Love entered, saying, 'You want me, boss?' Bill said, 'Yes, for a minute, Davey. You get about. You said you thought that those two fellas had scarpered after the car business?'

'Well, I did hear they went across the water down to North Shields.'

'Are you sure of that?'

'No, not sure, boss, it was just hearsay. It was in the pub.'

'You've heard about what's happening here to the fellas?'

'Aye, I've heard.'

'Well, you're on the pay-roll now, it could be you next.'

'No, begod! boss. I've got eyes in the back of me head.'

'Oh, you can be too clever.'

'Oh, 'tisn't a case of bein' clever; it's a case of whose walkin' behind you. I very rarely walk on the flags, I keep to the gutter or the road; cars are not half as dangerous as some people I know of, especially around our way. No, begod! I'll say.'

'Do you know anything about a man called Brown? He used to be a big pot in the town, lived in one of those houses facing

the Moor in Newcastle. Went to London some time ago, divorced and came back and took up with a woman he knew.'

'That Brown, boss?'

'Yes, that Brown.'

'Well, I know nowt about him, not really, but I know quite a bit about his one-time chauffeur-cum-odd-job man. He used to hire him when he was goin' out on a spree. He often had these bouts at one time, you know, goin' gettin' bottled up, mortalious, paralytic, the lot, oh aye, the lot. So Charlie Davison had the job of ferryin' him home. That was until Charlie saw my Betty, and once again it was love at first sight for her, and off they go together. Well, she had done it afore but not so brazenly. An' then she has the bloody cheek to come back, an' he follows her. God and His Holy Mother! was I rattled. Well, I followed him. The result was that holiday I told you about up in Durham, boss, y'know?'

Bill wanted to laugh. He wanted to bellow. He had just to hear this fellow talk and it was as if every other word he spoke was a joke. He had that way with him. But this business on his mind now was no laughing matter, so he said, 'Well, where is he now, this Charlie Davison?'

'As far away from me, boss, as he can get I should think, the way I left him.'

'Aye, yes, of course he would be. So you know nothing of Brown?'

'Not at the moment, boss; but I could find out. One thing's certain though: his type won't be livin' in Bog's End, even if he got his piece from there.'

'You never know; it might be her house.'

'Aye, there's that in it. But private house owners are few an' far atween around our quarter you know, boss. But as Alex said, his car was just an old 'un, no BMW, Volvo, or such, so he wouldn't be livin' up in Brampton Hill area, now would he? No; with a car like that he wouldn't. Middle town I'd say. Any road, I'll ask around. I'll have a talk with Kit Bradley at the pub. Aye, that's what I'll do. What he doesn't know isn't worth

learnin'. Anyroad, as soon as I hear anythin' you'll know of it, boss.'

'Thanks, Davey.'

'You're welcome, boss.'

'By the way' – Bill stopped him as he was about to turn about – 'both Dave and Alec seemed to remember that the fellas who attacked them were different sizes, a tall 'un and a short 'un. Now you seemed to think that there was a pair like that who pinched Tommy Turnbull's car, didn't you?'

'Aye, begod! I'm sure it was that pair. An' givin' it another thought, they could easily have slipped up from Shields to do their dirty work an' get back. Half an hour or so each way would see to it. Aye, it could be the same couple. And if it is it's a set-up job an' they're in somebody's pay, this fella Brown's. Is that how you see it, boss?'

'Yes, that's how I see it at present.'

'Well, we'll take it from there, boss, eh?' Nodding now, he turned and went out.

Yes, Bill said to himself; we'll take it from there. But once I find out where you are, Mr Brown, you can look out for sparks.

He was again pushing the paperweight around in circles. He had been in a few tight corners, business-wise, in his time but none so tight as this one. There was a time limit in getting these two houses finished and somebody . . . . Brown in fact knew what time limits meant and he was aiming to diminish his work force. And each of his men in his own way was an expert and worth three of any casual labour he might have to take on.

Then there was the thought that when this job was finished he'd be out on his beam ends if he didn't get that contract. And the more he knew about those who were in for it the more he saw it receding from him. He had heard that although Sir Charles Kingdom was out of hospital now he was still not a well man, so there was little hope of coming across him.

He rose from the chair and took his coat from the peg on the wall of the cabin, thinking as he did so there were businesses dropping like flies around him. Well, he wasn't going to go

down without a fight, and the first blow to be struck would be at Mr Brown.

Nell said, 'You look tired. What you want is a night out.'

'Well, I should think that would make me more tired. What I think I really want is an early night in bed.'

'We are of different opinions there.' And Nell cast a naughty glance at Fiona, then said, 'Get the big boy to take you out to dinner. And why you wanted to tack a new addition onto the squad I'll never know.'

'I've told you, Nell. I had no option.'

'But he stood at the door there and argued he had to come today because tomorrow's Confession and on his usual visiting day, Friday, he's got to stay on at school for some special "do" those nuns are organising and only announced this morning.'

Fiona sighed. 'Oh, I know; but there he was, wanting to be contradicted. I don't know what it is about him, he's an uncouth, dirty . . . no, he's not dirty, I will say that for him: however he's been brought up, his father keeps him very tidily dressed; but there's something about him.'

'Yes, I know there is, but I'm not going to let it get at me.'

'Oh, Nell Paget; there you were giving him the biggest piece of cake from the plate, filling his mug before it was empty. Oh, you're a hypocrite. Anyway, you tell me to get out, how can I when you're off tonight jitterbugging?'

At this Nell put her head back and laughed, saying, 'Oh, that's funny. Can you see Bert jitterbugging?'

'Yes, yes, I can; Bert to my mind is a deep well.'

'Oh, don't say that, Fiona.' Nell's face was serious now. 'I don't want to find out anything more about him than I know now, because if I put my bucket down the well it might bring up something nasty.'

'Not in Bert's case. He's a good nice man and . . . he's attractive.'

'I'm glad you think so.'

'Oh, come off it, Nell, you more than think so, you're positive of it. Has . . . well, has he spoken yet in any way?'

'No . . . Mrs Bailey, he hasn't spoken yet, but the minute he does you'll be the first to know.' She laughed now, saying quietly, 'It's odd you know, Fiona, but I feel like a daft girl, waiting you know, knowing what's going to come and a bit frightened of it. Well, well' – her tone altered – 'I suppose I would be after what I've gone through, because, don't forget, the late Mr Paget was also thought to be very charming. That sounded as if he was dead.' She gave a little giggle now, then added, 'I don't wish him dead; no, I wish him a long, long, long life and a houseful of bairns. Oh yes I do, because then there won't be any time for his wife to baby him, and he has been babied from birth. When we married, I simply took over from his mother. Ah well, it's all over, and I'll get away before the lord of the manor comes in, and also leave you to get rid of your guest.' She laughed now as she added, 'It's amazing how Willie's taken to him, isn't it? And he apparently to Willie. They both go to different schools; you didn't say how they met up.'

'Apparently on the football field. Master Samuel was warned off, or carried off, or sent off, or some such and roused Willie's admiration. They got on talking, as far as I can gather, and the next thing was that Mr Love junior was waiting for Willie coming out of school. He's at the convent along Mitchell Road. He's got to come some way from Bog's End to there.'

'He's at the convent!'

'Yes, he's at the convent. And by all accounts, if you've got to believe him, all nuns are not angels.'

'Oh, I can believe that. Well, as I said, I'll be off. But there's one thing you can say about this house, it's never lost for entertainment.'

She was going out of the door when Fiona said, 'Let me know if it happens, won't you?'

'What happens?'

'Oh, go on with you! Get out!' As she pushed Nell out, then closed the door, she looked up as she heard the pounding feet

crossing the landing, and she hadn't reached the kitchen door before it burst open and Willie came in, followed by Sammy.

'Ma, can Sammy come to my birthday party?'

'Your birthday party? That's weeks ahead.'

'Only three. It's the day after Easter Monday, you know.'

'Yes, I know, I know.'

As Fiona spoke she wasn't looking at her son but was returning the gaze of Samuel Love whose face had lost its wide expectancy and was now set, lips tight, the eyes unblinking. She heard herself say, 'Why, yes of course, if Sammy would like to come.'

'Oh, he'd like to come, wouldn't you, Sammy?'

It seemed that Sammy had difficulty in taking his gaze from his pal's mother. And when he did, his answer was abrupt and to the point: 'Aye,' he said.

'Oh well, that's settled.' Even as Fiona spoke she thought of Roland Featherstone who had been to tea with Mark just two nights ago and who spoke so beautifully; in fact, she was hoping that Mark would take a pattern from him. Not that her son did not speak well; but there was a difference between Roland's accent and that of the members of her own family. And the difference had been emphasized when Katie 'did him', immediately he left the room to depart, and then infuriated Mark on his return from setting his friend off to the bus by greeting him with: 'How d'you do? How d'you do, Mr Bailey?' and turning to Fiona, had added, 'I'm so pleased to meet you, Mrs Bailey.' And when Mark had struck out at her, she had come back at him with her toe in his shin. After she herself had remonstrated, Katie's last words were, 'Well, he gets up my nose. He's a cissy.' And she had further had to restrain Mark from dashing after the figure that was disappearing up the stairs. . . .

It was about nine o'clock that evening when Fiona, taking yet another cup of coffee into the study, said, 'Give over a minute. Sit back and leave that. Get your coffee and listen. You know Willie's birthday is looming up? Well, the latest is he's asked Sammy to come, and Mark has already asked Roland. Now imagine the party with those two, poles apart, present.'

'It should be fun.'

'What! With Willie ready to strike a blow for Sammy and Mark getting on his high horse if everybody doesn't admire Roland.'

'Well, if you want my opinion, Mrs B, if Master Roland doesn't like the set-up, he can lump it.'

'Oh, of course your sympathies lie with the poor down-trodden Sammy.'

'Huh! there you've got it wrong. My sympathies might lie with him, but he's no poor down-trodden Sammy. I'd like to bet he's got more spunk and intelligence in his little finger than Master Roland's got in his whole body. Although, mind, I like that lad. He's a civil enough kid, except of course that he speaks a different language.' He grinned at her now.

'Yes, yes, it's evident he speaks a different language.'

Leaning across the desk now, he poked his face at her, saying, 'And you would like your sons to speak the same as him, wouldn't you? Not common . . . like me and Sammy Love.'

'Yes, you're exactly right, exactly, Mr Bailey.'

'If I come round there I'll slap your lug for you. You're nothin' but a snob, you know that? I thought when I married you I'd knock it out of you, but I see I've still got a long way to go. You're your mother's daughter all right.'

The satisfied smile slid from Fiona's face and she muttered now, 'Don't say that, Bill. I mean, don't see me as you see my mother.'

He was round the desk and had his arms about her, saying, 'My God! woman, don't you know when I'm joking?'

She swallowed, then said, 'Yes; yes, I do; but oh, sometimes I get het up inside when I say something or do something and I tell myself that's just like Mother. And I can't help it but I don't want to be like Mother in any way. She's vicious and vindictive.'

'Now, now; forget about her. Give us a kiss.'

A moment later he pressed his head back from her, saying, 'That wasn't worth tuppence. Going cold on me, are you?

Somebody else in your eye? Oh, I know: you're jealous because Bert's going to pop the question.' He laughed; then went on, 'I wonder if he's done it?' And Fiona had just answered, 'She'll phone me if he has,' when there was a ring, but at the front door, and she cried, 'Oh lord! who's that at this time?'

'Likely she's bringing him the front way all correct an' proper.'

'No, not her,' she said as she turned to go and answer the door; but straightaway he said, 'Stay! It's after nine; who do we get at this time of night?'

When Bill opened the front door he saw whom they had got at this time of night. 'Hello, boss,' said Davey Love. ''Tis late, I know, but I've got a bit of news. I've just come across it, so it entered me mind that you might like to hear of it.'

'Come in. Come in, Davey. Come through here.'

'Evenin', Mrs Bailey. It's nice out; there's a full moon the night. 'Tis a beautiful sight, a full moon. But it does disturb some folks, so I'm told, at least they used to say in Ireland. But then there's some barmy ones over here an' all. Oh aye; begod! yes.'

'Is . . . is that so?' Her reply was stilted; Mr Love's conversation and even his greetings were different from the usual. 'Would you like a cup of coffee?' she said.

'I would that. Yes, I would that, Mrs Bailey, ma'am, if it's no trouble. But that's a daft thing to say; everything at night's a trouble. But I accept your invitation, kindly given an' kindly received.'

Fiona made her way towards the kitchen, her head making small perplexing movements.

In the study Bill said, 'Sit down, Davey. What's this news you've got for me?'

'Well, it's like this, boss. I was in the Mucky Duck.'

'The what?' Bill screwed up his face.

'Oh, that's me name for it. It's Kit Bradley's pub. It's called the Duck An' Drake, because, apparently, they tell me, years gone, donkey's years, there was a farm there where the pub stood, I mean stands the day.'

Bill made a small sound in his throat, then said, 'Aye . . . aye, I understand.'

And Davey went on, 'Well, I was doin' me little bit behind the bar, just washin' glasses you know – as I said, I'm not allowed to serve 'cos I would be thereby committin' a felony against the dole, but washin' glasses I'm only helpin' out a friend. Y'see? Well, there I was helpin' out a friend when this fella comes in. Now, I know every customer in that place as well as does Kit himself, an' when strangers appear they stick out like sore thumbs, as did them two fellas I told you about who pinched the car. . . . You've never heard any more about those, have you, boss?'

'Davey, come to the point, will you?'

'Oh, aye, that's me: I start meanderin' up a lane an' find meself in the middle of the A 1, an' drivin' on the wrong side. Well, I'll come to the point, aye I will. This fella asks for a large whisky, and he gets it. An' then he asks for another and he gets it. And I happen to go round the counter and pick some glasses up from an end table an' Joe Honeysett, that's the fella I know, he stops me and wags his head to the side an' he says to me, "He's out of the way, isn't he?" And I said, "Who?" And he nods towards the newcomer an', said he, "Brown, who used to be the big shot." So, of course, boss, as soon as he mentioned the name I said, "Brown? Brown who used to be the builder?" an', said he, "Aye. But he was never any builder, financier or somethin', but never any builder. He provided the money like. But his wife got rid of him an' he's back in the town." "D'you know where he lives now?' said I. "I only know one thing," said Joe; "he doesn't live round this quarter."

'So there I was boss, behind the counter again sayin' to Kit, "Can I have the loan of your jalopy for half an hour or so?" "What for?" said he. "I'll tell you when I come back," said I. And to that he said, "Well, take the jalopy, but drive it back in one piece. D'you understand?" Anyway, there I was sittin' in Kit's old banger that he takes more care of than he would a Volvo when this fella comes out and gets into his car. And it

was no great shakes either. An' so, as I trailed him, I felt like The Minder. And it was as Joe said, he didn't live anywhere in Bog's End, but in quite a nice part really, middle town. Seventy-two Drayburn Avenue, boss.'

'Drayburn Avenue, eh? Well, not a bad part as you say. Thanks, Davey. Look –' He put his hand into his back pocket and pulled out some loose change, four sovereigns amongst it, and when he handed them across the table to Davey, saying, 'Get yourself a drink from this side of the counter,' Davey Love rose to his feet and with a dignity that could have appeared comic at any other time, he said, 'Thanks, boss, but I'm not after expecting to be paid for a service like that. Anythin' I do for you outside workin' hours is to repay *you* an' your good missis for what you're doin' for me lad. Keepin' him off the streets an' showin' him a different way of life.'

For a moment Bill felt a twinge of guilt, knowing that the boy was only allowed into the house on sufferance. But in a way he could understand Fiona's reaction to the child because Willie was talking and acting more like his new mate every day, and this perhaps had amused him at first, but deep down he wanted his lad, as he thought of him, to be different, better than himself, at least where speech was concerned, and so he was now less amused. But he wouldn't for the world let Fiona know this. At the other end of the scale there was Mr Roland Featherstone. Now Fiona was more than willing to let her son copy Mr Roland Featherstone, oh yes. And wasn't he himself pleased in a way that Mark would pass himself and be able to converse like young Roland Featherstone? Oh, to hell! What was he thinking? He had Brown's number now and, by God! he'd have more than his number tomorrow when he saw him. Pocketing the coins again, he said, 'No offence meant, Davey.'

'None taken, boss, none taken. Well, I'll have to be off. An' now I've got the banger outside I'll go an' pick up that scallywag of mine from me ma's.'

He was making for the door when he turned and faced Bill again as if answering in protest some remark Bill had made: 'I

don't let him run the streets when I'm at the pub, don't think that. I push him along to me ma's; that's when she's in 'cos she's an old gadabout. But when I can, I make it worth her while to stay put. This is a very mercenary world, boss, we're in. God! I'll say it is. Although it's Himself made it. Yet there's times I have me doubts; and then I have to ask meself, if He didn't who did?'

'You're right there, Davey, you're right there. It is a very mercenary world.'

'Oh aye, I'm right there; you can get nowhere without money. Money doesn't only talk, it shouts, it bawls. By God! aye.'

He had turned away but now he turned yet again, and, a hand clasping the knob of the study door, and his voice lower now, he said, 'You'll never know how grateful I am for me job. And I can promise you this, you'll get more work out of me than you will out of a willin' donkey.'

'Aw! go on with you.' Bill gave him a push, and they both entered the hall laughing.

Bill opened the front door and was feeling almost thankful to be about to say a final good-night to his visitor when Davey, standing on the step and leaning towards him, said, 'You know something, boss? I can tell you where I wouldn't tell another soul, but I've made up me mind that I'm goin' to Mass on Sunday. 'Tis years since I stepped foot in a church, but that's where you'll find me on Sunday, first Mass, an' givin' thanks to God for straightenin' me life out for me, an' bringin' good friends into me son's existence. For only God an' His Holy Mother know that that kid wouldn't have had a rougher time if he had been brought up in Siberia. 'Night, boss.'

Bill did not reply. He watched the figure disappear down the garden path and through the gate; then he closed the door and stood with one hand pressed against it for a moment, his head bowed. And as he stood he stilled the desire to let out a bellow of a laugh because he knew if he had done another emotion might have welled up in him and contradicted his laughter.

Fiona, coming out of the sitting-room, said, 'I thought you

would be coming in for the coffee, but he's gone. What's the matter?'

'Nothing. Nothing, love.'

'What did he want?'

'He's found out where Brown lives.'

'Oh, Bill, you won't go and do anything silly?'

'Nothing silly, love. The only weapon I'll use is me mouth.'

'What's wrong?'

'Nothing. Nothing's wrong, love.'

'There is. Something's happened. Has he said something, something to upset you?'

'No, no; nothing to upset me. I'll tell you about it later, perhaps when we're in bed and the light out and our heads under the clothes.'

He bent forward, kissed her lightly on the lips, then made his way to the study.

Life was strange.

5

Bill did not visit Seventy-two, Drayburn Avenue until late the following afternoon, for as he saw it now Brown would surely be working and wouldn't be at home until tea-time. Yet this morning, when he arrived at the site and Arthur Taggart, the watchman, told him that Dandy, his dog, had been uneasy around one o'clock and when he let him go he had raced around barking his head off; he was sure the dog had disturbed someone on the site because when he reached the road he heard a car starting up, and there wasn't another house for a couple of hundred yards along the lane; it was then he had wanted to dash round to Brown's straightaway and to confront him.

He phoned Fiona to say he might be a little late. When she had enquired where he was going he had replied flippantly, to get blind drunk, so she had better look out and get the tribe to bed because he would be in the mood to play merry hell when he got in.

'I'll do as you say, Mr Bailey,' she had answered coolly; 'but should you find the door locked, there's always an hotel in the town, the one you went to before, you remember?' He had been able to smile as he put the phone down, but he wasn't smiling

when, a short while later, he rang the bell at Seventy-two, Drayburn Avenue.

Waiting for the door to open, he stretched his neck out of his pullover while telling himself he should have gone home and changed and smartened himself up before coming here. But what the hell! he just couldn't wait to get at this fellow.

The door had opened and he was looking at a woman well into her fifties: he was a good judge of age, and her tinted hair and well made-up face didn't deceive him; she wasn't a kick in the backside off sixty. Maybe she was the mother of Brown's piece.

'Yes?'

'I'd like to speak to Mr Brown, please.'

'He's not in.' The woman took half a step forward and pulled the door behind her and, her voice changing now, she said, 'And he won't be in to you, ever. I know who you are. You're Bailey, so get about your business. You've done enough harm, you.'

She almost fell back as the door was wrenched open and there stood Brown. But he wasn't the same Brown as Bill had last seen him; he had lost a lot of weight; yet his manner was the same. 'I've been expecting you,' he said.

'Well, you're not disappointed, are you? And you know why I've come?'

'Oh yes, I know why you've come. Your little tinpot business is being nibbled at.'

Bill clenched his teeth, then said slowly, 'You call being nibbled at leaving a man half dead, stealing a car, breaking into sheds, and last night aiming to sabotage me building?'

'Is that all that's been done?'

'Look, Brown; you're asking for it and you'll get it, not from me, for I wouldn't soil me hands on you, but from the courts because I'm puttin' up with this no longer. You must be a fool to think you can get away with it.'

'The only fool I've been is that I didn't bust you years ago when I could have done.'

'It was never in your power, Brown, to bust me, and you know it. In your wife's, aye. Yes, in hers, but never in yours. You're a little man. You'll always be a little man.'

The woman, in some agitation, pulled at Brown's arm, saying, 'Come in. Come in. Leave him; he's not worth it. He's not.'

Brown brushed off the restraining arm and said slowly, 'I'm going to tell you something, Bailey. You're barking up the wrong tree. I've got no hand in what's been happening to your tinpot business. D'you hear me? And this is the truth. No matter how much I'd like to see you and your little empire go up in smoke, I've never lifted a hand towards you, for the simple reason I've been too busy arranging my own business. No, you can take my word for it, whatever's happening to you, and will go on happening to you, oh yes, I can promise you that, it will go on happening to you, it's none of my doing. But you know something else? I wish it was. And yet it's good to stand on the sideline and see your dirty work done for you. So get the hell from my door. And if the things I wish for you come about there'll come a time when you'll wish you were dead.'

The door was banged, and Bill was left standing looking at it and not knowing what to think: he only knew what he felt and that was that Brown was telling the truth.

He'd have to look for another source, somebody else, some other firm that had it in for him. And there were a number to choose from, and more probably one of those that were in for the contract for the building of the estate. He got into his car, but did not immediately drive home; he stopped in a lay-by and sat thinking.

Three of the builders in for the business were known to him, and he felt sure they would never stoop to doing another down in the way that was happening to him. Would the big boys go to that trouble? Oh yes, yes; he could understand some of the big boys going to a great deal of trouble to wipe out an opponent. But why him? Oh yes; that was the point: they must think him worth wiping out; perhaps they had heard he had been favoured by Sir Charles Kingdom. . . .

Fiona greeted him with, 'Well, what have you been up to?'

'I've been to call on Mr James Brown and – Mrs Bailey – it isn't him.'

'What do you mean, it isn't him? He's not behind this business, all the things that are happening to the men?'

'No.'

'How do you know?'

'Because he said so.'

'And you believed him?'

'Yes; on this occasion I believed him.'

'Well, who could it be?'

'It can only be one of those in for the estate job. I must have opened me mouth too often about the good gang I have and that once they get goin' each one's as good as three of the ordinary floaters that's goin' about today. I should keep me mouth shut.'

'Yes, you should.'

'Oh, don't you start.'

'I'm only repeating what you said. Look there's masses of hot water; go and have a bath and change. It will make you feel better. I'll see if I can rake up some scraps for a meal, such as a meat pudding.'

'Meat pudding!' He pulled a face at her.

'Well, I don't know what it will be like by now or by the time you'll be ready for it. But go on, I'll have a talk to it.'

'Where's the tribe? There's no bustle, no yelling.'

'Oh, they're upstairs. Katie's in a mood. The bottom's fallen out of her world: she didn't come top in the mock exam; in fact, she didn't come second or third. She really can't believe it, so she's up there now digging into her homework, screaming at anybody who dares look at her. And Willie nearly got another twanking.'

'Why?'

'He came out with a polite "bloody". Something will have to be done about him and that boy.'

'Oh, the boy's all right. He'll learn.'

'*And so will Willie*, all the wrong things.'

'It's a phase; it'll pass.'

Detecting a weary note in his voice, she said, 'Go on, up those apples and pears.'

He grinned at her, saying now, 'I don't mind you turning common, that'll suit me, but it's got to be Liverpudlian common, or Geordie common, I draw the line at Cockney.'

He had reached the landing when he turned and called, 'Fiona!' And when she came to the foot of the stairs, he asked her, 'Any news about the love birds?'

'No. She said he never said a word. They had a lovely meal and went to a show, and that was that.'

'Silly bugger!'

And Fiona endorsed this as she walked towards the kitchen. Yes, Bert was a silly bugger.

It was about eight o'clock that night when the silly bugger came knocking at the back door. And when Fiona said, 'Come in, come in,' he hesitated, saying, 'She's not in, is she, I mean Nell?'

'No, no; she's next door.'

'Good. I . . . I'd like a word with you and the boss.'

'All right. Sit down. I was just going to take him in a drink; he's in the study.'

'No, I won't sit if you don't mind, Mrs B, it's . . . it's. . . .'

'Sit down, Bert. And stop fidgeting.' She laughed at him. 'Look; have that cup of coffee.' She took a cup off the tray.

'No, no.'

'Shut up and drink that; I can always make another.'

She now left the kitchen and hurried to the study and, pushing open the door, she said, 'Come into the kitchen for a moment, there's an employee of yours waiting to see you. And if you want any work out of him in the future, you'd better straighten out his love life.'

'Bert?'

'Yes, Bert.'

She gave an exaggerated whisper. 'And by the look of him he doesn't know which end of him is up. It's dreadful to reach that age before love hits you. He's had no practice at it.'

When Bill entered the kitchen Bert got to his feet, saying, 'I'm sorry to trouble you, boss, but . . . well, it's like this.'

'Sit yourself down, man, and finish your coffee. Where's mine, woman?'

Fiona handed him the cup, and he sat down opposite to Bert, saying, 'What's happened? Got home and found out you've been burgled?'

'No, nothing like that, boss. That would be simpler. Oh aye, that would be simpler. No; it's something I want to ask you. How long will this job take, boss? I mean. . . .'

'Well, you know as well as me, Bert, there's a time limit on it. We've got another eight weeks and then, if nothing comes up, we're all in the soup.'

'Aye . . . aye, I know that, boss, I know I'm asking the road I know, but have you nothin' in mind besides the big estate job?'

'Not a thing, Bert. Not a thing, at least so far. Of course there might be some odd bits and pieces pop up in the next few weeks, but they'll only be patching jobs, or gutting, because there's no spare land around here now, or very little, and what there is they want a gold mine for it. Anyway, Bert, you know the lie of the land, you've been with me long enough, you know I discuss everything with you all.'

'Aye, I know that, boss, but it's . . . er –' He drooped his head now and watched his fingers drumming on the table before he said, 'It's Nell. I want to ask her. Oh aye, I want to ask her. But what are me prospects if I'm finished after this lot? I own me own house, as you know, but there's rates and upkeep and you've got to eat, and in spite of all she's been through, she's lived a very . . . well, sort of middle-class life, so I can't ask her, the way things stand. It's come too late in life anyway.' He turned his head to the side, only to be almost startled by Fiona and in a voice that could have been attributed to Bill, crying, 'Don't be so damn soft and blind! Nell hasn't lived an easy

middle-class life; she's had to work all her days to help to keep that no-good husband of hers in comfort. So don't make that an excuse.'

'Oh. No! No! No!' He was on his feet now. 'I . . . I don't want to to make an excuse, I just . . . don't want to offer her something less than she's been used to and. . . .'

'You know what you are, Bert' – it was Bill speaking in a voice that was unusually quiet for him – 'You're a bloody fool. And I've known some good bloody fools being left on the shelf through the same ideas as you've got. And I can tell you this: if you wait any longer, when you do pop the question you'll be refused; 'cos she'll get the idea that you don't really want her. Women are like that, you know; they're bloody awkward.' He cast a glance at Fiona. 'They go as far as to tell their sons that they'll never marry, at least not fellas like brickies.'

'Bill!'

'Yes, Fiona? Well, you did. You did tell Mark that you'd never marry me.'

'Only because you kept pumping into me and everybody else within earshot that you were a middle-of-the-road man and that you would never marry anybody. Anyway, it's just like you to turn everything into a personal fight.' She looked at Bert now. 'Bert, you go next door this very minute and tell Nell what's in your mind and why you didn't pop the question to her last night when she was all dressed up and waiting.'

'You think she was?'

'I don't think, I'm sure. But, as Bill here said, women are queer cattle and you don't know what will happen just out of sheer pride.'

'But what if I'm out of work?' He was looking at Bill now and Bill's answer was a bark. 'There's always the bloody dole and social security and the odd scraps from our table here.'

Bert was smiling quietly now as he looked from one to the other, and his head wagged for a moment before he said, 'Well, if I never have a wife I'll always feel I've got two good friends.'

As he turned from the table, Bill said, 'What are you going to do?'

'Do what your Mrs B told me, go next door. But mind, me heart's in me mouth.'

'Well, spit it out and give it to her. Go on.'

Bill pushed him out of the door; and then, looking at Fiona, he said, 'I didn't know there were any of them left.'

'What left? What do you mean?'

'Just him, the likes of him, fellas who are afraid to ask a woman. He's an oddity.'

'Oh, I don't think so.' She went towards the kitchen door now, saying, 'I think there are many men like him. It's people like you who are the oddities, the brash individuals.' And she let out a squeal when he brought his hand across her buttocks; then hearing a door open upstairs she turned on him, saying in a whisper, 'There you are! Prepare yourself to meet the horde.'

There was only one solitary figure at the top of the stairs. 'Mam.'

'Yes; what is it?'

'Sammy's got a present for you. He's going to bring it on Saturday.'

'A present for me? That's very nice of him. What might it be?'

'He wouldn't tell me, but he says it's lovely.'

'Oh, I'll look forward to that. But he'd better not bring it in the morning because, as you know, we all go out shopping.'

'I told him that. I said early afternoon.'

'Oh, you did?'

'Yes, Mam. That O.K?'

'I . . . I suppose so.'

'Do you like Sammy, Dad?'

'Yes. Yes' – Bill nodded up at him – 'yes, I quite like Sammy.'

'I thought you did. I . . . I told him you would, I mean like him, because he's your type. I'm off to bed now. Good-night, Mam. Good-night, Dad.'

Fiona had hurried away, her hand across her mouth.

And they had just entered the sitting-room and Bill was saying, 'I see nothing funny in that, Mrs B,' when the phone rang, and Fiona, swinging round, said, 'That'll be Nell to give us the news.'

But a moment later when she lifted up the receiver and the voice said, 'Fiona,' she turned her head quickly and looked towards where Bill was standing in the doorway. And when she raised her eyes ceilingwards she heard him say, 'Oh, no!' as she herself said, 'Yes, Mother?'

'Now don't you get on your high horse, Fiona, at what I'm going to say. It's all for your own good. Well, I mean, the children's good.'

'What is for the children's good, Mother?'

'Well, to put it in a nutshell, the company they keep.'

'Oh. Well, as far as I know they all keep very good company.' She closed her mind to Sammy. 'Mark is very friendly with the son of a doctor whom I understand is a leading specialist in his own way, he's a gastro-enterologist; and Katie has a number of friends, and their parents, I know, would pass your scrutiny. One is an air pilot who I understand makes frequent trips to America.' She did not continue along this line to state that two of the fathers were unemployed, one having been made redundant just recently after twenty-five years managing quite a large business concern, she paused; and presently her mother's voice came over the line, saying, 'And Willie's friend?'

'Oh, Willie's friend is the son of a builder.'

'Son of a builder indeed! If I'm going on what Mrs Quinn heard, the "b" could stand for blaggard and bad language. She happened to be following them as they came along the street and she said, the . . . the b's punctuated every other word that boy said, and they were many and varied.'

'What a pity some of them didn't sting Mrs Quinn if there were so many flying about.'

'Don't be facetious, Fiona. And don't tell me that you've sunk so low that you condone your son's keeping company with dirty scum like that boy.'

Fiona held the phone away from her face for a moment; 'He's neither dirty nor scum! He is an unfortunate child who didn't have your opportunities or mine, as badly brought up as I was.'

'*Fiona!*'

'Yes, Mother; I say again, as badly brought up as I was. In fact, there's a great similarity between young Sammy Love, and that's his name, and myself, for Sammy, too, has never tasted mother-love as far as I can understand. And will you please tell Mrs Quinn that if she doesn't stop minding my business I might start looking into hers and why she's on her own so much.'

'Her husband works away. You know that.'

'Yes; but why does he work away? And where does he work away?'

'On an oil-rig. He's quite a big man.'

'Oh, I admit, he's quite a big man, at least in appearance; but men don't work on oil-rigs for nearly eleven months in the year. It's a long time since I've seen Mr Quinn. Now you tell her or I'll tell her myself. Yes I will; so don't bother, Mother, I'll do it myself. Good-night!' She banged down the phone, then turned to where Bill was standing close to her and he said quietly, 'Good for you, lass. Good for you.' Then, bending and kissing her, he said, 'Pick up the phone again.'

'I . . . I didn't mean, Bill.'

'Pick up the phone again and hand it here.'

Slowly she handed him the phone; and he dialled a number and when a polite voice said, 'Yes, Patricia Quinn here,' he said, 'Good-evening, Mrs Quinn. This is your neighbour but one, Mr William Bailey. We have just had a call from Mrs Vidler relating to us all the information you gave her concerning my son's companion. Now, Mrs Quinn, I want to tell you something. You interfere with our family life, my children's companions, or anything that happens in Number Sixteen, then I will start probing into the affairs of Number Twenty, and I'm sure that'll be very enlightening. Have you got my meaning, Mrs Quinn?'

'You . . . you're a dreadful man. Don't you dare threaten me.'

'Oh, Mrs Quinn, I wouldn't dream about threatening you; I'm just saying, should you interfere in our affairs, then, on a friendly basis too, we shall go about interfering in yours and bring to light, I'm sure, certain things that may be embarrassing. You understand me, Mrs Quinn? You see, I have ways and means of garnering information.'

A gasp came over the phone before it was banged down, and Bill, turning to Fiona, said, 'Have you noticed, Mrs B, my use of words when I'm on the phone, big words, unusual words? Garnering . . . that was a good one, eh? . . .'

'Oh, shut up! I don't feel like laughing, Bill.' She turned from him and hurried into the sitting-room; and when he followed her she said, 'I'm worried, really I am. I . . . I know you like Sammy, and in a way I do too, but he's no companion for Willie. I told you how Willie's letting words slip out as naturally as God bless you.'

'I know, I know, love.' He put his arm about her. 'But in a way I think Sammy's going to learn more from Willie than Willie will learn from him. And ask yourself, now ask yourself' – he brought her round to face him – 'have you it in your heart to tell that little chap not to come back here again and to stop seeing Willie? Now have you?'

Fiona moved her head impatiently; then she said, 'Well, something's got to be done. You've got to have a talk with him.'

'With which one?'

When the phone interrupted their discourse again, Fiona gasped, 'Oh no! I bet she's phoned my mother.'

'Leave it to me.'

'No, Bill.'

'Look' – he pushed her none too gently – 'you leave this to me.'

In the hall he grabbed up the phone. 'Yes? what is it now?'

When the voice came at him, 'Is that Bailey?' Bill held the mouthpiece away from him. He thought he recognised the

voice, but he didn't give himself time to think before he was answering, 'Yes, yes, this is Bailey, William Bailey.'

'Well, this is Charles Kingdom here.'

Oh, good God! He did not actually voice this but said it in protest against himself.

'You still there?'

'Yes, sir. Yes, I'm still here; and forgive me for my abruptness when I picked up the phone, I was . . . well, rather angry with someone.' He allowed his voice to fall to a confidential whisper and said, 'Mother-in-law.'

A slight giggle came over the line; then it rose to a laugh, and the voice came on a long chuckle, 'Mine's dead; but I know what you mean. How are you?'

'Oh, I'm very well, sir. And you? I heard you weren't too good.'

'No, I wasn't; but I'm back home now, under protest. Nobody wants me: here, they all say I should have stayed in hospital, and there, they were glad to get rid of me.' The voice dropped now as he went on, 'Wife's just walked out of the room.' Then resuming his ordinary tone, he went on, 'Like to see you, Bailey. Now, now, don't get big ideas. It's not about the margins, or the big business, but I would just like to see you and have a chat about . . . well, how you're going on. That all right with you?'

'Yes, sir, yes. I would like to very much.'

'How about Saturday afternoon?'

'That would do splendidly, sir.'

'What do you do usually on Saturdays?'

'Oh, well, it's usually a family day, shopping, you know.'

'Well, if it's fine bring them with you.'

'There's four of them, sir.'

'Yes, yes, I think I remember there's four of them. Well, I think the garden's big enough to take four. If I remember rightly there were five hundred at the last garden party here for some damn charity or other. But that was some time ago now when my wife was young and agile.' The voice dropped again: 'She's back in the room,' which made Bill smile when he recognised

that the voice wasn't low enough to miss his wife's ears; and it made him think they must be on very good terms, those two.

'Three o'clock suit you?'

'Yes, sir. Thank you very much. We'll be there at three o'clock and be very pleased to see you.'

'Daffodils are still out. Great sight in the woods. . . . Saturday then?'

'Yes, sir.' He heard the phone click before he put down his own receiver; then he turned and looked at Fiona who was standing a short distance from him and he said, 'Sir Charles Kingdom. Invited to Brookley Manor on Saturday for three o'clock . . . and the gang.'

'No!' She came up to him, her arms about his neck now: 'You've got it?'

'No. Apparently it's not about that. I don't know why he wants to see me but he made it quite plain it wasn't about the contract.'

'Oh.'

'Well, I told you, didn't I, he's not alone in this. There's quite a board. He might have a big say but, after all, he's only one.'

'But a very important one I should think.'

'Yes, yes.' He now walked her towards the sitting-room, saying nothing more until they were seated opposite the fire, when, leaning forward, his elbows on his knees and his hands dropped between them, he said, 'I wonder what he wants to see me about if not about that? It must be something important to ask me over there. He's a queer old card, with a mind like a rapier, for all his age. But you know what he said? He said, "The daffodils are still out. Great sight in the woods."'

'Did he really! The daffodils are out. Great sight in the wood. Sounds so nice. What is Brookley Manor like?'

'Beautiful, not all that big. I told you, I did a job over there, gutting one wing, and making it like another self-contained house. I really think he had it done for his tribe when they descend on him. By what he said he's not very fond of family gatherings, but perhaps that's only a front he puts on.'

Fiona caught hold of his hands now, saying, 'I feel excited already. And oh! won't the children enjoy it. Do you think I should go and tell them? They won't be asleep.'

'Can't see any harm in it. You can use it as a bribe to make them behave.'

'That's an idea.' She pushed herself up quickly and almost ran from the room; and Bill lay back on the couch, his mind again questioning: I wonder what he wants? He hasn't asked me over there just to say hello or to see the bairns. There's something in the wind. Ah well, I'll have to wait till Saturday afternoon, won't I?

It was as if the two words had brought him to the edge of the couch again and he repeated, Saturday afternoon. That's when little Sammy's going to bring Fiona her present. So what are we going to do about that?

Well, he told himself, the only thing to do would be to get Willie on the quiet and tell him to tell Sammy to get here before two o'clock, for if he was to arrive at Brookley at three o'clock, they would have to leave here by a quarter-past two, and if not forewarned about time Mr Samuel Love might arrive just as they were leaving. And what would happen then? Oh, he knew what would happen: Master William would see no reason why his pal could not join the afternoon outing. And that would be just too much for Fiona. So he must see that that emergency did not arise.

It should happen that Bill could do nothing about that particular emergency, for Willie was sick in the night, whether it was from excitement about the proposed visit or something that he had eaten, Fiona didn't know, but she kept him off school on the Friday.

Saturday came and Fiona took the children shopping in the morning while Bill continued to work with figures in the study. But he certainly knew that they had all returned home when Katie dashed into the study, crying, 'I've got a new dress, Dad. It's blue with a flared skirt and a white lace collar.'

'My! My!'

'And Willie's got new pants. He doesn't like them. They're long pants and he wanted short ones like Sammy. And he started to play up in the shop and Mam said she would leave him behind and he said that was all right with him.'

'Don't tell tales!'

Katie turned to Fiona who was now coming into the room and answered her:

'Well, you did. I mean, he did. He's always causing a fuss.'

'And, of course, you don't?'

The voice came from Mark who was behind his mother: 'Blessed Saint Katie of the enlarged mouth.'

'I'll hit you, our Mark.' But as she made a dive for him Bill, who had come round the desk, caught her by the collar of her coat and, swinging her about, he bent over her and said, 'D'you want to come with us this afternoon?'

She wagged her head, turned it slightly to the side, pursed her lips but said nothing.

'That means you do. So behave yourself, miss. Where's Mamie?'

'She's followed Willie upstairs,' said Mark. 'She's bought a dummy for her dolls. How she's going to get it into their mouths I don't know because her dolls are china ones.'

'Did you get anything new?' Bill looked at Mark.

'No, not a thing; I'm the last to be thought of in this house.'

'Poor soul.' Bill pulled a face as Mark grinned at him. Then Fiona, dropping down into the leather chair at the side of the desk, said, 'It would be very nice if somebody made me a cup of tea.'

'I'll do it, Mam.'

As Katie made to dash from the room Mark said pompously, 'There's good in the child yet,' which stopped her in her tracks, whereupon once again Bill had to say, 'Ah-ah. Now, now.'

And to Fiona, 'Tea you said?' And to Katie, 'Tea you would make; so, away woman!'

Then turning to Mark, he added, 'Stop teasing her so much. And I mean that, mind.'

'O.K. But she can't have all her own way, you know.'

'I know that, so does your mother.'

'Am I being told off?'

'Consider yourself so.'

As Mark went out shaking his head, Fiona muttered, 'Did somebody say the other night that this trip might blackmail them into being little angels or something similar? It's the worst Saturday morning that I can remember having with them. You should have heard Willie in that shop. I could have boxed his ears. I nearly did. And Mamie didn't want a small dummy; no, she wanted one of those great big monsters that clowns or drunks delight in sticking in their mouths.'

As Bill laughed, Fiona said, 'This has been a very funny week, in fact a very funny two or three weeks. Do you know, I was just thinking that nothing seems to have gone right since Mr Samuel Love showed himself in the garden; everything's gone topsy-turvy. People don't act somehow as you expect them to. For instance, Nell not phoning us; then coming in yesterday morning as cool as a cucumber and saying, "Oh, what? Yes, yes, he popped the question." And, "Oh, yes, I accepted him." It was like a damp.squib. You say that Bert looked as if he had lost a ten pence piece and found a new sovereign, and he was even singing. And you tell me the fellows were chipping him all day. Well, there was no such merriment here. You know, Bill, I feel that there's something not quite right there.'

'You mean between Nell and Bert?'

'No, next door. I just can't put my finger on it. Nell seems odd. She tried to be her usual self but somehow it seemed difficult for her. . . . Oh, thanks, Katie. That's lovely. And a biscuit too. And two cups!'

'I brought you tea, Dad, because I can never make the coffee properly. I know you don't like tea, but there it is.'

'You're not the only one who can't make coffee properly. You take after your mother. But thanks all the same, pet.'

Ignoring the remark, Fiona looked at Katie and said quietly, 'Go on up and get ready. But see to Mamie, first, will you? Wash her face and hands and put on her pink dress. Then you get ready. And in between times' – she leant forward now and touched her daughter on the cheek – 'say a kind word to Mark. I'm not asking you to apologise, just speak nicely.'

'Well, if I do that, Mam, he'll say, "What you after?"'

'Well, if he says that just you tell him, all you're after is civility.'

'Oh, Mam!' Katie turned away as if in disgust; and Bill said to Fiona, 'You do ask the impossible, don't you: a sister to say to her brother, all I ask is a little civility. Come on, woman, drink that tea up. And then you get upstairs an' all, an' plaster your face an' put your best bib an' tucker on.'

'What about you?'

'Well, from the moment I take the razor in me hand until I knot me tie the whole process takes me ten minutes, not an hour and ten minutes. So get yourself away.'

They were all ready and waiting, although it was only five minutes to two: Katie and Mamie were sitting on the couch; Mark was lounging in an armchair; Willie stood at the window looking down the garden; and Nell, coming into the room, put her hand over her eyes as if cutting out the glare as she said, 'My! My! I must have come into the wrong house or wandered into a BBC studio, the next programme will be fashions for children from five to fifteen,' and turned to Fiona, who was behind her, saying, 'Who's this lot?'

'I don't know. I've never seen them before, at least not like this; and not so quiet.'

Changing her tone now, Nell smiled and said, 'By! but you do all look lovely, smart. What time are you leaving?' Nell had turned to Fiona again.

'Quarter-past two on the dot we are informed; that's when we're all seated and strapped in. The journey takes forty-five

minutes, five minutes of which I am told covers the drive, and it's pretty rough in parts, it'll be like a military exercise.'

'And what are we going for? We haven't been invited to tea.' Willie had turned from the window for a moment.

'You haven't?' Nell showed her surprise.

'No, so Dad says; it's just a visit.'

'That's stingy, I'd say, after a journey like that.'

Nell had her back to the door when she asked, 'Where's your lord and master?' And when the voice came from behind her, saying, 'Her lord and master is here,' she turned and said, 'Oh, another one got up like a dog's dinner.'

Whatever response Bill might have made was checked by a cry from Willie, saying, 'Here's Sammy with your present. Mam, here's Sammy with your present.'

'Oh no. Oh no.' Not a startling response but a kind of whimper from Fiona. 'I'd . . . I'd forgotten,' and she put her hand to her brow, disarranging the veil that was attached to her small hat.

'Well, we've still got fifteen minutes. Don't get in a stew. Let him in, Mark.'

'No! I will.'

'You'll stay where you are, Willie.' Bill's finger was pointing down into the eager face; and Willie stayed where he was. They all stayed where they were and awaited Mark's entry into the room, accompanied by the visitor.

Sammy was carrying an unwieldy brown paper parcel. He was holding it in both hands and tightly pressed against his narrow chest, and it remained there as he looked around the company.

It was Bill who spoke to him first, saying, 'Hello there, Sammy. You've just caught us in time; we are all about to go out visiting.'

'Aye, I can see that, I'm not blind.'

Bill brought his lips tight together for a moment, whether with vexation or amusement couldn't be told. And now Sammy, looking at Willie, said somewhat accusingly, 'I told you I was

comin' on Saturday with the present. I told you to tell her.'

Fiona now forced herself to say, 'Willie hasn't been well, Sammy. I had to keep him in bed yesterday . . . He was sick in the night.'

Sammy made no comment; instead, moving the parcel from his chest, he held it out towards her, saying, 'This's for you.'

'For me?' Fiona made a good pretence of being utterly surprised, and she repeated, 'A present for me? That's . . . that's very kind of you.'

She took the parcel from the outstretched hands, then stood hesitating a moment until the presenter of it said, 'Well, aren't you gona open it?'

Walking to a small table, she pushed a glass dish aside and slowly unfolded the brown paper. Then there, exposed to her surprised gaze and not hers alone, was what had once been a silver-plated teapot. What little silver was left on it was bright; the rest of it was still bright but shining with a dull lustre. It had a beautifully curved spout and an ornamental lid; the handle too was ornamental. The whole could, at one time, have graced a Victorian tea-table; it still retained its beautiful shape except that the spout seemed to be leaning at a slight angle.

'Oh, it's . . . it's very nice, really lovely.' She glanced from the boy to Bill and the rest of the company who were now gathered round the table. Then remembering how Sammy had come into possession of her spoon, she asked him tentatively, 'Did . . . did your father give it to you, or . . . or your gran?'

That was as far as she got before Sammy told her in no polite tones that neither his father nor his granny had given him the teapot. 'No! me da didn't give it me, 'cos we've got nowt like this in the house; nor 'as me granny. I got it from the tip.'

Fiona glanced at Bill as if for help. And he came to her aid, saying, 'You go totting on the tip?'

'Aye. Aye, I do.'

'Which tip is that, Sammy?'

'The quarry where they're fillin' it in. Belmont Road. All the town's muck goes there.'

‘Oh! Yes; yes, that’s a big tip.’

‘Aye, it is. An’ you can get some good things off it an’ all. They bring barrows an’ carts, some with ponies, the ragmen do. Beds ya get, an’ chests of drawers, just with a leg off.’ He was talking to Bill now as to someone who understood these things. ‘Not long ago somebody found a tin box an’ it was full of money. But somebody claimed it. It had been thrown out by mistake, they said. There was a fight over it. Ya get all things. An’ I found that last week.’ He pointed to the teapot. ‘I had to fight for it. Another lad wanted it an’ he was bigger’n me, but I got it. An’ I’ve cleaned it up proper. I washed it inside an’ out. There’s no dirt on it. Ya can look.’

‘Oh, I’m sure there’s no dirt on it, Sammy. And it’s a lovely piece of work.’ Bill picked it up, making sure that he held the spout in place; and turning to Nell, he said, ‘I bet that’s poured some swanky cups of tea out. What d’you say, Nell?’

‘Yes, I bet it has at that.’ Nell looked down on Sammy. ‘It must have come from one of those big houses, the toffs,’ she said.

‘Aye, must ’ave. Don’t see many like that about; china ones with broken spouts, an’ brown ones, heaps of brown ones without lids or ’andles off, but nothin’ like that.’ He turned now to confront Fiona again. ‘D’ya like it, missis?’

‘Yes. Yes, I do, Sammy. I . . . I think it’s splendid. I’ll give it pride of place in the china cabinet. Put it on the top shelf in the china cabinet, Bill, please, will you?’

They all watched Bill gently move some Coalport cups and saucers to one side to make a place for the teapot. And after closing the door he stood back and said, ‘You’re very proud of your Coalport china, Mrs B; well, I’m sure at one time it had that very teapot to match it.’

It was noticeable that not one of the children as yet had spoken, and Bill, looking at Willie, whose face was bright as if with pride, said, ‘It’s good to have a thoughtful friend. What d’you say, Willie?’

Willie looked at Bill but didn’t answer. Then Bill, addressing Katie, said, ‘What d’you think of it, Katie?’

Katie looked at him, glanced at her mother, then, looking at Sammy, she said, 'I think it's very nice. And I think it was very kind of you, Sammy, to give it to my mother. It must have taken a long time to clean it up.'

'Aye, it did' – Sammy nodded back at her – ''cos it was black in parts.'

'I've got a nice teapot. I've got a whole tea-set; it's in my doll's house.'

'Yes, but those are toys.' Willie was almost spitting the words at Mamie now. 'This's a grown-up teapot. Well, what I mean is . . . well. . . .' But he couldn't express what he meant, and so Bill said, 'It's all right, laddie; we know what you mean.' Then looking at his watch, he said, 'Well, we must be off.' And now turning to Sammy, he said: 'As I told you, we've all been invited to visit somebody, so we've got to go now.'

'Well, there's nobody stoppin' ya.' The aggressiveness was back in the tone, the defence was up again, and as the small figure turned for the door Bill grabbed at his arm, saying, 'Hold your hand a minute and let me finish. You know, you've got as big a mouth as I have.'

This brought a titter from the children.

'You know what?' Bill was bending down looking into the stiff face. 'You'll grow up to be the same as me. Now you wouldn't like that, would you?'

'Don't know, might. You're all right in parts.'

Bill straightened his back, closed his eyes and turned his head away for a moment; then looking down at the boy again, he said, 'Well, the part that's all right is asking you if you'd like to come to tea the morrow?'

The boy didn't answer, but turned and looked at Fiona, his piercing eyes asking a question. And she nodded quickly at him, saying, 'Yes, that would be nice if you came to tea tomorrow.'

'Thanks, missis.'

'And thank you, Sammy, thank you very much for your present. I'll never forget that you gave me it, and I'll always take care of it.'

Sammy's face worked: it seemed that all the small muscles were vying with each other. His eyes blinked, his nose twitched, his lips moved from side to side, and his clearly marked eyebrows were pushed up as if trying to escape from his hair; then he turned from the company and marched through the hall. But just as he reached the door Nell's voice checked him, saying, 'Hold your hand a minute! Look, I'm on me own, at least I am till four o'clock when I have an appointment.' She sniffed now and tried not to glance in Fiona's direction. 'And there's one thing this lot who are going out don't know yet, and that is if they're going to be invited to tea; but I can tell you, you are.'

'Who with?' He glanced sidelong up at her.

'Me of course, next door. That's if you want to come. I've just made a cream sponge and it'll go begging, as this lot don't want it.'

There was a murmur from Katie, which was hushed by Bill's saying, 'Well, that's settled that. See you the morrow, young Sammy, eh?'

'Aye, all right. What time?'

Bill pursed his lips; then addressing Willie, he said, 'What time?'

Willie did not return Bill's look but, glancing at his friend, he said, 'Any time you like.' And on this he marched past Sammy and out of the front door, and the rest followed him, with the exception of Fiona who, turning to Nell, said quietly, 'Thanks, Nell.'

'You're welcome, Mrs B.'

'Will you lock up for me?'

'Yes. Go on, I'll see to everything. And in case you're not invited to tea, I'll bring what's left of the cream sponge round, that's if we leave any.' She was now looking down on Sammy. 'On second thoughts we won't leave any, will we? Will we, Sammy? We'll stuff our guts, eh?'

The small boy smiled up at the woman: she was speaking his language and he said, 'Aye. Aye, we'll stuff our guts.'

After Fiona clicked her tongue and said, 'I'll have a word with

you, Mrs Paget, when I return,' the boy stood watching her walk towards the car before, looking up at Nell, he said, 'That means you'll get it in the neck for sayin' guts.'

Nell put her arm around the small shoulders and pressed him to her side, and it was standing thus that the occupants of the car saw them as they drove out of the gate. And when Katie remarked, 'Look! Nell's hugging him,' Fiona wondered why the sight should create in her a guilty feeling; it was as if she had missed an opportunity of some sort.

They had been on the journey only two minutes or so when Katie, bending forward, tapped her mother on the shoulder, saying, 'Are you going to keep that teapot in the china cabinet, Mam?'

'Well . . . for a time, yes.'

'The spout's broken, did you notice?'

'Yes, she noticed, Katie.' Bill's voice was not his usual bawl, but there was a definite note in it that pressed Katie back into the seat as he went on, 'But spouts can be mended, and the whole can be replated and I'm going to see to it that it's done.' He did not add, 'And it'll probably cost twice as much as a new one would.'

'I know that tip, Dad, where he got it from,' said Mark.

'How *d'you* know it?' Bill half turned in his seat; then brought his gaze quickly back onto the road again. 'It's yon side of Bog's End; you've never been that way.'

'Oh yes, I have. Roland's father drove us round that way in the car.'

'Why?'

'Well, he said that Roland should know how . . . well, everybody should know how the other half lives. He has patients up that end.'

'I thought he worked in the hospital?'

'He does at times. He operates there. But he also sees people outside.'

'Private?'

'Roland says, some and some.'

'He sounds a man after me own heart.'

'It's an awful part, Dad: dreadful houses and the gangs rampage at night, Roland said.'

'Then you should thank your lucky stars you don't live there, Mark.'

'I wouldn't mind living where Sammy lives.'

This insertion into the conversation came naturally from Willie. And it was Fiona who turned round and said, 'Oh, you wouldn't? But then your wish is easily satisfied: you can pack your bag any time you like and go round there and live with him. Can't he, Mr B?'

'Well, I suppose so, if he wants to so badly. He could go an' try it for a time, anyway. It's not a bad idea.' He glanced at her; but Fiona, looking straight ahead, muttered, 'You know I was only joking.'

'What did you say, Mrs B?'

'I was merely talking to myself.'

'You know,' said Bill now, 'I don't think this is going to be a happy visit at all. The lady of the house takes them out and buys them things and nobody is satisfied; then some kind little fellow scrapes on a tip till he finds a present for the lady of the house, spends hours cleaning it, presents to her, only for it to be criticised from all quarters.'

'I'm not criticising it. I never criticised it. I think it was a very, very kind gesture.'

'I'm glad to hear it, Mrs B. But I haven't heard much approval from the rest of the family. The only one to my mind who seemed to have a real grip of the situation was Nell. She's another one who wants sorting out, but, you'll have your work cut out there. Whatever's happened to make Nell behave as she's doing she'll sort out herself; and mind, you'll not get to know what it is until she's ready. She's kept mum before, remember. Anyway' – his voice rose – 'let's forget about everything else but that we're going out for an afternoon's jaunt and have been invited to meet Sir Charles Kingdom. And let me tell you lot back there, it is an honour you are about to partake

in, for, as I sum up that gentleman, he doesn't scatter his invitations about. What d'you say to that, Mrs B. Am I right or am I wrong?'

'What I say, Mr B, is please keep your mind on the road else you'll still be bawling your head off when you drive us all under that bus in front.'

At the sound of explosive laughter from the back seat the atmosphere changed. . . .

From the moment the car left the long winding drive and swept round the large lawn towards the front of the house the children seemed to be struck dumb, even Mamie stopped her chattering. Not a word was spoken as they mounted the eight shallow steps to the stone balcony that fronted the house.

When Bill pulled the iron bell pull to the side of the black oak double door, Fiona had hardly time to cast a warning glance around them before the door opened and a smiling middle-aged woman dressed in a black dress and a small white apron said, 'Good-afternoon,' as she pulled wide one half of the door. And not one of them had hardly time to take in the huge hall with the stags' heads sticking out of the wall at each side of the broad staircase before a large woman came hurrying towards them and, holding out her hand, said, 'Good-afternoon, Mrs Bailey.' Then, 'Good-afternoon, Mr Bailey.'

These greetings exchanged, she then looked at the children and said, 'What a healthy looking quartet. Will you come this way? He's waiting for you, fuming as usual. You won't have to mind the smoke.'

Fiona, holding Mamie by the hand, followed their hostess, the other three children followed their mother in single file, and Bill brought up the rear. Then they were in a long room that seemed packed with furniture of all kinds, but mostly easy chairs and couches with little tables dotted here and there.

For a moment Fiona could imagine she was back in her own home as Lady Kingdom called out, and in no small voice, 'For goodness sake! Charlie, put out that cigar. Can't you leave them alone for five minutes? Here are your friends.' And before her

husband could make any response, she turned towards the company, saying, 'Sit down; make yourself at home. But you, Mr Bailey, better sit near his nibs because he'll want to chatter. Have you had a nice journey?' She was looking at Fiona.

'Yes, very pleasant, thank you.'

'You are much younger than I expected. From my husband's description I thought you must be in your forties, whereas you look as if you've just hit your twenties.'

The end of the compliment laid some salve on Sir Charles's idea of her age, and, looking up at the big hearty red-cheeked woman, she was tactful enough to say, 'I think Sir Charles was nearer the mark.'

'Nonsense. Nonsense. And now tell me your names.'

She addressed Mark first, and he, rising straight to his feet, said, 'I am Mark, Lady Kingdom.'

'Mark. That's a very nice name.' She inclined her head towards him. And now he took it upon himself to introduce the others by saying, 'This is Katie, my sister, and my brother William, and my adopted sister Mamie.'

'Katie, William, and Mamie, all nice names. I have a daughter called Katie.' She was bending over Katie now, but for once Katie had nothing to say. Yet, if she had spoken her thoughts she would have answered this lady, 'One day I'll have a house like yours, but I won't have so much furniture in the room. This is comfortable but cluttered.'

'What about tea?'

The intrusion caused Lady Kingdom to turn to her husband: 'All in good time,' she said. 'I thought you'd like a chatter first. And for goodness sake put that cigar out, will you! Every one isn't impregnated with smoke like I am. Some people can't stand it. You know what happened when Irene came, she was sick.' She turned now to Fiona, saying, 'Do you like houses? I know your husband builds them, but do you like looking over houses?'

'Yes, I do indeed, especially houses like this.'

'Well, come along then and leave them to have their chatter before we have a cup of tea. I won't say I'll give you a guided

tour but I'll show you the main rooms, and then Jessie can take the children around the rest.'

Bill watched his squad, as he thought of them, rise quickly from their chairs, all their faces looking bright with expectancy, and he knew it wouldn't be long before their tongues were loosened.

The door closed, he now turned and looked at the old man propped up in a long basket-chair, with, to his side, a table on which stood a box of cigars and an outsize ash-tray.

'You don't smoke, Bailey?'

'No, sir.'

'Drink?'

'Oh yes, sir; I like a drink.'

'Well, what's your poison?'

'Whisky as a rule, and neat.'

'Like one now?' He pointed across the room. 'There's a bottle in that cabinet there.'

'If you don't mind, sir, I won't at the moment. I try not to when I'm drivin' and especially when I've got five passengers.'

'Well, yes, you're right. I see your point. There'll be tea in shortly. Ah now. Well' – he sighed – 'I'd better get down to the reason I asked you here today. First of all, mind, I wish it was to say that you've got the contract, I do really, yes I do, but that remains to be seen. I never thought there'd be so many firms interested in it; but of course it's a concern that will take some long time. It'll put somebody on their feet. But, it's about the trouble you've been having.'

'Trouble?'

'Yes, trouble with your men, things happening.' Bill's lower jaw fell slightly. 'You . . . you've heard about that?'

'Oh yes, yes.' The old man grinned wickedly. 'I have my ear to the ground. I can hear a horse galloping five miles away, or words to that effect. You know what I mean?'

'Not really, sir. Why should you have come to know what's been happenin' in the yard to my men?'

'Because things like that get about, Bailey. You know as well

as I do, one firm can't blink but the other one hears about it. And I was very sorry to hear when one of your men was hurt, attacked, mugged they call it now, don't they? And then a car was stolen; and another one had his place broken in to. And it could go on if it's allowed to go on.'

'You know who's behind this, sir?'

The old man reached forward, took a fresh cigar from the box, tore off the band, took up something that looked like a pair of pliers, used it to nip at the end of the cigar, then lit it, before he replied, 'Yes; and it wasn't Brown as you imagined, although it's the kind of thing that I wouldn't put past him if he had enough money to pay the culprits.'

Bill had moved to the end of his chair and, leaning forward, he said, 'It's someone that's in for the contract, then?'

'No, no. They wouldn't do things like that. But on the other hand I don't know. . . . No; not in this case, no. You're a sharp fellow, you know, Bailey, the kind of fellow who would say to himself, there's no flies on me; yet, you don't seem to have an inkling who's at you?'

'No, I don't, sir. Except for Brown, I don't know of anyone else who would have it in for me.'

'Don't you? Have you heard these words: Hell hath no fury like a woman scorned?'

Bill's jaw actually did drop now. His mouth went into a gape, his cheeks pushed up, his eyes narrowed, his mouth even went into a wider gape before he said, '*Never!* Not her?'

'Yes, her. You should never say to a woman that you wouldn't touch her with a barge-pole, no matter what you might think of her. That's what you said to her, didn't you? Whatever happened in your workmen's hut that day, you insulted her, you made her feel small, and that was something she had never been made to feel in her life. She admitted so much to me. She had offered you a position in London and you took it that she was offering herself.'

'*She was.* Believe me, sir, she was.'

'Oh, yes, yes, I believe you. But on the other hand it takes a

lot to make a woman like Eva Brown cry. I had never seen her cry, not even after she had let herself down with Brown and had to allow herself to marry him. She didn't cry unless it was in the privacy of the night. But I happened to come across her not less than half an hour after she had left you that morning. And she was still white-hot with rage. You know, you're not a very tactful man, Bailey. All right, you didn't want her, you preferred your wife, but you could have let her down gently.'

Bill gulped heavily before he managed to say, 'Sir, you weren't there, you don't know what happened. She laid herself open to me. I've had experience of a great many women in my time, I must admit, but not one so brazen as she was. And then I asked her what about Brown, and she said she was divorcing him. And next I asked her if all the businesses she wanted me to manage were in her name and she said, yes every one of them; Brown had just been a sort of manager. She inferred she had let him play the big man but she held the strings and wore the trousers. And then the final note was when she said that if he were to sue her he would get less than she was going to give him in redundancy pay. That was the word, redundancy pay. No matter what the man was, and I can say now, I hate his guts, always have done, but at that moment I was sorry for him and for the life he'd had to lead with a woman like her, a calculating cold fish: she hadn't taken into consideration my wife or the children; she had been used to getting her own way, stepping on people. It was then I told her that if she was the last woman on earth I wouldn't touch her with a barge-pole. It's a well-worn saying that, common if you like, but I meant every word of it. And I still do; I don't take back anything I said that morning, tact or no tact.'

The old man blew out three large puffs of smoke before he said, 'Well, putting it like that shows a different complexion, at least from your side. But I know what kind of a life she's had to lead and it hasn't been easy. Power's been her only pleasure. But power's an empty love and a cold bed. Come to think of it, though, I'm not without blame, at least where your men are

concerned, because I can recall telling her that you had a gang of the best men throughout the area which showed itself in the work they had turned out, especially those houses above Brampton Hill. And she then likely saw one way of getting at you was to disrupt your gang. She's a ruthless woman, I admit. Oh yes, she's ruthless. But I know one thing, she disliked Brown, in fact she might have hated him, but not with the fervour that she hates you, to go to the length of engaging scoundrels to do dirty work, as she has. Anyway, I sent her a wire and told her that it had to stop; and then wrote to her and told her I was aware of her little game. But apparently the letter didn't reach her. I understand she's gone abroad on holiday.'

'But what makes you so sure she's behind this, sir?'

'Oh, a hunch, and the way she told me if it was the last thing she ever did she would ruin you one way or another, for she meant it. She also said that if I voted for you to get this contract she'd never speak to me again. And she meant that too.'

'But, sir' – Bill had now risen to his feet – 'I'm not going to let this go on; I'm going to the police.'

'What can you prove? Nothing until they catch the fellows.'

'I can say who's behind them.'

'You've only my word for it, Bailey. And sit down, sit down, you look ferocious standing there. Do something for me: put on another nightwatchman just for the time being. If you do I'll pay his wages, so don't worry about that. You see, there's two or more of these other blokes and your single man and a dog won't be a match for them because they're dirty players. And another thing, if they should cause any more damage, I'll make it right.'

When Bill resumed his seat he sat quiet for a moment; but he certainly wasn't quiet inside, he was raging. He wanted to strike out at something or someone. That bitch of a woman. Never would he have imagined that she would go to such lengths. It was criminal. She was worse than any gangster. And this he voiced now, saying, 'It's criminal. She's worse than any gangster. Look, sir, as much as I admire you, I can't promise

to keep my tongue quiet if I can nab those fellows. Anyway, like all thugs of that type, they'll squawk once they're caught.'

'Well, until they are, Bailey, let's say that any damage they do to your works or your men's property will be covered . . . I'll see to it.'

'Money won't buy a life, sir, and they nearly did for Barney McGuire. He's a man of fifty, and tough. And they almost got Dave McRae. What about if they kill somebody, sir?'

'Oh, they won't go that far; they'd be afraid of the consequences.'

'Do you know who they are, sir?'

'No, I don't, Bailey; and if I did, I'm afraid the frame of mind you're in I wouldn't tell you, because that would involve Eva straightaway. And once I get in touch with her she'll stop this. I'll see to it.'

Bill got abruptly to his feet again, and he walked the length of the long rug towards the big open fireplace; and there he stood for a moment in silence.

When he turned, he looked at the old man and said, 'I can't believe it, sir; I can't take it in. That some firm had it in for me through competition; yes; yes, that would be quite feasible; but that she would take it on herself to get back at me like this . . . well, as I said, I just can't believe it.'

'You said a moment ago you'd had quite a few dealings with women in your life, and I can believe that. Well then, you should have learned that they are the more dangerous of the species. Sit down. Sit down. You get on my nerves popping up and down. And I'll tell you something about women, something that happened in this very house. My great-grandmother was the daughter of a farmer, what you'd call in those days a gentleman farmer. She had her eye on this house and all that was in it, I was told, and she set her cap at my great-grandfather. Now he was a lad of many tastes and his tastes ranged from the kitchen, through various farm barns, to the wife of his best friend. Now, my great-grandmother must have known all about this before she took him, but when she found him in one of the

attics with the housemaid she went almost berserk. And later, when the girl was known to be pregnant, she made her marry, at least she paid this man, a horse dealer, to marry her. And this particular fellow was known to be cruel, even to the dog he was supposed to care for. He was never seen without a whip in his hand and he whipped his bride from the day he married her. It was said he was ordered to by my great-grandmother. And when my great-grandfather discovered what had happened . . . he really wasn't a man who bothered with anybody's business but his own, but he had the decency to take the girl away before she was flailed to death. He installed her in a cottage with a woman to look after her. It was only half a mile from the house – the foundations can still be seen, overgrown with weeds but they can still be seen – but the day after the child was born the cottage was burnt down and the mother and the child and the woman who was looking after her were burnt with it. It was rumoured that the window had been nailed up and so had the door. The horse dealer disappeared. It was also rumoured that my great-grandmother had paid him to do the deed. Anyway, from that time my great-grandfather never slept with his wife; but he made hay all round the countryside and she could do nothing about it. It was said, too, that he was heard to say while laughing at her, "You can't go round burning all the barns down, Cicely." It became a catch-phrase I understand: "You can't go round burning all the barns, Cicely." Women, Bailey, are the very devil. I've been lucky. Oh yes, I've been lucky: Bertha is a good woman; she's been a great helpmate and companion. But, you know, we've bred one hell-cat of a daughter. She could be great-grandmother Cicely over again.' He laughed now and his lower set of false teeth wobbled in his mouth. Then he said, 'You know people think nothing happens in the country. Let me tell you, the country makes the patterns for the towns. And, you know, it isn't the day or yesterday that I've thought Eva Brown could be the reincarnation of great-grandmother Cicely. Ah, here they come.'

The door opened and the children actually ran up the room,

only to come to a stop at a respectful distance from the man in the basket-chair. But he cried to them, 'Come here! Come here! Well, what do you think of this little cottage?'

They all laughed, and it was Katie who said, 'It's beautiful, lovely.'

'Would you like to live in a place like this?'

Katie glanced first at her mother then at Bill, and her answer was diplomatic: 'When I grow up,' she said.

'Clever girl, clever girl. You like your own home?'

'It's a beautiful house, sir.' The old man looked at Mark and asked now, 'What are you going to be, career-wise?'

'Well, sir, I would like to do physics; and I'm rather good at maths, you see; yet on the other hand I have a fancy for being a doctor, so I might have to take biology, I'm told. I haven't fully made up my mind yet. It all depends on how I do in the exam.'

'Well, it's good to hear that somebody knows what road their life's going to take. Either one of those sounds good. And you, young lady, what are you going to be?'

'An actress.'

There was a quick exchange of glances between Bill and Fiona because it was the first they had heard of it.

'An actress? My! My! Stage or television?'

Katie hesitated just a moment before she said, 'I'll be able to do both.'

The old man put his head back and let out a wheezy laugh, which caused his wife to wag her finger at him and say, 'There you are! You're laughing now; you didn't laugh when Annabella made that statement some years ago, did you?'

'A lot of water's gone under the social bridge since then, woman. Ah, here's Jessie with the tea.'

At this they all turned and looked towards the door where a maid was pushing in a large two-tier tea-trolley, the top laden with tea things, the bottom shelf holding plates of scones, sandwiches, and a fruit loaf.

'By! you've taken your time, Jessie; my mouth's as dry as the desert.'

'That's caused by cigar smoke, sir.'

'Now, don't you start.'

Fiona watched a mingling of glances between the mistress and the maid; then Lady Kingdom, now addressing Mark, said, 'Take the things off that small table there, will you, dear, and bring it here? This room's full of tables, and for what? Just to hold stupid cups and trophies. And who notices them?'

'I do. It's all I've left in life.'

'Poor soul. Poor soul.'

Again there was an exchange of glances, this time among the children. They were amused; this sounded just like home.

When Mark had duly brought the table to her, Lady Kingdom set it in front of Fiona, saying now, 'Do help yourself, please; I've long since given up being polite and handing plates around. You see, when the family descends upon us it's a free for all. And so I generally let them get on with it. I can assure you of one thing, the sandwiches will be very nice: they are fresh cucumber, pre-season, brought forward in the greenhouses. I said to a certain person' – she now closed her eyes and nodded her large head – 'that we should start a market garden, but no. Has everyone got a cup of tea? Well then, it's a free for all. Move along, dear; I'm going to sit in between you.'

Willie hitched himself along to the end of the couch, and when the big woman as he thought of her sat down on the big cushions beside him he bounced slightly. Then, with some surprise he watched the big woman bite into a scone, taking half of it in one mouthful.

He looked at the tea trolley. On it, there was a large silver tray and on the tray was a silver teapot and a matching sugar basin and milk jug, besides a small tea strainer on a stand.

'How old are you?'

When Willie didn't answer, Lady Kingdom followed his gaze and said, 'Would you like another cup of tea?'

'No, thank you. It's the teapot.' he pointed.

'The teapot, you like it?'

'Ah-ha; I mean yes. It's just like the one my friend Sammy brought my mother today.'

'It isn't!' The strong denial came from the other end of the couch and brought all eyes on Katie. 'That's a beautiful teapot, the other one's broken. He . . . he got it off the tip.'

It was evident that both Katie and Willie had forgotten just where they were for the moment because Willie, bending across Lady Kingdom's knee, hissed, 'I know where he got it, but it's still a lovely. . . .'

'*Willie! Katie!*' Bill's voice brought them both back to where they were. 'Apologise to Lady Kingdom.'

'Oh, no! No! No!' Lady Kingdom was laughing now, as was Sir Charles, and they, looking at each other, said, 'It could be Rachel's lot, couldn't it?'

'Yes, to a tee, to a tee.'

'Well, what about this teapot?' Sir Charles was looking at Willie now. 'You say, at least your sister says, he got it from a tip. What do you mean he got it from a tip? Somebody tip him off to buy it?'

Willie hung his head for a moment; then, jerking his chin upward, he stared straight at the old fellow in the funny basket chair and said, 'No, sir; he hasn't got any money to buy silver teapots, he's very poor. He's from Bog's End. But they're filling in the quarry in Belmont Road.'

'Oh, that tip! where they're filling in Murphy's quarry. And so your friend found a silver teapot there?'

'Yes, sir. And he cleaned it up inside and out and brought it to my mother for a present.' He glanced at his mother's very red face.

'Well, to my mind, that seems very kind of him. Is he a school-mate of yours?'

'Well' – Willie hesitated – 'he doesn't go to the same school. I go to St Oswald's, it's a private school, but Sammy goes to the convent school, he's taught by nuns but he doesn't like them.'

'He doesn't like the nuns? Why now, why? I thought nuns were all holy ladies.'

It was evident in the glint in Sir Charles's eyes that he was enjoying this conversation. He had even brought himself more upright in the chair and had stopped puffing at his cigar. 'Why doesn't he like the nuns?'

'Well, sir, Sammy says they've all got hosepipe hands.'

'What hands?'

'Hosepipe hands, sir.' Willie had made his voice loud and clear as if he was talking to somebody hard of hearing.

'Hosepipe hands? Nuns with hosepipe hands? What does he mean by that?'

'I suppose it's because when they whack him across the ear it's as if he was being hit by a piece of hosepipe. His dad went for one of the nuns . . . put the wind up her. . . .'

Of a sudden Sir Charles had a fit of coughing and at the same time his wife seemed to be wriggling in her seat. Willie did not look towards either his mother or Bill, he kept his gaze directed to the funny old fellow. He liked him. He thought, somehow, Sammy would like him, and he would like Sammy an' all.

The bout of coughing over, Sir Charles wiped the spittle from his lips with a napkin; then, looking at Willie again, he said, 'He sounds a very interesting chap, this friend of yours. How did you meet him if you go to different schools?'

'Our school played them at football, sir.'

'Do you like football? Are you a good footballer?'

'Not very.'

'What about him, your friend?'

'He's not very good either, sir. He was pushed off the field that day.'

'What for?'

'I don't quite know, misbehaviour I suppose.'

'You mean fouling?'

'Could be, sir.'

'So you and he are pals?'

'Yes, sir.'

Sir Charles now looked at Bill and Fiona and noting the

consternation on Fiona's countenance, he said, 'With your parents' approval?'

Lady Kingdom had also noticed the look on Fiona's face and, now pulling herself with some effort from the deep cushion on the couch, she addressed her husband, saying, 'Mind your own business, Charlie Kingdom. You should know by now that children pick their own friends, and they're often better at it than parents. Now, do you want anything more to eat?'

'No, ma'am, I don't.' And he turned to one side so he could once again see Willie, and in a loud whisper he said, 'Do you get bullied like this?' And Willie, smiling back at him, said, 'Yes, sir.'

Sir Charles's voice changing, he looked up at his wife and said quietly, 'Bring me the children's box will you, dear?' And she turned from him and went to a cabinet at the far end of the room and returned under the watchful eyes of the company and placed a box on her husband's knees.

'Have you had enough to eat?' He looked from one to the other of the children. And when they all spoke at once, saying, 'Yes, thank you,' he said, 'Come here, then.' And when they stood in a line at the side of his chair, he opened the box and said, 'This was my father's children's box and each week he doled us out a certain amount according to our age. I was the second in line and I got ninepence. My brother, the eldest who is now dead, he got a shilling. The baby got a penny. There were seven of us altogether. So I propose to do the same with you as I do with my grandchildren. You Mark, are the eldest. Well, here you are.' He picked out a pound coin from the box and handed it to Mark, who said with evident gratitude, 'Oh, thank you, sir. Thank you very much indeed.'

'Now you, Katie. Well, I think it will have to be fifty pence for you.'

'Thank you, sir. Oh, thank you.'

'And Willie. Well, what's half of fifty, Willie?'

'Twenty-five pence, sir.'

'Well, let me see.' He now counted out twenty-five pence and handed it to him.

'Thank you, sir.'

'And now the little one. Maisie you say her name is?'

'No; Mamie, sir.'

'Oh . . . Mamie. Well, Mamie, ten pence is your allotment.'

'I have a money box, a piggy bank.'

'Have you? And are you going to put that in?'

'Well, some of it.'

'Say thank you, Mamie.' Fiona was standing behind the child now, and she said, 'I have, Mammy B.'

'No, you haven't.'

'Oh well. Thank you, Mr . . . sir.'

'You're welcome, Mamie.'

'I suppose you'll be making for home now?'

It wasn't a note of dismissal but a note of enquiry and Fiona answered, 'Yes, Sir Charles, straight home. We wouldn't want to spoil the memory of this visit with anything else.'

'Nicely put. Nicely put. Well, it's been my pleasure too.' He now shook hands with the childen one after the other. And they all said again, 'Thank you, sir.' And then they turned to Lady Kingdom, and as they thanked her she patted their heads; at least she patted three, with Mark she did him the courtesy of shaking his hand.

It was as they were all trooping out Sir Charles's voice called, 'Willie!'

Willie turned quickly and looked back up the room to see the funny old man leaning forward in his chair, saying, 'The next time you come to visit us, bring your friend from the tip. Will you?'

Willie's smile spread from ear to ear. '*Yes, sir! Yes, sir!* I'll tell him.'

Lady Kingdom bade them a warm farewell at the front door and said that they must come again.

The car had hardly started to move before Willie exclaimed loudly, 'Did you hear what he said?'

Before he could continue, however, Fiona said, 'Yes, I heard what Sir Charles said, but he was joking.'

'He wasn't, Mam. He meant it.'

'Yes, he might have meant it, but merely to be able to laugh at Sammy.'

'Oh, no, Fiona.' Bill cast her a hard look now. 'He'd laugh with the lad but not at him. He's not that kind of a man.'

'Dad's right.'

'Be quiet! Willie.'

'Oh, Mam' – there were tears in the boy's voice now – 'Don't spoil the afternoon.'

Fiona turned round now and angrily retorted, 'If the afternoon was to be spoilt, Willie, it was you who contributed mainly towards it. You had no right to bring up the matter of the teapot.'

'Enough! Enough! It was a natural thing for him to do.'

'Oh, Bill.' She turned and stared out of the window, thinking, as she had done once before, there had been no peace in the house since that boy had entered it. She would have to do something. But what? She couldn't think at the moment. And then the perpetrator of her irritation himself swept it away from her when his hand came on her shoulder and his voice in her ear muttered, 'I'm sorry, Mam. I really am. I didn't mean to spoil anything. It's been a lovely time.'

It was some seconds before she could turn her face round to him and say, 'I know you didn't, dear. It's all right. And it was a lovely time, wasn't it?' Then she forced herself to go a step further and make them all laugh by saying, 'And isn't it wonderful we're going to have an actress in the family.'

When the laughter subsided, Bill said, 'Many a true word spoken in a joke, eh Katie?'

'Yes, Dad. I'll surprise them all one day. And when I'm picked for the Royal Variety Show. . . .'

'Oh lord! she's going to be a comedian.'

'No, I'm not, our Mark. And anyway, you've got it wrong, a woman can't be a comedian, it's comedienne.'

'There you are. And she's right, too; what's wrong with being

a comedienne? Look at Penelope Keith in *To The Manor Born*; she's marvellous.'

'I like Olive and Popeye,' put in Mamie.

Again there was general laughter; then out of the blue Willie enquired, 'Why did we go there this afternoon, Dad? What did Sir Kingdom want?'

'Oh, only to talk about a bit of business.'

'You're going to get the big estate job?'

This was from Mark, and Bill answered, 'No, no; that isn't settled yet. It was just a bit of other business.' . . .

From Bill's tone and the look on his face, Fiona couldn't wait until they got home to know what this other business was. But it wasn't until the children had changed their clothes and got through another more substantial meal and were now settled round the television that she managed to be alone with him in the study. And she opened by saying, 'Well, what was it all about?'

He didn't answer immediately, but when he did what he said surprised her: 'I'm sick in my stomach,' he said.

'Why? What's made you like that?'

'What Sir Charles told me with regard to who's got it in for me.'

'He knows?'

'Yes. Oh, yes, he knows.'

'Well, tell me. Who is it? One of those in for the contract?'

'I wish it was; I wouldn't feel so bad. No.' He paused, then looking into her face he said quietly, 'Mrs Brown, that was.'

'What d'you mean, Mrs Brown that was?'

'Brown's wife.'

'She? But . . . but why would she want to cause havoc in your business?'

'Well, isn't it evident? She's out to break me in one way or another.'

'And Sir Charles knows?'

'Yes. Yes, he knows.'

'But does he know the reason why? Or do you know the reason why?'

'Yes, of course I do, my dear. Don't you remember? Just before that time you went into hospital she came to the office and held out high prospects if I'd go to London and work for her, but in more ways than one.'

Fiona screwed up her face. Yes, she remembered something about it now; but she had been in such a state, thinking she had cancer, and, too, Bill had made fun of the incident. Her voice was a mutter now and held some incredulity: 'You mean, because of that she would go to the length of . . . well, engaging men . . . thugs? She must have.'

'Yes; yes, she must have.'

'But . . . but aren't you upset? Surely, if she's gone so far she'll stop at nothing.'

'She'll stop all right, or, as I've told him, I go to the police. And yet, as he pointed out, I've no proof, and I won't have until I catch those buggers. All I hope is I'm not alone when I do come up with them because I'll want to do for them meself.'

'What is he going to do about it? Has he any influence with her?'

'Well, quite a lot I would have said at one time, but apparently not enough. She's out of the country at the moment but she's due back soon. He sent her a wire and a letter, so he tells me, and he's also offered to pay for any damage she does. But as I said, he can't pay for a life. And if it had been Harry Newton that was set upon instead of Barney she would have had a corpse at her door because Harry's had one slight heart attack already. Barney's the oldest of the lot, but he's got a constitution like a horse, and so it's just as well.'

Fiona turned away from him, her hands gripping each other as she said, 'She's a dreadful woman, to go to those lengths all because you rebuked her.'

'Aye. Well, you can imagine just how I rebuked her, can't you? Because, believe it or not, I was really sorry for Brown at the time and told her so. I also used the term, barge-pole.'

'You mean you said you wouldn't touch her with a barge-pole?'

'Just that.'

'Oh! Bill.'

'Now don't worry. Don't worry.'

'That's a stupid thing to say, don't worry. And you're worrying. I knew something had happened as soon as I got back into that room; you looked as if you'd had a shock.'

'Well, you're right there, I did have a shock. And you've just got a shock, haven't you? But there's one thing I'll say to you: I know you talk to Mark as one adult to another, but don't give him any hint of this. He'll probe to know what business it was, not out of mere curiosity, I grant you, but just to know what's going on. I've always tried to make him feel important and in charge of the others; but he's as sensitive as a woman in some ways. So, I'm telling you, don't let on. Think up anything but the truth.'

She went to him now and put her arms around his neck and, looking into his eyes, she said, 'If you had still been the middle-of-the-road man when she put her proposal to you, would you have accepted?'

'No; knowing then the set-up between her and Brown, no.'

'But if you hadn't known about the set-up?'

One corner of Bill's mouth took on a quirk and he put his head back as if considering; then, looking at her again, he said, 'I might have, being a middle-of-the-road man and havin' an offer like that made to me by an attractive woman, because, say what you like, she was attractive.'

Her hands snapped from around his neck and she pushed him with both of them on the chest, saying, 'I ask myself at times why I bother with you! You can lie like a trooper about other things, why can't you lie to me?'

'Because, love, you wouldn't want me to. Aw, lass' – he pulled her towards him – 'don't take the pet. 'Tisn't you.'

'Then why can't you be tactful?'

'It wouldn't be me. I've always been honest with you. Anyway,

how many times have I told you it was from the minute I saw you in that paper shop that I knew I'd have you, and not just as a landlady either. But I had to work me way in, hadn't I? By! that was hard. Come on, lass, smile. I've got enough on me plate without worrying about our love life.'

'Oh, Bill, you're incorrigible.'

'I like that word, I must remember it. I'm collecting words, you know. I hope you've noticed. . . . Oh! there's the phone. You know, that phone never seems to stop ringing. What time is it? Ten minutes to seven.'

Bill was making for the door when he turned, saying, 'Oh, someone's answering it. That's likely Mark.'

A moment later Mark pushed his head round the study door, saying, 'It's Nell, Mam.'

'Nell?'

Fiona went quickly past them now. She picked up the phone, and Nell must have realised this, for her voice came to her saying, 'I knew you had all come back. Are you going out again?'

'No, no, Nell. Why?'

'May I come round for a moment?'

'I wish you wouldn't be so silly, woman, may you come round for a moment! Whatever it is, get yourself round; and don't ever ask again.'

She put down the phone and turned to Bill who had come into the hall and said, 'It's Nell. She wants to come round for a moment.'

'She's daft, that woman. Why on earth does she have to phone?'

'It's all because of you. I told you; she hates to disturb your slumber. Anyway, apparently she wants to have a talk, and I'm glad because she's been acting very odd, at least she has for someone newly engaged, so will you keep them out of the kitchen?'

'Leave it to me.'

Fiona was only in the kitchen a minute or so when the back

door opened and Nell came in. She was dressed for out and looked very smart, and Fiona, making the obvious remark, said, 'You're going out?' and so she got the obvious answer: 'Yes, yes, I'm meeting Bert at half-past seven. I was round at his place this afternoon, but now we're going out to dinner.'

'Nice. I'm glad. Sit down.'

They both sat down, but when Nell didn't speak and bit on her thumb nail, Fiona said, 'Come on, come on. Unload.' Then reaching across, she gripped Nell's hand, saying, 'What is it, dear? Oh, don't cry; it'll make a mess of your make-up. What is it?'

'You never know people, do you?'

'No, I suppose that's true.'

'I've lived with Mam and Dad since . . . well, since we moved next door, and before that I was always dropping in, seeing to things for them. Well, I thought they knew how Bert felt about me and how I felt about him . . . well, I knew Mam did. But whenever Dad spoke of it I realise now he did it as a sort of joke. Well, to cut a long story short, when things were coming to a head, I mean between Bert and me, and I knew he was going to ask me, once or twice I heard Mam and Dad arguing, and I couldn't believe it really because they seemed such a happy couple. And then the very night we got engaged I found out why. He . . . he ordered me out.'

'He what! You mean, Mr Paget?'

'Yes, yes. I . . . I couldn't believe it. He said if I was going to marry that man – in fact, he suggested that we were already married except in name – I had either to go to his place or to my friends next door.' Nell's head was bobbing now and her eyes were bright with tears. 'Fiona, I just couldn't believe it. It was a bigger shock than when Harry walked out on me. It was, really. He said that after all they had done for me he expected me to stay with them for life and look after them, especially Mam, being she's not well. He gave me no option: pointing to my ring, he said, "Either give that back to him this very night or don't come back here." Mam had to intervene.'

'I can't believe it. He seemed such a nice man, and thought the world of you.'

'So thought I. But I know now that his kindly manner had been hiding a sort of religious mania or moral mania. When Harry left me I thought his father was taking a very strong note when he said that he would never speak to him again as long as he lived. But last night, he told me that he considered me still married to his son: his son may have sinned but I was still his lawful wife. He tolerated you, Fiona, I gathered, because your husband had really died. That made the difference, you see; yet not altogether, because you had been married in a registry office. It all came out. I really couldn't take it in.'

'And I can't either, not what you're telling me. Anyway, why didn't you speak about this before? Why didn't you come straight round here?'

'Oh, I just couldn't. I felt it would be taking advantage of good nature; and anyway, I was sort of . . . of stunned. Do you know, it had a really worse effect on me than when Harry walked out.'

'Have you told Bert about this?'

'No. How could I?'

'Well, you must, woman. Now, this very night you tell him. And you're not going to be swayed, are you?'

'Oh no, Fiona, I'm not going to be swayed because I realise that I've never known what . . . well' – she looked down towards her hands again – 'what real love is; and I have it for Bert, and I'm sure Bert has it for me.'

'Well, there you are then. There's a house all ready waiting for you; forget about engagements and go and get married straightaway. I know he's a churchman, but the minister might be one of those who won't marry divorced people. If the church won't do it, there's the registry office, and so get yourself to it and don't wait, dear, because if Mr Paget's turned out to be the Jekyll and Hyde that he is he could play on your feelings until you do give in. Oh, I've heard of such, and I've had a bit of it,

you know, through Mother. But again I cannot understand why you didn't tell me straightaway.'

Nell smiled now and said, 'Well, there was another obstacle. You've just mentioned Jekyll and Hyde. Well, my father-in-law has certainly turned into that all right, because, you know, after telling me to get myself across here he informed me that if I said a word about his attitude he would know and he would come across and tell. . . .' She paused here and repeated, 'He said he'd come across here and tell Bill what he thought about him as a man, and so on, and so on. And by the sound of it his opinion wasn't high, and never has been. And just look back to the times that he's been here for a meal. Remember Christmas? Could you remember a nicer or more jolly man?' Her voice and face changed now as she said, 'I . . . I think he must be mental, schizophrenic or something, one of those. And I think Mam has been aware of this for a long time, because since this has happened I can recall her coming downstairs at times, saying, "Dad's lying down. He's got that headache again." And when I've offered to take him a drink, she's said, "No; I'll do it," although she could hardly get upstairs with her bad leg.'

Nell rose to her feet now and looked at her watch, saying, 'I'll have to be off,' and Fiona went to her and, putting her hands on her friend's shoulders, she said, 'Now, listen to me. You'll tell Bert all this, won't you?'

'Yes; yes, I will.'

'And if it gets too hot for you next door you come back here, because I can easily shuffle those beds around upstairs. If the worst comes to the worst you can take up your abode in the playroom. That old couch is as comfortable as any in the house.'

'Oh, Fiona.'

'Now, now; don't cry; you'll mess up that make-up. I've told you. And you look fine, like a young girl. I'm not kidding. Go on now, and no matter what time you get back, pop in and tell me that it's all settled, that you're going to be married next week.'

‘Oh, Fiona, that’s jumping the sticks.’

‘Well, it’s about time you did. Go on.’ She now pushed Nell out of the door, but within a minute she was in the sitting-room and beckoning to Bill as she said, ‘Here!’

‘Shhhh! Mam.’ The command for silence came from Mark and Katie; and Bill whispered, ‘It’s a Western. They’re going to get him.’

‘I’ll get you if you don’t come now.’

Bill made a great pretence of dragging himself away from the television. And when he reached the study close on her heels he said, ‘Well, what’s the news?’

‘Sit down. You won’t believe this.’

It took her all of five minutes to relate what Nell had said, for she interspersed this with her own comments. And when there was no response from Bill she said, ‘What d’you think of that? Eh?’

‘What do I think of it? I think we’ve got a psycho next door all right. And when I come to think of it now, there have been times when he’s utterly ignored me and I thought he was slightly deaf. I spoke to him over the fence one morning. He was doing something in the garden. His back was half turned towards me, but my voice, as you say, carries to the end of the street, and he didn’t move a muscle. I thought it was funny at the time, and I remember thinking he must be deaf in one ear, but recalling that he hadn’t seemed to be deaf when he had been in here at various times before that. And that wasn’t the only time that he seemed to ignore me. I still put it down to this being deaf in one ear business though. Poor old Nell. She does get it, doesn’t she? Likely his son took after him and she had that to put up with too. By the way’ – he wagged his finger at her – ‘didn’t Mrs Paget say he was from Ireland, and I remarked it wasn’t an Irish name? Remember?’

‘Yes, but what has that got to do with it?’

‘Only these things seem to link up. You know, Liverpool floats on the Irish population and in our street we felt like foreigners with so many of them. And I remember a sort of

discussion, well, it would often come up, about two families where the daughters of the house never married and that in both cases they had looked after their parents. And I can hear me dad saying, jocular like, that Ireland was full of bachelors 'cos Irish parents demanded that one daughter stay at home to see to them in their old age. And you know, he was right. These two were very nice and presentable middle-aged women who only seemed to get out of the house when they went to Mass or Confession or what have you. Aye' – he nodded – 'me dad said it was an Irish strain, and if the only girl in the family should walk out an' let them fend for themselves, it was as if she had committed a crime. Now, there you have it, the strain is next door.'

'Oh, that might be part of it, Bill, but it's more than that. From what she said, it's religious mania, and that in a twisted sort of way, too.'

'Well, I can tell you one thing, love: if she doesn't tell Bert the night I will in the morning, and tell him to get cracking. There's nothing to stop them going to the registry office on Monday if it comes to the push. You know, there's one thing you can say for this lower middle-class avenue, and that is, there's always something going on.'

'Why stick on the lower?'

'Because that's what it is. There's a lot of pretence along this street, you know. Look at our dear Mrs Quinn. And there's the two redundant managers further up. You said yourself you were invited to one of their coffee mornings.'

'Well, I suppose they could still afford a cup of coffee.'

'Aye, I suppose so in that case; but what about that bloke at the top inviting us to a meal and suggesting at the same time we take a bottle.'

'Well, if I remember rightly, we didn't get a second invitation after your refusal of the first. You know, you are an uncouth individual at times.'

'Look, Fiona' – he again pointed at her – 'don't use that word on me. I'm a big mouth and I'm brash but I'm not uncouth. I know you were smiling when you said it but I still don't like it.'

'Oh, I'm sorry, Mr Bailey.' She went to turn away and he got hold of her none too gently and pulled her tight against him, saying, 'An' don't take the pet. And that means, ever, because if I can't speak me mind to you, then I'm all at sea.' And his smile widening now, he went on, 'And me rudder's gone and me outboard engine's bust; I didn't bring any oars and there's a leak in the bottom of the boat. Dear Agony Aunt, what must I do?'

'Oh! Bill Bailey.'

'Don't spit at me when you say my name like that.' He made great play of rubbing his hand across his mouth. 'Anyway, you say that Nell's going to let you know how things go when she gets back. Well, that could be all-hours. But we'll wait up. And there's a certain way we can fill in the time, isn't there, Mrs B?'

She pressed herself from him, saying, 'You know, with all these other things on your mind, I'm amazed at the space you reserve for that one thing.'

'Well, what's life for, love, if not for that?'

'Oh you!' She thrust him away none too gently, and as she went out she said, 'I'm going to have a bath, and I don't want to be disturbed for the next hour. Will you inform the crew?'

'I'll give you half an hour, woman. That's long enough for any bath and titivating.'

When she had gone he sat down at the desk and for a few moments his mind dwelt on Nell's situation; but then he was back to the main happening of the day, and once again he was experiencing the feeling that had arisen in him when Sir Charles Kingdom informed him who was behind his present troubles. But added to it now was an emotion he hadn't experienced before, and it was fear. Fear of that woman; and this in itself was frightening, for never in his life could he recall being afraid of a man.

6

It was Willie's birthday, Tuesday, April the first.

Two more things had happened to Bill's men in the intervening time. One: Jos Wright's allotment had been stripped and trampled flat. And Jos being a leek fanatic, this had really depressed him. As he said, they could have mugged him and he wouldn't have minded so much.

The second incident had to do with Morris Fenwick's pigeons. It was known among the pigeon fanciers in the district that Morris had great hopes for one of his birds winning the continental race. But in the middle of the night before the special day the birds had been let out from their lofts at the bottom of the garden, and Maurice and his wife had been woken up with the flutter they made as they circled the house.

What Morris and no one else could understand was how the birds had been let out, because the coops had been locked, for it wasn't unknown that attempts could be made to steal prize pigeons, or, as some vandals had done of late, to kill them. It would seem in this case that the interlopers had had keys to fit the locks.

In both cases the police had been informed; Sir Charles Kingdom, too, had been informed and by a very angry Bill who

had promised him that just one more thing, just one more, and he would go back to the police and spill the whole story. What Sir Charles had said, was, 'Don't do that, Bailey. As I said, I'll make everything good; but don't do that, not at this late stage because you'll spoil your own chance if you do.'

When Bill had asked him what he meant by that he got no answer for the line went dead. . . .

But now it was Willie's birthday. All the April Fool tricks that could be played had been played on him and by him. Excitement in the house was at a high pitch waiting for the party to begin at half-past five, when Bill would join them, and also Bert.

It was a special day for Bert. He hadn't been to work, for he was getting ready for his wedding to Nell on the morrow. But now here they all were, ten people sitting round the table: Fiona at one end, Bill at the other; Sammy Love to Bill's right hand and Willie to his left; next to Willie was Roland Featherstone, and opposite him Katie; Bert's seat was next to Katie, and opposite him was Nell; next to Nell sat Mark, and opposite Mark, to Fiona's left, was Mamie.

The children had got through sandwiches, sausages on sticks, a variety of small cakes, ice-cream and jelly. Now they were waiting for the cake to come; and when Fiona paused in the doorway holding her son's birthday cake topped with nine fluttering candles, there was a concerted cheer from those at the table. And when she placed it on the table before Willie, he looked up at her and said, 'Oh! Mam; it's a big one. Where've you kept it?'

'Never you mind. Aren't you going to blow the candles out?'

His face glowing, Willie puffed twice and the candles were snuffed out; and Katie's calling across to him, 'Look what it says; it's got writing on all sides,' caused a stretching towards the cake and pointing now as different ones read out the words: 'Happy Birthday'; and then again 'To Dear Willie' which was written on the top.

'Well, go on and cut it, man,' said Bill; 'We're all waiting just to see if your mother's a better hand at making a cake than

she is at brewing coffee.' And he now nodded towards Roland, saying, 'She burns the water when she makes coffee, she does.'

'She doesn't, Dad! It's you, you want it so thick,' countered Mark.

'You would take her part, wouldn't you?' Bill was nodding down the table at Mark when Fiona, looking at Willie, said, 'Give your dad a piece of cake, will you, Willie, to keep him quiet.'

As Willie placed a piece of cake on Bill's plate he said, 'It'll take more than that, Dad, won't it, to keep you quiet?'

'Never a truer word spoken, laddie.'

His eyes still on Bill, Willie asked, 'What's it taste like, Dad?'

Bill chewed on the cake for a moment, then nodded, first at Willie then down the table at Fiona. 'Lovely!' he said. 'The best she's ever made.'

Fiona smiled back at the man sitting at the head of the table. She knew that her husband had no sweet tooth and that one thing he disliked was fruit cake; but there he was, munching away and grinning widely.

Everyone had been served, and Willie, looking across at his friend, said, 'You like it, Sammy?'

'Aye.' Sammy nodded. 'It's good; not scrimped on the fruit,' which brought a laugh from the company.

The ceremony of the cake over, Fiona now pointed to the two pyramids of crackers in the centre of the table. They were the left-overs from Christmas and she said so, then told Willie to pass them round.

With each motto being read out there was the accompanying laughter. First, Nell. When she hesitated to read hers, Mark said, 'Well, go on,' and Bill added, 'What's keeping you?' And Nell, pink in the face, looked at Bert and read, 'You will shortly meet and marry a handsome man and live happy ever after.'

'And that's true. That's true, Nell.'

'Aw! Bill, man.' Bert's head was wagging.

But when Mark read his: 'I'm a little fairy flown from the wood, may I join your party if I promise to be good?' and added

in baby talk: 'Twinkle, twinkle, little star, how I wonder where you are? Up above the earth so high like a diamond in the sky,' Willie and Katie fell about.

Then one and another cried at Bill, 'Read yours! What's the matter? Read yours!' But he pulled a face, saying, 'They're daft things,' and crumpling the tiny piece of paper, he thrust it into his pocket, which for a moment caused a silence to fall on the table until Bill said to Sammy, 'What's yours say, Sammy?'

'It's daft an' all.'

'I know. They're all daft, but what does it say?'

'Look.' He handed it to Bill, who read out, 'You're a man after my own heart; don't break it.'

This brought the laughter back again, and when Willie read, 'You will soon be offered a high post, jump at it,' Katie put in, 'You could never jump a flag-stone, Willie.' And he, flapping his hands towards her, replied, 'Oh you! Just you wait.'

There followed a desultory flatness that had to be lifted, so Willie, looking across at Sammy, said, 'You tell them the Pat and Mick story.'

'Aw! I couldn't.'

'Well, you told it to me.'

'Aye; that's different.'

'What's this Pat and Mick story?' Bill was nodding down to Willie now, and Willie said, 'Well, Pat brought his mother over from Ireland and she was very tired; and he was a big fella, so he carried her through the town. And she said, "Why don't you go into one of them places, Pat?" And he said, "How can I, Mother? They all say rest . . . yer . . . aunt, but there's no place says rest . . . yer . . . mother."'

The laughter was forced but it was loud. Then Roland's cultured tones brought all attention on him when he said, 'I have an uncle, in Scotland. He's a minister in the Church of Scotland and he tells the funniest jokes. He has the congregation rolling in the aisles, so to speak, when he's in the pulpit.'

'You're kiddin'?' Bert looked across at Roland. 'The Church of Scotland minister telling jokes from the pulpit?'

'Yes, it is perfectly true, Mr Ormesby. People have to go very early to get a seat. His church is always full.'

'I must go and hear him one day.' Bert smiled across at Roland.

'Oh, you wouldn't need to go to church to hear him, you could hear him at a wedding or a little party. The only thing he draws a line at are funerals. But for weddings and christenings, people always invite him. He told a very funny one at my cousin's wedding a short while ago.'

'Well, let's have it.' Bill was nodding at him.

'Oh, well, it was very funny, but it takes him to tell the jokes. Like the comedian, it's how he tells them.'

'Don't be so bashful; and you're not bashful, so don't tell me you can't tell a joke. Go on, let's have that joke.'

Roland looked round the table; then his eyes rested on Fiona and she too said, 'Go on, Roland.'

'It's . . . it's a very odd joke.'

'We like odd jokes.'

'Well, you see, my cousin was being married and you know the husband always has to stand up and reply. Well, the weddings I've been to, the new husbands always seem very bashful and the best men who speak for the bridesmaids they're always very dull, I mean, in their replies. And it should happen that this day the groom was very nervous and the best man, to my mind at least, pretty boring because he was reminiscing about his sporting childhood with the groom. Anyway, my uncle stood up and everyone became quiet because, you see, a lot of people there were strangers to him. He had come from far away in Scotland and this was London and moreover he had a dog collar on. Well, he began by congratulating the bride and groom in a very funny way that made people titter. Then he got on to his jokes and –' Roland bit on his lower lip and said, 'Well, this is the one I like but it's . . . well, it's –' He turned now and looked at Bill and said, 'It's not really naughty.'

'Oh, that's a pity,' said Bill; and having glanced at Fiona, he went on, 'Well, we're nearly all grown up here, except one.'

And he nodded towards Mamie who was still munching at her second piece of birthday cake. Then he said, 'Go on, lad. Go on.'

So Roland got on with it: 'Well, I'll use the Pat and Mick names,' he said; 'they're easier than the Scottish ones. Well, there were these two Irish farm-workers. They were on a half-day holiday and they had to take a message for the farmer to the village a mile or two away. It was very hot and they had got half-way along the road when Pat said to Mick, "Aw, I'm not going no further, Mick."' Roland had dropped his southern accent and was into broad Irish. '"You go on," said Pat, "and I'll have a kip here until you come back." "I'll do that," said Mick; "I don't mind walkin'. You have your kip." And so off went Mick to the village, and Pat lay dozing in the ditch by the roadside. Well, it was just half an hour later when he was brought with a start from the ditch because there was Mick, sitting in, of all things, a great big Volvo car. So he rushes up to him and says, "Mick, where on earth did you get that? You haven't nicked it?" "No, no," said Mick. "You see, it was like this. I was on me way back from the village and this young woman stopped and asked if I would like a lift, and I said, 'Thank you very much, ma'am. I'll be very obliged for it's hot it is.' So into the car I got. But she didn't keep to the road, she turned off into a thicket and out she got and, Pat, believe me, before God! she stripped off to her bare pelt, took every stitch off her, she did, and there she was, naked as the day she was born. And she comes up to the car and she says, 'Irish farm boy I'll give you anything you want.' . . . And so . . . well, I took the car."'

There was a great splutter, a clatter in Bill bringing his hand quickly to his mouth to help soften the explosion, and in doing so he upset his teacup which was half full; and this seemed to accentuate the laughter. Nell was choking. Bert had his hand tight across his brow shading his eyes. Mark and Katie were both doubled up; Willie and even Mamie were smiling. Of course, they were just following the pattern. The only one who hadn't

a smile on his face was Sammy. But Roland was waving his hands, flapping them and saying between gusts of laughter, 'It . . . it isn't finished, it isn't finished.'

'Oh, my lord!' said Nell; 'there can't be any more after that, boy.'

'Yes, there is. There is. Listen. Listen.' Roland was choking with laughter himself and as soon as there was comparative quiet he said, 'When Mick said, "Well, I took the car," Pat said to him, "You did right there, boy, you did right, 'cos her clothes wouldn't have been any use to you."'

Both Nell and Fiona rose from the table, but as Nell did so she brought Roland a clip across the head with her hand, gasping as she said, 'You'll go far, but where to I don't know.'

'I must get something to wipe up that mess,' Fiona said as she passed down the side of the table.

Bill had a hand across his forehead, his elbow resting on the arm of the chair. His body was shaking, and it sounded as if he was in pain.

'Move your carcass out of that.' Fiona had returned and was sopping up the tea from the table-cloth. And as she did so she looked at Roland, saying, 'You know I don't believe a word of that parson-uncle of yours.'

'Oh' – the boy's face was serious now – 'it's true, Mrs Bailey. Oh yes. If I may I'll bring him to see you the next time he comes down.'

'Well, I'll believe it when I see him.'

'And you'll believe it when you hear him too.'

A few minutes later, seated at the table again, Bill said to Sammy, 'I noticed you didn't laugh at that joke, Sammy. Mamie didn't know what it was all about but she laughed.'

'I knew what it was all about; it was about a whore.'

The whole table seemed to freeze. Every eye was on him. Bill had no immediate answer, and the boy went on, 'Women who take all their clothes off are whores. Me da says they're bad women, and me da says a wife can be a whore, but not a mother.'

Even the gulp Bill made in his throat was audible; then he nodded at Sammy and said, 'Yes, yes, your dad's right in a way: mothers are precious things; wives can make mistakes but never mothers, at least from the man's point of view. Yes, I understand your father.'

While he was speaking one part of his face seemed to be sending signals up the table to Fiona who had half risen from her seat, and also to Mark. He now glanced at Willie. Willie's face looked blank; he knew that Sammy had blotted his copybook again. He wasn't quite sure whether it was a four-letter word or not, but it was one that hadn't to be used. Then all eyes, as if in relief, were turned on Bert, for he was saying, 'I know this game; the lads in the club love it. You can all sit where you are, but we'll have to be divided into two teams. Mrs Bailey will take that side of the table and Mr Bailey will take this side of the table that includes Sammy, Katie, and Mamie and myself. It's to do with words. Now you have three choices, you lot over there.' He was pointing to them. 'You can either choose actors and actresses, or towns, or countries. The words start with A. Say you pick actors and actresses, well you must name as many surnames of actors starting with A during the time we at this side count twenty seconds. And we do it loudly. You know how to count a second: one-and, two-and, three-and . . . like that. We'll get a pencil and we'll put down how many you get. You start first, Willie, with A. And then Roland will have to take B. And Nell will have to take C. And Mark D.'

'That isn't fair.'

Bert looked at Katie. 'Why?'

'Well, they're all older and they'll know more. Mamie won't know any and I doubt if Sammy will.'

'I ain't daft. I know towns and countries as well as you. And I go to the pictures on a Saturda' mornin', so I know actors and actresses an' all.'

'There you are,' said Bert loudly now. 'We'll not only match them but we'll beat them.'

Fiona looked down the table towards Bill; then they both

looked at Nell. Nell was smiling widely as if with pride. Her husband-to-be was not only a good man, he was a diplomatic man; he had saved the birthday party. Oh yes, indeed, because Fiona had been ready to blow her top. Mr Samuel Love's oration on morality and on the filial piety of mothers from a son's point of view had obliterated Pat and Mick and the Volvo car. Oh, she must remember that one.

When the phone rang Fiona put her hand up, checking Bill from rising, saying, 'I'll see to it.' And as she passed the bottom end of the table, Bill pulled her towards him and, above the noise of the counting, he said, 'Tell her where to go to.'

Fiona picked up the phone. He had been right, it was her mother. 'Fiona?'

'Yes, Mother.'

'It's Willie's birthday and as he hasn't called for his present and I have not been invited to his birthday party, it remains here until he comes.'

'Mother, the birthday party is for children, and if I remember rightly you expressed the opinion that you can't stand children in a horde.' She almost added, 'You couldn't stand one, singular.'

'If I'd been invited I could have looked in for a moment. I . . . I feel very isolated, Fiona. And it's your doing, and . . . and . . . and that person's.'

'I've warned you, Mother, that if you do not refer to Bill either by his name or as my husband I shall refuse to talk to you, even on the phone.'

'You're hard, Fiona. You don't take after me.'

No, thank God. Again she'd had to restrain herself from voicing her thoughts, but she said, 'You're not very isolated, Mother, when you can play bridge three times a week, go to the theatre on a Saturday night with your cronies, have your coffee mornings and your weekends away for relaxation. Your life hasn't altered a bit over the years, Mother. You don't need me. You never have; all you want to do is to disrupt my way of living, my life. Now, look, I've got to see to the children. I'll

send Willie tomorrow after he comes from school. Good-night, Mother.'

'*Fiona.*'

As she thrust the phone down the term 'serpent in heaven' came into her mind. The party had been going beautifully, and she had to ring. What was she talking about, going beautifully? That child had nearly ruined it. Something would have to be done. But what? And his father talking to him about whores. Really! If only Willie wasn't so set on the boy. Well, she'd have to put her foot down; that association couldn't be allowed to go on.

Bert's game was a great success; and it went on for a half-hour or more, until Bill gave the signal for an end to festivities, at least in the dining-room, by rising from the table, saying, 'The slave women want to get this table cleared, so the rest of you up aloft and see what you can do with Willie's computer. Only don't break it.' And pointing his finger down at Willie, he warned, 'That cost me a packet.'

'Yes, I know, Dad. And thank you very much,' Willie said as he put his arms around Bill's waist; and Bill ruffled the boy's hair as he muttered, 'Later on tonight you come back and tell me it's bad manners to say what you paid for a present, because if you don't your mother will; and I'd rather it came from you.'

Bert and Nell helped to clear the table and wash up, after which, when everything in the dining-room was shipshape again, they returned there to discuss the big event of the morrow. And it was as Bert was saying, 'I can't help feeling guilty, boss, in taking leave at this time, when everybody's working all out to get the places finished,' that the phone rang again. And Bill, stopping Fiona from rising, said, 'It can't be her again so it'll likely be for me, although I don't know who'll be ringing unless it's more trouble.'

His expression was blank as he picked up the phone: 'Fellburn 7843,' he said.

'Hello, Bailey. This is Sir Charles here.'

'Oh. Oh, Sir Charles? How nice to hear you. How are you feeling?'

'Very well at the moment, at least in my mind. If my body was as good as my mind I'd be running races.'

'I'm sure you would, sir. You know about the latest attack, about the pigeons?'

'Yes, you told me at the time, and I said I'll make it all good. But that isn't what I've rung you about.'

'No, sir?' Bill's voice was still flat.

'Are you standing up or sitting down?'

'I'm standing up, sir.'

'Well, put your hand out and hang on to something.'

'I'm sorry, sir.' Bill gave a slight laugh. 'There's nothing within reach that I can hang on to, except a chair here, but that's rather fragile. I rarely sit on it in case I snap the legs.'

There was no response to this, jocular or otherwise, only silence on the line, and he was about to enquire, 'Are you there, sir?' when Sir Charles's voice said, 'You've as good as got the contract, Bailey.'

Bill's hand did shoot out now and grip the back of the chair.

'Did you hear what I said?'

Still Bill could not answer for a moment; then he muttered, 'Yes, sir. Yes, I heard what you said.'

'Well, there's been a meeting here today, the whole crew of them, and I can tell you I had to resort to a little wangling, a bit of persuasion, and in one or two cases perhaps a bit of threatening. One big boy wanted to know why such an important project should be given to a small builder, to which I replied that that small builder's work was better than any other's I'd seen.'

Again there was a pause before Bill could say, with a break in his voice, 'Oh, thank you, sir. From the bottom of my heart, thank you. If I can ever do . . . well, it's not easy to say this from where I'm standing, but if ever I could do you or your family any service you've only got to to say.'

'Oh, well; that you might be able to, if that madwoman of

whom I'm rather fond doesn't let up, and if those rascals are found she might be in need of help. Then whether the case comes up or is dropped will be up to you.'

Bill didn't answer for a moment; but his tone was thoughtful as he said, 'Well, I never break a promise.'

'Good man. Now, what you must do is be in Newcastle tomorrow at the Civic Centre at three o'clock. I'll be there, if I've got to be pushed in a wheelchair. But I can manage the car now, so never fear, I'll be there. Put on your best bib and tucker. And there's no need for me to ask you to answer straight because you always do that; but on this occasion, not too straight. Try a little diplomacy here and there, for there's a couple on this finance board who would still have their own favourites. You understand?'

'Yes, sir. Yes I do. And oh; thank you very much, and not only on my behalf but on behalf of my men, especially the ten that have stuck by me all these years.'

'Well, you'll need many more than ten when you start on this project. It's a big deal, Bailey. You'll need to take on supervisory help, you know that. And also you'll need to have a long talk with your bank manager . . . oh, yes indeed.'

'Oh, aye. Yes, sir, I've worked it out, just in case;' and he smiled at the phone as he said, 'Night after night for weeks now, I've gone over and over it: who I would need, and what I would need. You can't work a project like this on your own. But I have the men in mind: two of my own men will be site managers; and two others will take on gangs. These are the ones who don't mind responsibility. Others are good workers; but after work they consider they've earned their clubs, and darts, and snooker. Oh, yes; I've got it all worked out, sir. And again and again, I thank you.'

'Well, see you tomorrow. Don't let me down.'

'I'll never do that, sir.'

'Good-night, Bailey.'

'Good-night to you, sir.'

He stood for a moment with his hand pressed tight down on

the receiver, and actual tears welled up in his eyes, which he slowly rubbed away with his handkerchief.

He did not run into the sitting-room, he walked in quietly, and straight to Fiona, who was looking at him enquiringly.

He pulled her from the couch, then drew up Nell, and, when Bert, too, got to his feet he put his arms as far around them all as he could, clutching at Bert; then his head drooped between them and there was a break in his voice as he said, 'I've got it, the contract.' Then, his manner changing, he threw his head back and let out a 'Whoop!' and amid cries of, 'Wonderful! Marvellous!' he took Fiona into his arms; and when she buried her face in his shoulder he patted her, saying, 'There now. There now; I feel like that meself, but I'll wait till I get into bed.'

Looking at Bert, who was holding Nell and whose face, too, was showing emotion, he said, 'We're set, Bert. We're set. Work for the lads for some years ahead; and for others an' all. Oh, yes, dozens of them. Oh, let's drink to it.'

Gently now, he pressed Fiona onto the couch; then on his way to the cabinet in the corner he turned towards Bert and said, 'I'm not going to tempt you, but would you?'

'No thanks, Bill. No thanks. I can get high as a kite on orange juice.'

Amid the laughter Bill said, 'How about you, Nell, sherry?'

'Yes, please.'

He brought the tray to the couch, on it the two glasses of sherry, the orange juice and a whisky. And as their glasses clinked, he said, 'Let's drink to an outsize in miracles because, believe me, when I knew how many were in for this, although I kept struggling and hoping, I felt I really hadn't a chance.'

'God's good.'

Looking at Bert, Bill said, 'I'll believe it after this. You take it from me, I'll believe it after this.' . . .

It was eight o'clock when Bill drove Roland and Sammy back to their homes, homes set well apart in the town's layout. Roland had been effusive in his thanks for the wonderful party, and Bill

had said that he had gone a long way towards making it a success, and assured him that he would never forget that story; he also hoped that one day he would bring his uncle to see them.

When he dropped the boy before the iron gates at the entrance to the short drive leading to the white stuccoed house that faced The Moor, Roland turned and said to Sammy, 'Be seeing you again, Sammy.' And Sammy's mouth opened and shut twice before he answered, 'Aye, O.K.'

Having watched Roland walk towards the gate, then turn and wave, Bill started the car, and Sammy leaned over the back seat and said, 'He said he'll be seein' me. Think he meant it?'

'Of course he did; he's a very nice boy that.'

'Not snotty?'

'No; no, he's not snotty.'

'Like some.'

'Well, in life you'll always find there's some and some, Sammy; young and old, there'll always be some and some. But the real ones, the real gents and ladies, they're never snotty.'

Bill drove through Bog's End and when he stopped at the block of flats he said, 'Will your dad be in?'

'Don't 'spect so. But I've got a key.' He dug his hand into the bottom of his pocket, pulled out the door key, and Bill looked at it for a moment before he said, 'Would you like me to come up with you and see you in?'

'No. No, I can go by meself; I always do.'

'Yes, aye, of course. Did . . . did you enjoy the party?'

'Aye. Aye, it was good. Nice food. An' . . . an' did ya think that Willie liked me present?'

'He loved it.'

'I didn't get it off the tip. Me da give me the money for it, and he helped me pick it. He said it was the best model car on the market.'

'It is; it is that. And I know one thing, it'll start Willie on collecting them.' Bill now leant over and opened the back door, saying as he did so, 'Good-night, Sammy.'

'Good-night, mister.'

The boy was standing on the pavement now, and he said, 'What have I got to call ya besides mister?'

'What about Mr Bill?'

'You won't lose your hair if I call ya that?'

'Well, I've just said so, haven't I?'

'Aye. Night then.'

'Night, Sammy.'

Bill watched the small figure open the paint-scratched and scarred door that led into the hall of the flats before starting the car, saying to himself, 'God above!'

He, too, had had a rough childhood but nothing like that kid's. His own mother had always been at home waiting with a meal, even if her hand might be outstretched towards his head if he wasn't on time to sit down with his dad and her; and when he was younger she would always kiss him good-night after he'd had a playful slap on the backside from his father. He didn't know why he felt so concerned about this little fella, but he was. Yet it was obvious Davey did the best he could for him: he was well shod and clothed and likely got plenty to eat; and it would seem that he tried to instil a certain morality into him, even if it was about the whores. Eeh my! He grinned to himself. He had thought he would collapse when he heard him, and he wanted to bawl even louder than he had done at Roland's Pat and Mick story. And by! that was a corker an' all. My goodness! what kids came out with these days. But that lad; he would like to do something for him, and he would. Yes, he'd do it through giving his dad plenty of work that would enable them to get out of that hole and into a decent little house.

Work. He was set. Set for years ahead; for once he had done a job like that the world would be his oyster 'cos he'd build those houses like houses had never been built before. There'd be hardly two of the same design. He'd fight to get his ideas through. But then, they must have liked them in the first place to give him the contract.

Dear Lord – he was swinging the car round into the drive –

he had never felt like praying but at this minute he wished he was going into a church where he could kneel and say thanks to whatever was there. He did that.

A bubbly feeling rose in him and his step was so light that he almost danced into the house, only to realise straightaway that the party atmosphere was changed.

Nell was coming down the stairs and Fiona behind her.

'What's up?'

'I've . . . I've been thrown out, finally.'

'Come and sit down.' Fiona put her arm around Nell's shoulders and guided her into the sitting-room, Bill following, saying, 'The old devil threw you out?'

'Literally.' Nell sniffed, then blew her nose. 'Mam tried to stop him, but he nearly knocked her on her back. He had my cases and everything lined up in the kitchen, with the ultimatum that either I gave up this mad idea and stayed where I belonged or else I could go to my fancy man now and he never wanted to set eyes on me again.

'I went to pick up the cases, and he actually punched me in the chest; then, one after the other, he threw my things outside. I called over the fence for Bert, and when he saw what had happened he wanted to go in to him, to reason with him. But I told him you couldn't reason with that man, or at least the man he had become.'

'Where's Bert now?'

'He got a taxi and took my things along home. Funny . . . I already think of it as home.'

'He should have waited; what's my car for?'

'He . . . he didn't know what time you'd be back. Anyway, you've got a lodger for the night.'

'My God! I've a good mind to go over there and give him the length of me tongue, if nothing else.'

'It's no use, Bill. It's as if the devil or something has got into him. I can't understand it. He's . . . he's become a frightening creature.'

'Well, this time tomorrow you'll be away from it all. Look,

now that things are settled for the future, why not make Bert take a week off. What's two days for a honeymoon?'

'All I want, Bill, is to come back into that house and know that I've got a real home and a real man at last.' She now turned to Fiona, saying, 'And yet I won't feel safe until after the ceremony tomorrow morning; I've got the feeling that something will happen, that he'll do something.'

'He'll do nothing of the kind, because we won't let you out of our sight until the deed is done and you're on that train. So don't worry. And look, Mrs B' – he turned to Fiona – 'go and make some of your rotten coffee, and lace it with a little brandy before Bert gets back, because if he sees her having the hard stuff he'll think we've already got her off the straight and narrow.'

As Fiona passed the bottom of the stairs two voices hissed at her, 'Mam! Mam!'

She looked up to see Katie and Willie, and in stage whispers they said, 'We heard Nell.' And it was Katie who took up the conversation now. 'I saw Mr Paget going up and down his garden. He seemed to be talking to himself. All the lights were on in the house. Willie saw him an' all, and he came for me.'

'It's all right. Go back to bed and get to sleep or else, mind, it'll be school for you tomorrow and no wedding. Go on now.'

'What's the matter with Mr Paget, Mam?' This was from Willie.

'He's . . . he's not very well.'

'Then he should go to bed, shouldn't he?'

'Yes, he should. Now both of you get back to your beds; I'll be up in a minute.' And hearing them dutifully scampering across the landing, she turned and went towards the kitchen to make the coffee.

This was made and she was about to lift the tray with the three cups on it when there came a knock on the back door. It was a hard knock, and she wondered why Bert hadn't come the front way, as he had been doing of late.

She unbolted the back door, pulled it open, then stood gaping at the man confronting her, for she did not recognise John Paget:

the man who was always meticulously dressed was wearing only his under-vest and trousers and slippers. He did not attempt to come into the house; in fact, he stepped back from her as if, it would seem, to give his arm and finger more length to point at her as he said, 'You tell her she's got to come back. Do you hear? She owes us that much. My wife needs her. I'm sorry we ever saw this house, and you and your big-mouthed man, because it's him that's the cause of this. Yes, it is. Yes, it is. He pushed his low-type workman at her. He did it to spite me because he never liked me. But he'll pay for it. Oh yes, I'll get him. Oh yes, I'll do for him, or I'll burn him out and the lot of you.'

Gasping for breath, she banged the door in his face; then stood holding on to it as if to get her wind after a long run. Even after she'd heard the back gate bang it was still a full minute before she could move to the table and onto a chair.

That was how Bill found her when he entered the kitchen, saying, 'Have you gone to Brazil for that coffee? . . . What's up? You've got a pain? What's up?' He had his arms about her. 'You look as white as a sheet. What's happened? Tell me. Tell me.'

Twice she made an effort to speak before she could bring out, 'He . . . he came, Mr Paget. He . . . he threatened.'

'What d'you mean, threatened? What did he say?'

She stared into Bill's face but couldn't say, 'He threatened to do you in and burn us out,' because Bill would have gone round there and God only knew what would happen. So what she said was, 'Oh, he was on about Nell and that she had to go back and . . . and that one of your low-type workmen had got her. And so on, and so on.'

'Come on.' Bill pulled her to her feet. 'Look, come on, pull yourself together. And we mustn't tell her that he's been for she'll not close her eyes tonight. And I won't sleep very heavily either, I can tell you. By the sound of it that old fella's gone off his rocker and should see a doctor, a special one at that. Here! look; before you go in there, take a gulp at that coffee and let's

get some colour in your cheeks.' He patted each side of her face. 'Then we're all for bed. Now, as arranged, Nell will sleep with you, and I'll sleep down on the sofa.'

'It isn't long enough.'

'You leave that to me. My God!' – he picked up the tray now – 'talk about situation. Who would believe that old fella could turn out like that?' He paused as he was going towards the door and, looking at Fiona, he said, 'If he can change as much as he has done in the past few weeks I don't think it's something new. I'd like to get to the bottom of it.'

They got to the bottom of it at eleven that same night. After Bert returned they had sat talking in the sitting-room until nearly eleven o'clock, when both Fiona and Bill left the room to let the couple say good-night and to part for the last time before their marriage.

As they went into the kitchen Bill said, 'Now I won't be ten minutes running him home, and you don't open the door to anyone, not even God himself. D'you hear?'

'Don't worry. Don't worry about that.'

'But while I'm away, if you're frightened or he comes back to that door, dial 999. This, I think, has become a police matter.'

A few minutes later, after Fiona had locked the front door after the two men, she went upstairs with Nell. In the bedroom she said, 'Now get yourself to bed and go to sleep; I'll be up as soon as Bill comes back. That brandy should do the trick.'

'Yes; I think it's starting already.' Nell gave a weak smile. 'It was more than a drop; he said it was.'

Of a sudden Nell put her arms around Fiona, saying brokenly, 'What would I have done without you? I'll never know.'

'Well, you're not going to do without me. Things will go on just the same, at least for half days only. It's all arranged, now isn't it? So there's nothing more to worry about. And no more talk; get into that bed and go to sleep,' and saying this, she went to push Nell towards the bed, but Nell, her old manner returning for a moment, pushed back at her, saying, 'Well, let's get me

clothes off first,' which caused them both to laugh and left Fiona feeling easier in her mind when she went from the room to do her nightly round of looking in on her children before going downstairs again.

But she had no sooner entered the kitchen and reached the stove and was about to put the kettle on when she heard a tap on the kitchen door.

She swung round and stared towards it; then slowly, as if sliding past someone, she was making for the hall again when a small voice said, 'Fiona, it's me, Mrs Paget.'

Fiona put her hand to her neck as if to assist herself to breathe. Then she hurried to the back door and was about to unlock it when she stopped at the thought that he might be behind her. And so she called, 'Are you alone, Mrs Paget?'

'Yes, yes, I'm alone.'

When she'd opened the door, Mrs Paget, a coat pulled over her dressing-gown, stumbled into the kitchen, and Fiona locked the door again before saying to the elderly woman, 'Sit down. Sit down.'

'Oh, Fiona, what can I say? What can I say? Where's Nell?'

'She's in bed, Mrs Paget.'

'I would like to have seen her, but . . . but perhaps it's better not. Will . . . will you give her this?' She brought from her dressing-gown pocket a narrow black case, saying, 'I . . . I couldn't get out; he . . . he wouldn't take me out to buy her anything, a wedding present. Tell her that it was my mother's. It's the thing I value most and I want her to have it because I value her too.'

'Why has your husband turned so much against her, Mrs Paget? He never was like that.'

'Oh, my dear –' The pale pink face seemed to crumple and the older woman had to fight for control before she said, 'He's been like that many times, my dear, but he's never had such a long spell since Nell came to live with us. He seemed to change altogether after Nell came, and it's been like a small miracle, no, a large miracle. He . . . he's a good man really, the other

side of him. If he hadn't been I would have left him years ago. When he comes to himself he's like a child, so sorry. But I've never seen him as bad as this before.'

'Have you told the doctor?'

'Oh, the doctor knows about his spells; but he's threatened what he would do if I ever call the doctor in. I need the doctor for myself as I haven't been well. I'm never well when he's like this. It's nerves you know; nothing physical, just nerves.'

'Oh, my dear.' Fiona took a seat by the side of the troubled woman and she asked, 'Nell mustn't have known anything about this?'

'No, no, she didn't.'

'Didn't her husband tell her? He must have known.'

'Oh, he wouldn't have. Harry wouldn't have told Nell; he was ashamed of his father having these turns.'

Remembering the threat the man had levelled at her a short while ago, Fiona put the question tentatively now as she said, 'Has he ever become . . . well, dangerous in his manner?'

Mrs Paget sighed before she answered, 'Yes, twice, and . . . and he was in the hospital for almost a year after that.'

'How long do these turns last?'

'It's strange, but I've known them go as quickly as they come. Other times he's got to have medication for a lengthy period. Once he . . . he went for a man, quite a big man, and the man felled him with one blow. And when he came round he had his senses back too. The doctors found this very interesting.'

The thought went through Fiona's mind that it might perhaps have been a good job if she had let Bill go round there, for his medicine might have brought the man to his senses again. But then it would take a lot for Bill to hit an old man.

'You must get the doctor to him as soon as possible,' she said.

'I will tomorrow, no matter what happens. But he watches me, my every movement, and whenever I go near the phone it seems to agitate him. When he's like this he does not realise he's ill. Yet he does realise he can be put away; and oh dear, that's pitiful.'

'I'm so sorry, Mrs Paget. I never guessed that you were in this trouble; you were always so bright, seemingly happy.'

'Yes, I was because . . . well, Nell was there. To him she was like a cure. But please, oh! please, don't think I don't want her to be married, and he's a good man. Will you tell her I wish her all the best in the world? I love that girl. I must go now, but . . . but I wanted you to understand.'

After unlocking the back door, Fiona turned before opening it and said to Mrs Paget, 'If your husband has to go into hospital and you're on your own, well, remember you won't be on your own: Nell will be coming here half days and we will all be at hand to help you in any way we can.'

'Thank you, my dear. That is something to know anyway. You will give my love to Nell? And will you tell her what I've told you?'

'Yes, right away. She'll understand then. Good-night, Mrs Paget.'

'Good-night, my dear.'

The older woman now touched Fiona's hand, saying, 'You've got a good man. Take care of him.'

When the door was closed once more Fiona stood with her back to it. You have a good man. Take care of him. It was Bill who took care of her and of all of them. But yes, she would take care of him.

7

It was done. Nell was now Mrs Ormesby. They came out of the town hall, Bert and Nell, Bill and Fiona, Mark, Katie, Willie, and Mamie, dressed in their best. And that wasn't all. Barney McGuire had taken the morning off, so had Harry Newton and Jos Wright. Amid laughter and chaffing they piled into their respective cars, Bill and Fiona taking the bride and groom, the children divided between Harry Newton and Barney McGuire.

It was only a short run to the hotel where the wedding breakfast was awaiting them, but before Bill drew up in the forecourt he said over his shoulder, 'The first thing you'll get, Bert, is a car.'

'I can't drive a car, boss; you know that.'

'No, but your wife can.'

'Can you drive a car?' Bert looked at Nell.

Their faces were shining and Nell laughed as she said, 'Of course I can drive a car.'

'You never told me.'

Bill was quick out of the car, and first went round and opened the door for Fiona; then addressing Bert again, he said, 'Lad, you're in for some surprises. You never told me, you said. You'll be kept awake at nights with the things she'll tell you and that

you didn't know. I never got any sleep for the first month.'

'Oh Bill, shut up!'

So laughing, they entered the hotel.

They laughed a lot during the breakfast and when, an hour and a half later they all stood on the station platform saying goodbye to the happy couple, there was still much laughter.

Nell, hugging Fiona, now said, 'Tell Mam I'll be seeing her soon. . . . Give her my love. Tell her I'm happy. And things will work out all right now that I know about Dad. Oh, you don't know what that's done for me, to know I haven't been the cause of his illness.'

The train was moving off as Bill yelled to Bert, 'Make it a week. I've told you.'

'Not on your life, boss. Be back on Friday.'

'Come back on Sunday night.'

Nell's head was thrust out of the window and she yelled at the top of her voice, 'You mind your own business, Bill Bailey.'

This caused more laughter and comments from the men, Barney saying, 'Well, now you know, boss; somebody's tellin' you straight.'

'Don't they always!'

And so, amid chaffing, the wedding party divided, Bill addressing his men, saying, 'I'll be changed and back on the site within an hour. If any of you are a minute late it's the sack. So you know. So long.'

'The same to you, boss, the same to you. But I thought you had the big meeting this afternoon, boss. Have you forgotten?'

'Don't be such a . . . don't be such a fool, Harry. As if anybody could forget that.'

'Then you won't be changin' your clothes, will you?'

'You're too clever by half. Anyway, get back on that job. I'll be looking in afore I go on to Newcastle.'

'We'll see about it,' said Jos Wright. 'Might stop and have a pint or two, then on top of that champagne, you never know the effect it'll have on us. Do you, lads?'

In the car again, Willie said, 'They're funny men, aren't they, Dad?'

'You said it, Willie, they're funny men. And I don't know whether it's funny ha-ha or funny peculiar.'

'Have we got to change our clothes, Mam?' said Katie.

'Of course you've got to change your clothes. You're not going to lounge around in that dress for the rest of the day.'

'Why not? She'll shortly be able to have a new one for every day of the week.'

'Will I, Dad?'

'No, you won't, miss,' Fiona answered for Bill quickly and definitely; 'so sit back there and behave yourself. And take Mamie on to your knee because Mark's leg's in the cramp. It is, isn't it?'

'Yes, Mam.' Mark was pushing his foot against the back of the seat.

'I don't want to go on Katie's knee; I'll sit on Willie's knee.'

'You'll do no such thing. I don't want you on my knee. If you don't sit on Katie's you can sit on the stool.'

'I'm too big to sit on the stool, and I'll stop loving you shortly, Willie Bailey, 'cos you're always at me.'

There was a quick glance between Fiona and Bill. That was the first time since that little girl had come under their care that she had spoken out against Willie and his manner towards her.

'Well, well. Good for you, Mamie. It's about time you told him where he stood.' Mark was patting Mamie on the head now and she smiled up at him from the cracket where she was crushed between their feet, and she said, 'You're nicer than Willie.'

'What's the matter with you? Gone daft?' Willie was definitely perturbed: his sole female admirer preferring his elder brother and telling him off in front of the family.

'Revelation.'

'What do you say, Mam?' Willie was bending forward.

'Nothing.'

'Well, I'm going to say something, Mam. I'm going to wait

for Sammy coming out of school, then I'm going to his house.'

'You're doing nothing of the kind; you're staying at home. If you don't want to play in the garden or in the playroom then you can sulk in your bedroom.'

'Dad, can I go and see . . . ?'

'No, you can't!' Bill bawled at him. 'Don't you dare start that prank, Willie Bailey. If your mother says you can't do a thing, you can't do it. You could talk to her and try to make her see it your way, but don't you come to me expecting me to countermand her orders. Never do that. Do you hear? And that goes for all of you.'

It was some moments later when a lone voice said, 'Happy wedding.' But no one laughed or made any comment on Mark's statement.

At half-past one Bill left the house. He had arranged to give himself time to visit the site and be in Newcastle well before three. In the privacy of the bedroom he had held Fiona in his arms and said, 'Lass, I'm shaking like a leaf inside. Facing and talking to Sir Charles is one kettle of fish, this board will be another.'

'But you've got it; he said you've got it.'

'Yes; but I've still got to put myself over to the board, to gain their confidence in me, because there's only two from the old board on this one and by the sound of it there's a dozen or more altogether.'

'You'll win them over, all of them. You know your job and you won't lie or prevaricate.'

'What's that? Prevaricate? Oh, I must add that to the list, prevaricate.'

They had kissed and clung together; then she had set him to the gate and watched him drive away in the car.

It was half-past five when he phoned her from Newcastle, saying, 'How does it feel, Mrs B, to be the wife of a building tycoon?'

'Just the same feeling as it was when I was the landlady to the

fellow who had risen from a brickie; it hasn't altered. I don't think it will. I'm not the impressionable kind. . . . Oh! Bill. Everything went well?'

'Yes, yes. A bit tricky here and there. Questions flung at me that made me want to, well you know me, spit back. But I kept me cool an' convinced them that I was the man for the job. Sir Charles was delighted. He shook my hand after. But what was more impressive than words, he didn't speak at all, he just kept shaking my hand. And now, Mrs Bailey, I have been asked to join five of the men at dinner in their hotel, so don't expect me home yet awhile. If you go to the paper shop and ask Mrs Green for a late edition of the evening rag you'll likely find a report of the outcome of the meeting because there were a number of newspaper men around. And I saw a TV crew, too, so it might be on Look North with Mike Neville. Look love, I don't know what time I'll be home, but I'll get away as soon as possible.'

'Don't hurry, dear. Don't hurry. Enjoy your meal. Enjoy your success.'

'I never enjoy anything without you. Now if you were here we'd make a night of it.'

'Will Sir Charles be there?'

'No, no. He went off early. He's still pretty groggy, I think, but his secretary will be standing in for him, so he said. I think the secretary is a relation. He lives in the house. I never knew he had a secretary. But, of course, with all his business he's bound to have. He's a nice fellow, not unlike Sir Charles when he was young I would think. Oh, Fiona, I don't know whether I'm on my head or my heels. But one thing I do know, there's a lot of hard work before me, and worry. Oh, aye, and worry. But if I can get a crew together even half as good as my lot, then we'll manage. You know, I'm that excited I want to do a hand-stand, or jump up and click me heels, do something daft like that; and I will do once I get home. You wait and see: I'll get all the kids up and I'll slide down the bannister.'

'You'll do no such thing, because they'll be after you, and they'll break their necks.'

'Don't be daft. Nobody's broken his neck sliding down a bannister. But that's what I'll do as soon as I reach home, I promise you. I won't even look at you; I'll go straight to the top of those stairs and slide down that bannister, and the noise I'll make will bring them all flyin' out of their beds.'

'Oh Bill, I'd let you do that now if you were here this minute.'

'Well, it's going to be an early dinner, and I can promise you that, as I'm driving home, I'll be steady on the liquor. I must go now. I love you, Mrs B.'

'And I have a strong affection for you, Mr B. Hurry home.'

She put down the phone; then went straightaway upstairs and told the children the news.

'Will we be rich now?' asked Katie.

'No, we won't be rich, but we'll have a little more to get by on.'

She knew Katie's tongue and she could imagine her going to school and saying, 'My father's going to be rich and he's a friend of Sir Charles Kingdom,' and so on, and so on.

And their excitement seemed to revolve around that little bit more, and so she left them jabbering about what they wanted; except Mark. He followed her to her room, saying, 'I'm glad for him, Mam. And I'm glad you married him.'

'Oh, Mark.' She put her arms about him, and he clung to her as he used to do when he was smaller and not the twelve-year-old budding man.

'You know something, Mam?'

'What?'

'I . . . I like Bill. You know, inside I always think of him as Mr Bill. I like him better than I liked my father. I remember my father well.'

'Oh, don't say that, Mark.' There was a sad note in her voice now, but he went on, 'He never played with us, and I can remember him going for you. But from the minute Bill came into the house, he noticed us, he did things with us and for us.'

'Look, Mark Bailey, get yourself away else you'll have me in tears. And if Bill, or Mr Bill, or your dad, whatever, hears you,

his head will be more swollen than it is at present. But' – she gently touched his cheek – 'thank you for what you've said, I mean about Bill, because he's a very special person.'

'Yes, yes, I think he is, too.' And then laughing, he added, 'Anybody who can bring in a kid who is about to throw a brick through a window and give him tea must be a very special person.' They were both laughing loudly now as they went downstairs. But in the hall Fiona stopped and in a quiet voice she said, 'But something must be done about Sammy and Willie, because, you know, that child is impossible. I can't imagine him ever changing; all he can do is get worse, and he's not a fit companion for Willie.'

'I shouldn't worry about Sammy, Mam. You know, I can't help it but I like him too.'

'Well, I'm glad you haven't got a counterpart and you've picked a boy like Roland.'

'I'll tell you something, Roland likes him.'

'Oh, go on with you.' She pushed him away and hurried towards the kitchen, saying now, 'Take some ice-cream up to them to celebrate.'

She, too, celebrated, singing and humming to herself for the next hour. And when she heard a scream from above which caused her to jump from Bill's chair in the study where she had been sitting musing about the bright future, she rushed out to meet the horde tumbling down the stairs, Mark holding out his transistor, calling to her, 'Listen! Listen, Mam. They're talking about Dad.'

They seemed to be hanging above her, clinging onto the bannister, while Mark, on the bottom stair, held up the transistor and, with an ear-grinning smile, looked into his mother's face and listened to a voice, saying, 'This is a triumph for a small company. It is understood there were fifteen firms applying for this contract, and so it must say much for Mr Bailey and his particular small firm that they have succeeded against bigger firms more experienced in this form of contract. It is understood

that he'll be able to set on at least a hundred men, and this comes at a time when only this week Brignall and Patten have closed down with the loss of seventy-five jobs.

'Tune in again this time tomorrow for more up-to-date news of what is happening in your street, your town, and your area. This is YS, YT, YA, signing off.'

'Isn't it wonderful, Mam!'

Her smile was as wide as Mark's. 'Marvellous!'

'It'll likely be on the news, nationwide.'

'No, no, it won't be on there, dear. Perhaps on BBC North.'

And it was on BBC North. They all sat around the television staring at Mike Neville, the jovial practised presenter. He opened the programme with a repeat of the closing down of Brignall and Patten and the loss of seventy-five jobs. He spoke of the busmen refusing to drive after a certain time at night because of the hooliganism and the threatening attitude of young gangs. He next told of the attack on a crippled seventy-five year old woman as she was returning from drawing her pension. And this apparently took place in a quiet suburb where up till then residents thought they were quite safe and that such incidents happened only in the lower end of towns. Then, his face stretching into a wide smile, he said, 'Now for the good news of the evening. David and Goliath are not dead, for today David, in the form of Mr William Bailey, a building contractor of Fellburn, brought off a scoop. He put a stone in his sling, and fifteen other firms, among them half a dozen big boys, fell. There are still Jack the Giant killers kicking around. . . . Pardon my puns.' He made a face at himelf. 'Mr Bailey will be celebrating with his eleven good men and true, as he told our David. These eleven men have nearly all worked for him for the past twelve years. They are, he said, the foundation, and there could be no better workmen in the country. Mr Bailey is a Liverpudlian by birth but a Geordie by inclination. And he couldn't have been more forthright if he had been born a Geordie, because he said, "Yes, I'll be taking on quite a number of men, but they'll have to be those who'll pull their weight and know that

when we start at eight, it doesn't mean quarter-past; and when we finish at half-past four they don't start to get ready for that at half-past three." Mr Bailey knows what he wants and he's the kind of man who will get it. That's how he's pulled off this very choice deal . . . I wonder if he'll set me on; I could run round with the tea.'

This must have brought forth a quip from the cameraman, which couldn't be heard but which Mike Neville made use of in his own inimitable way: 'Well, Mr Bailey admits he started as a tea-boy. And what one can do another can. . . . What do you mean, there are exceptions?' . . .

'Isn't he funny, Mam?' Katie was looking up at Fiona where she stood behind the couch.

'Yes, he is.'

'He's had a bad leg, that's why he was off and couldn't come and talk.'

'He doesn't talk with his leg, stupid.' Mark pushed Willie now. 'And it was his foot not his leg.'

'Now, now, Willie.' Fiona leant over and grabbed her son's flailing arms.

'I wish Daddy B was in. He would have liked to hear that, wouldn't he?'

They all looked. at Mamie now and laughed. Then Fiona ruffling the child's hair, said, 'Yes, he would have liked to hear that, but –' She turned and looked at the clock, saying, 'Just about now he'll be going into a slap-up meal in a posh hotel in Newcastle.'

'Mam.' Katie was kneeling up on the couch, looking into her mother's face. 'Will you be going out in the evening all dressed up in new things? To dinner and parties and such?'

'Well, I might be going out to a dinner now and again, but I'll not always be wearing new things.'

'Well, you couldn't go to a dinner two weeks running in the same dress. And you'll have to have a fur coat that you can take off and hand to the waiter, and he'll put it on the back of the chair or hang it up.'

'My dear girl' – Fiona was bending over her now – 'I won't have any fur coat that a waiter can put on the back of the chair or hang up. Now get that into your head. And now listen to me, and not only you, but all of you: life will go on much the same for a long while, except that very likely we won't see so much of your dad, because he'll be working all hours. There'll be treats but they certainly won't be every week; nor will you be any better dressed than you are now. Your dad's bought you two rig-outs in the last few months, you know. So things will go on pretty much the same for a time.'

'How long?'

Fiona looked down on Willie. 'I don't know, Willie, but when your dad comes back you must greet him with, "What am I going to get out of this?"'

'Oh, Mam!' Mark got up, saying, 'They didn't mean that.'

'I know. I know. I don't know whether I'm on my head or my heels either. Look what I did, sending all that ice cream up to you. I never meant to do that.'

The giggles now turned to high laughter when Mamie, addressing no one in particular, said, 'I want a big pram and a talking baby.'

'She wants a big pram and a talking baby' built into a chorus which followed Fiona out of the room.

A talking baby. She wanted a talking baby too; and she had hardly dared to think about it these last few days because she had gone past her time. She had gone past her time before and nothing had happened, but this time she prayed it would, for she wanted to give Bill something of his very own. She was only thirty, and so there was plenty of time; but she longed to give him two, three, or four. No; she would stop at two. But oh, how she longed to see that man's face when he held his own child, because he gave so much to others.

She stopped by the telephone table. Her mother hadn't phoned today; nor was it likely that she would now because she was bound to have heard something of this, if not on the radio or the television, then certainly from Mrs Green's paper shop;

for Mrs Green didn't only sell papers, she gave away, free, the local gossip.

Looking at the phone, her face spread into a smile; her mother hadn't phoned her but she could phone her mother. Oh yes, yes, she could phone her mother.

As if the thought had lifted her to the phone, she already had the receiver in one hand and was quickly dialling a number with the other. And when the sweet voice came on the other end, 'This is Mrs Vidler's residence,' she pressed her lips tight to quell the sound of laughter from being in her voice when she would say, 'Mother, it's me, Fiona.'

There was a slight pause before the voice said, 'Fiona? This is an unusual occurrence, you phoning me.'

'It's an unusual day, and I have unusual news, Mother. But I'm sure you've heard about it already.'

Another and considerably longer pause now before the voice said, 'I don't know what you're talking about.'

'Oh, Mother! If you hadn't the radio, you have the television on every night, as well as, if I'm not mistaken, your routine taking you to Mrs Green's gossip shop at least once a day.'

'Fiona! I needn't listen to you, you know that. I can put the phone down.'

'Yes, you can, Mother, but you won't, will you? Because you must have heard about my husband getting this wonderful contract and the praise that's been doled out to him on both the television and the radio. He's been referred to as David, and as Jack the Giant killer.'

'Well, his mouth is big enough to hold either of those characters, I should imagine.'

Fiona did not retort to this; instead she said, 'You can't bear it, can you, Mother? to know that this brickie, as you call him, or that man, or that person, has pulled off one of the biggest deals in building in this area for a long time. And what is more, he is a friend of Sir Charles Kingdom.'

'Oh, well, there you have it. As I said, it's who you know, and if you can suck up to a title.'

'So, you've already expressed your opinion on my husband's success. But let me tell you, Bill didn't get this contract through the people he knew, but because of his good work and because it is known that he has a trained group of sound workmen.'

'Well, what you've got to remember, Fiona, is the old adage, you can't make a silk purse out of a sow's ear.'

Fiona's teeth pressed together: her mother was winning as usual, boiling her up. But she couldn't let her get off with it this time. 'It's a pity distance doesn't cut off the phone because I don't suppose we'll be staying here much longer; Bill's had his eye on one of those big houses in Gosforth, one standing in its own grounds. He had said if he got the contract that's where we would move to. He's also considering buying a chalet type of house in Barbados, where we can slip over two or three times a year for a break. And when we make these moves, Mother, I could also change our phone number, in fact, I've been thinking about being put on ex-directory, the particular type, you know, where no one can get through, no matter how much they press or ask. Good-night, Mother.'

She walked into the kitchen and stood at the sink looking down the garden. The sun was casting long shadows over the lawn from the one big tree growing there. She loved this house; she never wanted to leave it. As for Newcastle, she couldn't bear the thought of living in the city, not even on the outskirts, all that traffic buzzing about. And Barbados, well you could keep Barbados for her. If she was going anywhere she would like to go to America or Australia, but certainly not Barbados. Lying on a beach all day would bore her to death. Oh!

She turned from the window. She wasn't going to let her mother spoil this. The children were settled, so she would go up and have a bath, give her face one of those ten minute mudpacks; put on another dress, the blue one that Bill liked; it showed off her figure, he said. What time was it now? Just turned seven. He'd likely be in the thick of that dinner now; but he shouldn't be later than half-past nine or ten.

She almost skipped from the room, ran across the hall, and

put her head round the door of the sitting-room, saying, 'I'm going to have a bath. Behave yourselves.'

'You going to do your face up with that lemon pack, Mam?'

'Yes. Yes, I might even do that.'

'Well, I'll come up and watch you.'

'You'll do nothing of the kind.' Her arm was thrust out, the finger pointing. 'Give me half an hour to myself.'

As she turned away, she glimpsed Mark's hand pulling Katie back onto the couch, the while saying, 'Sit down, hussy!'

And Katie's strident tones, likely telling her brother what she thought of him, followed her up the stairs.

Oh, she was happy, happy in all ways. Just that one fly in the ointment. But her mother had always been a fly in the ointment, so why worry?

It was just on nine o'clock when she thought she heard the car turning into the drive, and she went into the kitchen because she knew he would come in the back way.

When she didn't hear the garage door bang she went into the hall again and looked through the small side window but it was too dark to see as far as the gate. Yet she had heard his car stop there.

The night having turned chilly, she put on a coat; then she walked down the drive in the shadow of the cypress hedge. But she stopped where the hedge finished, for there was a car drawn up to the kerb and so parked that no car would be able to enter the drive. The car wasn't theirs; Bill's was a silver-grey Volvo, whereas this car, as far as she could make out in the light from the far street lamp, was either a dull reddish colour or brown. She detected a movement inside; so she stepped back a few paces before turning and making her way back to the house again. Bill would have something to say to them when he found he couldn't get into his own drive. He had often remarked on the snoggers finding their way to the avenue when it was dark; it wasn't all that brightly lit and was certainly quiet.

About half an hour later she thought she heard a commotion

in the street, and she told herself that would be Bill telling the occupants of that car where to go to. She didn't go out, but waited in the hall. However, when there was no sound of the car coming up the drive, she once again went down and stood in the shadow of the cypress hedge. The car was gone. Somebody else had likely complained and there had been a bit of an altercation. That's what she had heard. She did not go out of the gate into the street but returned to the house.

At eleven o'clock she began to worry. The children, having become tired of waiting for Bill's return, were in bed and asleep. The house was quiet.

There was the sound of a car, but it was from next door and made her wonder why Mr Paget should be returning so late. He very rarely went out in the car at night and in his present state of mind she imagined his driving would be anything but safe.

At half-past eleven she was standing in the hall rubbing one hand against the back of the other, telling herself that he wouldn't have stayed so late without having phoned her. Whom could she get in touch with? Sir Charles' secretary? He lived at the manor, apparently. But Bill had said he was at the dinner as well.

She whipped through the pages of the directory, and then she was dialling the number. She listened to the bell ringing and ringing, but she wouldn't put the phone down. Then a woman's weary voice said, 'Yes? Yes, what is it? Who is it?'

'May I speak to Sir Charles Kingdom's secretary, please?'

'Who . . . who's speaking?'

'This is Mrs Bailey.'

'Oh. Mrs Bailey. Well, this is Lady Kingdom here. What is wrong?'

'My husband hasn't returned from Newcastle. I . . . I understood he was having dinner with Sir Charles's secretary and others and he said he wouldn't be late, but it is now nearing twelve o'clock and . . . and. . . .'

'Oh, my goodness me! Yes, yes. Wait a moment, I'll get up.'

'Oh, I'm very sorry.'

'Don't worry. Don't worry. I can contact Rupert on the intercom.'

She waited, one hand holding the receiver, the other tapping her lips in agitation. When a man's voice came on the phone, saying, 'Mrs Bailey?' she said, 'Yes. Yes, it's Mrs Bailey.'

'Lady Kingdom has just told me that . . . but . . . but your husband should have been home ages ago. He had a very early dinner. It was over by. . . . Oh well, I'm not quite sure, about half-past eight, perhaps quarter to nine. I left him in the foyer talking to Mr Ramshaw and Mr Pilby.'

'Are . . . are they Newcastle men?'

'I think so. Yes, I think they both live in Newcastle. Look . . . what time is it now?' He paused. 'Twenty minutes to twelve. What I should do first of all is ring the police and see if there's been an accident.'

'But they would have let me know surely; he always carries papers on him.'

'Yes, yes, that's right. But nevertheless I would do that. Then perhaps you could ring me back when there's any more news.'

'Yes. Yes, I'll do that.'

Her hand was shaking visibly as she phoned the police station.

'Have there been any accidents on the road from Newcastle this evening?'

'No, madam; not that I know of. Who's speaking?'

'Mrs Bailey. My . . . my husband hasn't come home, and it's just on twelve o'clock. He's the builder, and he went to a dinner, but he said he'd be back about ten.'

'Ah, Mrs Bailey. Yes, I know Mr Bailey. I shouldn't worry; he'll turn up. Would he have gone on to another function?'

'My husband would have phoned me, officer, if he had been going on to a further function.'

'He would?'

The question seemed to say, Well you're a lucky woman, and she answered it as if she had heard it: 'Yes, he would. He's that kind of man.'

'Yes, all right. All right. What is your address, Mrs Bailey?'

She gave him the address. Then he said, 'Well, there's bound to be a patrol car somewhere near. I'll get in touch with them right away and they'll give you a call.'

'Thank you.' She put down the phone. Celebrating indeed. Bill would never celebrate without her if he could help it.

It seemed to her that she had been walking the floor for at least half an hour before the bell rang; but the clock told her it was only five minutes past twelve. When she opened the door there were two policemen standing on the step.

'Mrs Bailey?'

'Yes.'

'About your husband.'

'Yes. He . . . he hasn't returned home. It's very unusual and. . . .'

'May we come in, Mrs Bailey?'

'Of course, yes, yes.'

They passed her and stood in the hall; and then the taller one said, 'I am Constable Anderson and this is Constable Burrows. What make of car does your husband drive?'

'It's a grey Volvo.'

'And can you remember the number?'

'Oh.' She looked from one to the other, then round the hall, before she said, 'I'm dreadful on numbers. It starts with a JR.'

'That's all right. That's all right.' The police constables looked at each other, and then one said, 'Sit down, Mrs Bailey.'

'Why should I sit down? Look, please tell me what's happened or what you know.'

'Mrs Bailey, your husband's car is outside on the road.'

'*It's on the . . .* !'

'Yes, it's on the road. But your husband isn't in it, and I'm afraid, there is evidence of something very wrong. It isn't locked, the ignition key's still there, and parcels that were presumably on the front passenger seat are trampled on the floor. There are bits of broken glass there and a sort of a child's toy and various other articles which we haven't as yet examined. And what is

more. . . . Please do sit down, Mrs Bailey.' The taller of the two men took her arm and led her to the hall chair, and when she was seated her voice was just a whisper as she said, 'You said: what is more.'

'Yes. There's evidently been a struggle because there's . . . well, there is a splash of blood on the dashboard, and more on the pavement. But the blood on the pavement is near the boot of the car. Do you want a drink of water, ma'am? Get her a drink of water.'

'Where's the kitchen?'

She brought up her drooping head and put out her hand, saying, 'I'm all right. I'm all right.'

'Have you any relatives living near who could come and stay with you?'

Her mother was the last person on earth she wanted at this moment, and Nell wasn't here, so she shook her head.

P.C. Anderson said to his partner, 'Ring the office and see if Joan Wallace is free. Ask them to send her round straightaway; and while you're on you'd better tell Sergeant Nichols to inform the inspector.'

'He'll have gone home.'

'Yes, I know that.' The words were a hiss. 'Well, he can just come back from home or from wherever he is. You tell them.'

There was a great silence in Fiona's head, yet she could hear the policemen talking. They were at the far end of space; they were disembodied voices. And one of the voices floated over her head and spoke to her, saying, 'Have you any children?'

The silence seemed to explode as she pulled herself to her feet, and she said, 'I have four children.'

'Young?'

'The eldest is twelve. He's very sensible. I'll go and wake him.'

'No. No, I wouldn't ma'am, not yet. A policewoman will be coming to keep you company, and the inspector an' all because. . . .' But she didn't wait to hear why; she walked to the phone and dialled the Brookley Manor number again.

It was Sir Charles's secretary who spoke, saying, 'Yes, Mrs Bailey?'

She went to open her mouth but found she couldn't speak for a moment and she turned and looked at the policeman and, her voice again like a whimper, she said, 'It is Sir Charles Kingdom's secretary. He . . . he was at the dinner with my husband tonight. Will . . . will you tell him, please?'

Constable Anderson took the phone from her hand, and he said, 'This is Police Constable Anderson here from Fellburn. We have found Mr Bailey's car outside his own gate. There are signs of a struggle. That's all I can tell you at the moment, sir.'

'Well . . . well where is he? I mean, Mr Bailey?'

'We'd like to know that, sir. He wasn't in the car. We are just going on what we saw there.'

'*My God!* I'll come across.'

'I don't think there's anything you can do at the moment, sir, but we'll keep you informed. Mrs Bailey would like that.'

The policeman put down the phone and, turning to Fiona, he said, 'The less there are moving around the car at the moment, the better, ma'am. You understand?'

'Yes, yes. But . . . but what do you think? Oh' – she put her hand to her head – 'I . . . I can't believe it. Who would want to do that? But there. . . . Yes, yes, there was a car outside from just after nine blocking our drive. There was someone inside, a courting couple I think, but I didn't like to go onto the pavement to enquire further.'

'Are you sure of the time, ma'am?'

'I think it was nine. I'm not sure. I'm not sure of anything at the moment. Then I heard Mr Paget come in at eleven. No, no; it wasn't quite eleven.'

'He is your neighbour, this Mr Paget?'

'Yes. Yes, he is our neighbour.'

'We could speak to him. We'll do that when the inspector arrives.'

'No, no.' She shook her head. 'He's not well. He . . . well, his mind's gone a bit funny lately and. . . .' She stopped and

stared across the hall, and it was as if her eyes were seeing through the kitchen into the back garden and into the house next door. My God! He had said he would do for Bill. And he was more than slightly mad. Had he?

'What is it, ma'am?'

'Mr Paget, he . . . he was angry with my husband.'

'What was he angry about?'

'Because his daughter-in-law was to be married to one of my husband's men. She was divorced from his son. He didn't want to lose her, and he blamed Bill. Yes, yes; he blamed Bill for being the means of them losing Nell. He's been going funny lately. He's. . . . Oh my God!' She put her hand over her mouth and rushed towards the kitchen and just managed to reach the sink before she vomited.

Constable Anderson was about to follow her, but he turned to Constable Burrows, saying, 'Get on that phone again and see if they've got the inspector yet. There's more here than meets the eye. I want to know if I should go next door or not. . . .'

It was half-past one when the inspector and Police Constable Anderson rang the bell next door. When there was no response to the second ring the inspector kept his finger on the bell, and this time it was answered by the opening of a window.

'What is it? What is it?'

'Mrs Paget?'

'Yes, yes, I'm Mrs Paget.'

'Would you mind coming down a moment, please?'

'What do you want?'

'We are the police. We just want to speak to your husband for a moment.'

'He's in bed, sound asleep.'

'Would you please come down, Mrs Paget?'

The window closed with hardly a sound, and a minute or two later Mrs Paget opened the front door, then stood pulling hard at her dressing-gown belt.

'May we come in, Mrs Paget?'

She stood hesitant for a moment, then said, 'What . . . what can you want with my husband?'

'We just wanted to ask him a few questions.'

'What about, and at this time of night?'

'Would you ask him to come down, please?'

'No . . . no, I can't. He's not well.'

'Mrs Paget' – they were standing in the hall now – 'Mr Bailey has gone missing. His car is outside his gate. There is evidence that he has been attacked: there are bloodstains on the pavement and signs of a struggle inside the car.'

'But . . . but what has my husband to do with that?'

The inspector did not answer this question; instead he asked one of his own. 'What time did your husband return home tonight?'

'I . . . I don't know; I was asleep. I haven't been very well.'

'Do you know what time he went out?'

'About seven o'clock, I think.'

'Do you know where he was going?'

'No, no. He often goes for a drive. It helps to soothe his . . . well, it helps to soothe his nerves.'

'I'm afraid, Mrs Paget, I must ask you to go and wake your husband and bring him downstairs.'

'But why? Why? My husband wouldn't have anything to do –' She put her hand to her mouth, then said, 'What has Fiona been saying? I mean, Mrs Bailey.'

'Mrs Bailey is very distressed. Her husband has disappeared after apparently being attacked. She recalls that your husband was very abusive to her and threatened what he was going to do to her husband. Now I would like to see your husband and have this accusation confirmed or denied. If you don't bring him downstairs, Mrs Paget, I'm afraid I'll have to go up and question him there.'

The poor woman almost stumbled up the stairs, and it was a full ten minutes later when she reappeared in the hall followed by her husband who, on the sight of the police, began to tremble.

'He's not well. He's under the doctor. But he would never do such a thing. Come and sit down, dear.' She led the shivering

form into the sitting-room, and the two officers followed. Looking at what appeared to be a tall frail man, the inspector had difficulty in believing that this man could overpower a fellow like Bill Bailey, because he knew Bill Bailey and he was a tough guy altogether. One blow from him should have knocked this fellow flying. But from what he had heard from Mrs Bailey, this man was a sort of Jekyll and Hyde. He bent towards him now, saying, 'Where did you go when you drove your car tonight, Mr Paget?'

'I don't know. Well, I just drive. It . . . it soothes me, doesn't it? Doesn't it, Bella?'

'Yes, dear, it does, it does. He . . . he hasn't been very well. . . .'

'I know. I know, Mrs Paget.' The inspector silenced her with a small movement of his hand. Then looking at the man again, he said, 'Did you stop and speak to Mr Bailey when you were out?'

'No, no, I didn't. I never saw him. His car was at the gate though when I came in, and I felt bad against him. I remember that, yes, I do, but not any more.'

The policemen exchanged glances.

'Did you not get out of your car and speak to Mr Bailey?'

Both men watched the older man blink his eyes, nip on his lip, then look up at his wife before saying, 'No, no, I never did. I never did.'

'No; of course, you didn't, dear. Of course, you didn't.'

The inspector now spoke to Mrs Paget, saying, 'Who is your doctor, Mrs Paget?'

'Doctor Nelson. He . . . he knows my husband's case.'

'What do you mean, your husband's case?'

'Well, he's been under him for five years. I have too. That's what I mean.' There was an icy touch in her tone now. 'What are you trying to insinuate? My John wouldn't hurt a fly. He gets angry at times when he's not well, but, as I said, he wouldn't hurt a fly.'

'What are you getting at? What are they getting at, Bella?'

'Nothing, my dear, nothing.'

'I'm afraid we are, Mr Paget.' The inspector once more leant forward. 'As I've already said, Mr Bailey is missing. There are signs of a struggle and blood was spilt. And we just want to know when you last saw him and if you spoke to him with regard to what you were angry about.'

'No, no, I didn't. I haven't done anything. I didn't. I wouldn't. I'd never go as far as that, never. Would I, Bella? Would I?'

'No, no, you wouldn't, dear.'

'Take your husband back to bed, Mrs Paget. We'll have another talk later. I'm sorry we disturbed you. I'd get in touch with his doctor, and perhaps he will come and see him in the morning. I may be round again, too.'

Both men left the room, and when Mrs Paget followed them it would seem she hadn't the strength to open the door; and the policeman, putting his hand on her shoulder, said, 'Don't worry, missis, don't worry; it's just an investigation. We have to ask these questions. You understand that?'

She nodded, but was unable to speak. And when the door closed on the two men they walked slowly down the drive and into the street again and stood looking at the Volvo and the stain on the pavement near the boot.

'What d'you think, sir?'

'I can't see him getting the better of Bailey in any way. Yet if he's schizophrenic . . . they can get the strength of ten men when the mood's on them. Remember that young lad last year from Boswell Terrace, a respectable family, father a solicitor? Look what he did. He's out again now, but I understand the mother's in a breakdown because she's hardly let him see daylight since. To my mind he should never have been let home. And that's what the girl's parents are saying too. Still, by the look of that old fellow he won't do much more harm the night. But if he has gone for Bailey, we've got to find out where he's dumped him. We'll have another go at him first thing in the morning. By that time we should have his doctor's report. But we had better go in now and see if Burrows and Wallace have been able to calm down Mrs Bailey. She's in a state. I think we'll have to

have a doctor there an' all. In the meantime I want this car ringed round; somebody on duty all the time. And it looks as if our next visitor will be Sir Charles Kingdom's secretary, if not Sir Charles himself.'

'I thought he was ill, sir, I mean, the old man?'

'No, I understand from the papers and the radio report of the meeting that put Mr William Bailey in the big money that the old fellow was there today, and very much in voice.'

They were going up the drive now when he stopped and said, 'We might be jumping to conclusions about that old fellow next door. Disappointed rivals, you know, can become nasty. And they say there were twelve or more of them in for that big slice of cake. Yes –' He stood now under the outside light of the front door and, nodding to the constable, he said, 'It looks as if we'll have a number of interviews tomorrow besides the old schizo boy next door. But there's one thing I'm going to have and that's a couple of hours shut-eye before we have them. So I'll send Parkins and Steel round; they can see that nobody fingers anything. We'll leave Burrows here with Wallace. If it's a kidnapping job, and you never know, there should be somebody near that phone. In the meantime I want you to go back to the office and tell Pringle to get names, addresses, and phone numbers of every man that was at that meeting yesterday, that's those on the board and also every firm that applied for the job. Names, addresses, the lot. Anyway, nothing much can be done till daylight, and since I've been up since six o'clock yesterday morning preparing for the minor Royalty that was flitting through, it's more than twenty hours since I had my head down, and I need at least four hours a night or I get nasty.'

When they entered the house they heard the sound of crying coming from the sitting-room; and when they entered the room it was to see Mrs Bailey holding a young boy tightly to her and saying, 'It's all right. It's all right. He'll come back. You know Mr Bill, don't you, no one gets the better of Mr Bill. They never have and they never will. You know that. You know that, Mark, no one gets the better of Mr Bill.'

8

It was nine o'clock the next morning. The car had been taken away; a policeman was standing just inside the gate and a number of reporters on the pavement outside. The news had spread early up the avenue, and there had been a crowd of sightseers to see the car being driven away. But it had thinned somewhat by the time Barney McGuire forced himself through to speak to the policeman. 'I'm Mr Bailey's foreman,' he said. 'We've just heard. I must see Mrs Bailey.'

'What's your name?'

'Barney McGuire.'

'Stay where you are a minute.'

The policeman went up the path; and when he returned he opened the gate, but as he did so a reporter tried to slip in, only to be grabbed by the collar and pushed back onto the pavement again. And the policeman, an extremely tall young man, said, 'We don't want any rough stuff, do we? Now I've told you, if there's any news from inside you'll get it, but you'll get it standing on your own side of the gate.'

The door was opened for Barney by a red-eyed Katie who said, 'Mam's in the sitting-room, Mr McGuire. Have . . . have you heard anything?'

'No, hinny. No.' He took off his cap and walked on tiptoe across the hall and into the sitting-room.

Fiona was standing in front of the fireplace. It was already quite warm outside but she had the electric fire on. She said, 'Hello, Barney.'

'Hello, Mrs B. I can't believe it. I just can't believe it. We're all stunned. The fellas all wanted to come and see what they could do, but, as I said, the job had to go on. That's what he would want. We had to keep at it until he came back. Oh. . . .' He stopped, lost for words.

'Why should it happen to him, Barney?'

Her voice was breaking. 'Who would want to do this? And he must have put up a fight, there must have been more than one. I . . . I thought last night in my distress that it might have been Mr Paget next door because he's been funny lately and going on about Nell marrying Bert, because he didn't want her to leave them. And he had said quite threatening things to me, what he would do to Bill. But when I thought about it, Bill would have knocked him down with one hand. The only thing is, if he had an implement. But then he would have had to lift or pull Bill into his car and take him . . . somewhere. Oh, I can't help it.' She turned now and faced the fire. 'I can't help it, Barney. I keep thinking aloud all the time, talking, talking. I think I'm going to go mad.'

He was standing at her side now, his hand on her shoulder. 'Look, as the lads said back there, he's a tough guy, the toughest, they don't come tougher than him. He's not going to be knocked out with one blow. It's likely somebody's done this for money, kidnapping you know because they've heard he's got the big job. And you'll see, you'll get a phone call shortly. But as we all said, if that was the case we'd skin our hides to help you meet it, we would that, because there'll never be another boss like him. And they all know it. Who, I ask you, would make it into a sort of partnership as he did last year on that other job and give us a percentage of the profits at Christmas? Not many, not many I can tell you.' His voice was rising as if he were addressing

a meeting. Then he turned as the door opened and Mark came in.

'Hello there, son.'

'Hello, Mr Barney. Have . . . have you heard anything?'

'No, lad; we've only just got to hear of it back on the houses. We couldn't believe it.'

'Sit down, Mam.' The boy came and took Fiona's arm and, as if she were an old lady, led her to the couch. Then looking at Barney, he said, 'Sit down, Mr Barney.'

'No, lad, I won't stay. He'd want the job to go on, as I said to your mam. And I'll see it goes on. Aye by God! I will, because he'll be back. You'll see, he'll be back. And you know what I just said a minute ago, Mrs B, about blackmail, you know, of being kidnapped; well, as the lads were sayin', if that's the case it's been done by those blokes who mugged me and took Jack Mowbray's bike and levelled Jos Wright's allotment, not to mention Morris Fenwick's pigeons. Then there was Alec Finlay's outhouse and all his tools, and the whole thing started with Tommy Turnbull's car being pinched. D'you remember? Now they've been through us all, and it seems to be the same two fellas, they've turned to the boss, and it'll be money they're after this time, blackmail, as the lads said. By God! If we could only get our hands on them they wouldn't live, I can tell you, not to go to court. But . . . but as Davey Love, the new Irish fella, said, "Blokes don't do things like that off their own bat except they're gettin' paid, 'cos there'd be no money in it, would there, for levelling an allotment and letting out pigeons?" No, there's some big bloke behind it. But that fella Love's got his head screwed on the right way, and he seems to think everything stems from the fellas who took the car. He remembers what those blokes looked like, Mutt and Jeff, he said, one big and one small, well, not over-small, but contrast like, you know.'

She wished he would stop talking. She wished he would go away.

There was a bit of commotion in the hall, and she rose from the couch and put her hand out towards Mark's and gripped it

tightly. But she didn't move from where she was standing: she kept her eyes on the door expecting it to open and Bill to walk or stumble in. But it was Katie, who said, 'It's Sir Kingdom, Mam.'

She drew in a long breath, then said, 'Oh, show him in. Bring him in.' Then turning to Barney, she said, 'Thank you, Barney. If . . . if you hear anything at all you'll let me know, won't you? And if we have any news we'll phone you.'

'Thank you, ma'am. Yes, thank you.' He edged his way to the door but had to step back when Sir Charles, followed by his secretary, came into the room, the old man saying, 'They didn't tell me a word of this, Mrs Bailey, not a word did I hear until after breakfast. A lot of nincompoops. My dear. My dear. What can I say?'

He turned and looked at Barney who was aiming to get out of the door and said, 'You . . . you one of the workmen?'

'Yes, sir. I'm the boss's gaffer.'

'Oh, well, he'd want you to keep on working, wouldn't he?'

'Yes, sir. Yes, he would that. Good-day to you, sir.'

'Oh my dear.' He was moving towards Fiona now, his hands outstretched. 'What can I say? I feel responsible. Oh I do, I feel responsible.'

'Please sit down, Sir Charles.'

'Thank you. Thank you.'

The old man dropped into a chair; then looking up at his secretary, he said, 'I'll never forgive you for keeping this from me; nor my wife either, because . . . because I feel responsible for it all. I should have done something before now. Yes, I should. I should.'

'What could you have done, Sir Charles, that could have prevented this?'

'Oh, my dear' – the old man put his hand to his head – 'I should have gone to the police and told them what I thought she was up to. What did I do? I said to Bailey I would make good all the damages to his men. But as he pointed out to me, oh yes, and truthfully, you couldn't pay for a life.'

'What are you saying, Sir Charles?' Fiona's eyes were wide, her mouth slightly agape; then she went on, 'You know . . . you know who has done this? You know where my husband is?'

'No, my dear; the latter I don't know, I don't know where your husband is. I'd give all I own at this moment to be able to say to you, yes, I know where he is. But her thugs must have got at him.'

'Her?' She could not believe what her mind was thinking. Her, he had said. Her voice was small when she said, 'Your niece, you mean?'

'No, she's not my niece, dear, she's my godchild. Strangely, I've thought of her as a daughter and put up with her whims and antics for years; in fact I've condoned them, but not this, not this. I warned her, but she went abroad and I couldn't locate her. I tried again this morning only to be told that she's gone off again. Rupert here' – he wagged his finger towards his secretary – 'got in touch with her accountant, and what he was told, well, I could hardly believe. Over the past months she has sold most of her businesses and now plans to live abroad. Where, nobody seems to be able to tell me. But you can't escape in this world for very long, and if anything happens to Bailey. . . .'

Fiona turned from him, her hand shading her eyes, saying as she did so, 'Please! Please, sir, don't even suggest such a thing. I . . . I can't bear it. Anyway, you should know her and I'm sure you don't think she would be capable of . . . of anything like –' she couldn't say 'murder', but instead said, 'anything awful just because my husband refused her advances and told her plainly he wouldn't leave me for her. That's what it's all about, isn't it? Hurt pride, someone dared to refuse her something. But . . . but even so, she would surely stop at ordering someone to really hurt him, murder him, wouldn't she? Wouldn't she?' Her voice had risen almost to a scream, and both Katie and Mark rushed to her side and put their arms about her.

The next moment, however, she became full of contrition as she saw the old man bow his head and the secretary put his arm

on his shoulder, saying, 'Can I get you something, sir?' And he turned to Fiona, saying, 'May I ask if you have any spirits, a little brandy?'

'Oh yes, yes.'

'I'll get it, Mam.'

Mark hurried to the drinks' cabinet in the corner of the room, and when he returned with the glass half filled with brandy the secretary smiled wanly at him, saying, 'That looks like a treble, but thank you.' Then taking the glass from the boy, he turned to Sir Charles, saying, 'Drink this, sir,' and the old man, with a shaking hand, took the glass, looked at it for a moment before drinking half its contents, then sat back in the chair, his head resting on the rail. Presently, looking at Fiona, he said, 'Nothing you could say to me, my dear, could come within miles of the condemnation I'm pouring on my own head at this moment.'

'I'm sorry, Sir Charles, but I'm so upset. He was, I mean he is,' and she stressed the last word, 'such a good man. He loves my children as if they were his own. He may be rough of tongue but he would not do an underhand or dishonourable thing.'

'I'm sure of that, my dear. Yes, I know that. I had great respect for him.'

'Sir, may I speak?'

'Can you tell me who has ever been able to stop you if you wanted to, man?'

'Well, you seem to have come to the conclusion that this happening is solely at Mrs Brown's door. But last night I seemed to think it could have been done by the neighbour next door. Isn't that so, Mrs Bailey?' After a moment's hesitation, Fiona said, 'Yes. Yes, that's right. I understand Mr Paget is schizophrenic or something similar.'

'And you know, sir, such people can have dual personalities; they can do the most outrageous things when their character changes. They can have uncommon strength and be wily with it. So I don't think, sir, you should take it for granted that Mrs Brown is solely behind this. Then again, as has been hinted, it

could have been the work of a disappointed contender for the estate project.'

A little of the strain seemed to go from the old man's face, and he looked fom his secretary to Fiona, saying, 'Yes, he could be right. He could be right. I only hope that he is. But whatever, the main thing now is to find out what has happened to your husband.'

'But we can't find out that, sir, can we, until we know who did it?'

Their attention was all on Mark now, and the secretary said, 'Yes, you're right, you're right. But the police are hard at work looking into every possibility; they are not just following one lead. The inspector said to me on the phone this morning that this case is turning out like a piece of tapestry, there are so many threads to it.'

Sir Charles now drank the remainder of the brandy; then looking at his secretary he rose to his feet, saying, 'You've eased my mind a little, Rupert. You have the habit of doing that. I suppose you get that from your mathematical mind.' Then looking at Fiona again, he held out his hand to her, and when she took it he patted it and in a low voice he muttered, 'We will keep in close touch. I . . . I will phone every hour.'

'Thank you, Sir Charles.'

'Oh, don't thank me for anything, my dear, don't thank me.' His head still shaking, he went out, and his secretary, after exchanging a glance with Fiona, turned and followed the old man. . . .

The next visitor was Mr Paget's doctor. He stood in the hall, saying, 'I've had a long talk with him. Quite candidly he doesn't really remember what he did last night when he went out in the car. This often happens in cases like this. I've attended him for years and he hasn't had a bad turn, well, not for some long time. But they were pretty frequent at one time. He seems to have been better since his daughter-in-law came to live with them. Really he's been a changed individual. It's been only since she talked of leaving them to get married again that he's

reverted. Even so, the once or twice I've looked in on him recently he hasn't seemed too bad. Of course, in cases like these they can become very sly and appear quite normal when talking to a professional man. But I can say he is greatly distressed this morning. He says he saw your husband's car there as he drove into his drive, which surely points to the fact that, whatever happened, happened before he arrived home, because your husband, naturally, would drive straight into his garage, wouldn't he?'

'Yes, yes, he would.'

'But then, of course, he could have said he saw the car there. I don't know, I really don't know, except that if the police get at him and wear him down he might own up to things that he's never done out of sheer fear, and so confuse the issue. This also happens. Anyway, I'm glad they're leaving him where he is for the time being. And his poor little wife is so upset. Now she is, physically, not well at all. I know how worried you must be about your husband, Mrs Bailey, but I do hope that whatever has happened to him isn't laid at Mr Paget's door, because all his life he's been a frightened man. He knows what's wrong with him and he's afraid of it. But when he has these turns he takes on an aggressive attitude as if to make up for the fear and timidity that has filled the best part of his life. We never know what the other fellow is thinking, do we, Mrs Bailey? Anyway, I'll be looking in on him later in the day. I'll tell you what transpires then.'

'Thank you, Doctor.'

It was around twelve o'clock when the next visitor appeared after having had an altercation with the policeman at the gate. Mark opened the door to him and the visitor said, 'Could I be seein' yer ma, son? I'm Davey Love; you know, Sammy's father.'

'Yes, yes. Come in, please. Will you come into the sitting-room? My mother's upstairs; I'll call her.'

A minute later Mark knocked on Fiona's bedroom door, calling, 'Mam.'

'Yes? Come in, Mark.'

'Sammy's father's downstairs.'

'Mr Love?'

'Yes.'

'Oh. Tell him I'll be down in a minute.'

She had turned her face towards him, and he knew that she was crying and he went out and walked slowly down the stairs. He too wanted to cry, like he had wanted to in the night, but, as his mother had said, she had only him to rely on until Mr Bill came back. He felt more in touch with him when he thought of him as Mr Bill rather than as Dad. He was wonderful as a dad but he had been more wonderful still as Mr Bill. He had come into their lives like an explosion, a burst of fireworks. In those early days he had longed to get home just to hear his voice. It was different now he was their father. But it was a good difference. He supposed it was a difference without the fear that he might get up, pack up and leave as he had done once before, when he was a lodger. He entered the room to see Mr Love sitting on the sofa holding Willie's hand and saying, 'You take me word for it, yer dad's comin' back. We'll scour the town and as far afield as it takes, but we'll find him, and whole. An' the next thing you know he'll be bawlin' his big head off at you like he does us at work. Oh, God in heaven! I'd love to hear that bawl this minute, indeed to God I would that. You know, boy' – he now looked up at Mark – 'I've just joined the troop, so to speak, but I've never worked with a more decent lot of men, and I've never before worked with men who had a good word for their boss. Not that they're angels, they're always on the grouse. Well I mean, if we didn't grumble what would we have to talk about? Now I ask you. But when the chips are down that lot would stand on their heads for him. . . . Oh, there you are, ma'am.' And he rose to his feet as Fiona entered the room. 'It's me dinner hour. I thought I'd come round and have a word with you.'

'Thank you, Mr Love. It's very kind of you.'

'Kind? Not at all. If it wasn't that that big-mouth gaffer Barney says we've all got to stick at it, 'cos that's what the boss would

expect, I would've had the half-day off, or the whole day, since I heard the news. I have me own ideas where I could put me fingers on two blokes, the two that've been playin' havoc with the gang. But o'course there's no proof that this could be tacked on to them. They were up to their eyes in piddlin' things like stealin' bikes, lettin' pigeons out, an' things like that, annoyin' things. But I don't know if they'd be up to kidnappin'. They're sayin' now there's so many suspects fallin' over themselves, the police don't know which end of them's up. There's an old bloke next door gone off his head, they say. An' then there's those that were after the big job. An' you know some blokes can't take defeat. Up to every trick in the book. Oh aye, begod! I know some of them. Don't I now. But anyway, I just want to tell you you've got all me attention and as soon as I finish on the job the night I'll be lookin' for those two blokes, and if it's only one of 'em I find, I'll kick his backside from here to hell before handin' him over to the polis. Ma'am, can I ask you somethin', personal like?'

'Yes, Mr Love, anything.'

'It's about me young 'un. He missed seein' Willie yesterday, an' this bein' Thursday he's bound for Confession. But what in the name of God! he has to confess I won't be knowin', except his four letter words, an' they've dropped off of late. It's surprisin'. I know what state you're in but d'you think that the morrow he could come round and have a word with yer Willie there. It's amazing, 'tis, how the lad's taken to Willie. An' you like him an' all, Willie, don't you?'

Willie's face was unsmiling as he said, 'Yes. Yes, I do like Sammy.'

'There you are then. How will it be, missis? He won't be in the way, he knows better. I've threatened to knock his brains out an' slap his face with 'em if he doesn't behave himself when he's in yer house. But that boy's as miserable as sin when he can't see the young chap here.' He jerked his head in Willie's direction. 'I've never known him to be like this, not in all his life. Such a change in him. He was always askin' when his ma

was comin' back, an' when I said, never I hope, I'd find him cryin' in bed. So I had to tell him she'd come in the door one day: she'd pop in just like the bad penny she was. But lately, not a word about his ma an' no cryin' in bed. So, if you wouldn't mind. I feel that I'm imposin' upon you in yer trouble, but. . . .'

'Of course, Mr Love, he may come round.' Anything, she was thinking, only go.

'Thank you, ma'am. Thank you very much. Well, I'll be off now. I'll have a bite and a pint afore I start again, but I tell you I'll be hot on somebody's trail the night if it takes me to dawn. I have me own ideas about this. Oh aye, I have. Goodbye to you.'

'Goodbye, Mr Love. Will you see Mr Love out, Mark?'

'It's a fine family you have. I don't begrudge you them, but I can't help wishin'. No harm in wishin' is there?'

'No, Mr Love, there isn't. No, there isn't.'

'No, there isn't. And I know what you're wishin' at this minute, and it'll come true. Believe me, it'll come true.' He had reached the sitting-room door when he turned and added, 'I'm a very bad Catholic, and a bad Catholic is worse than a heathen, there's no hope for them. God forgives them who doesn't know any better, like heathens, Chinese, Indians, and Baptists' – he grinned as he said the last word – 'but for a bad Catholic there's no hope, 'cos you know, we should know better, we've been given the faith. But I'll tell you what I'll do the night afore I start on me rounds after those two bug . . . blokes, I'll go into church, before God I will! and I'll make a bargain with Him and I'll give you three guesses as to what that bargain will be. Now I'll be off, rightly this time I'll be off. Good-day to you.'

Fiona didn't answer, 'Good-day.' She only wished that she could laugh, but she would never laugh again. No, she would never laugh again. . . .

The inspector called in the afternoon to tell her how things were going. His men had made a house to house call in the district. They had police scouring the fields on the outskirts of

the town and Brooker's woodland. He didn't mention that there were divers in the river, nor did he say that they'd had an anonymous call from someone who had likely put in for the contract, to say that he had heard a certain man, whom he named, saying that he would like to put a bomb under Bailey's car. That was another thread in the tapestry of this case but they were following it up.

At seven o'clock in the evening Nell phoned. They had just heard the news; they had been out all day. They were coming back straightaway.

'Oh, Nell, Nell,' Fiona had almost wailed over the phone; 'I think I'm going mad. I can't eat. I can't close my eyes. Oh, Nell, Nell, I'll be glad to see you.'

'I'll be with you soon,' said Nell. 'But there's no train from here until six o'clock tomorrow morning, but we'll be on it.'

At eight o'clock her mother rang. 'Fiona. Oh, my dear, my dear, I've just heard. I'd been on a trip, I'd been to Harrogate with the bridge four, you know we go on a little trip now and again. Oh, my dear, I am, I must say it, I am extremely sorry. Believe me, dear, I am. We had our differences I know, but for this to happen. Have you heard any more news?'

'No, Mother.'

'What do you think could have happened to him?'

'I don't know, Mother. It's all in the papers or on the radio. It will be on the nine o'clock news again, I suppose.'

'I'll come round, dear.'

'No, Mother, please wait until tomorrow morning; I'm . . . I'm going to take a sleeping tablet.'

'But the children?'

'The children are wonderful, Mother. Mark is managing them and Nell will be back in the morning.'

'Oh, Nell! I suppose you prefer others to your own kith and kin.'

'Please, Mother, please.'

'All right, dear, all right, I won't. But . . . but I'm distressed for you.'

'Thank you, Mother. Thank you.'

'Fiona, I think it only right that I should come round now.'

'Mother, do this for me, please: let me sleep tonight.'

'But . . . but, my dear, I wouldn't disturb you. I can sleep downstairs on the couch.'

'Mother, you'd never rest on the couch, you know you like your own bed, but I appreciate what you're offering, what you're saying. I do really.'

'I'm so glad you do, dear, and I mean it. I'm really deeply sorry. And after he had got that wonderful contract. Someone's done this out of spite, I'm sure of it. They hate to see people get on.'

Fiona closed her eyes. How could people change like that? Her mother talking like a normal caring person, a normal caring mother, when only two days ago Bill's name was like a firebrand to her. If only she didn't talk as if Bill was dead and she herself already a widow.

'Good-night, Mother,' she said. 'Thank you for calling. I'll see you in the morning.'

'Good-night, my dear. Good-night.'

She had said she was going to take a sleeping tablet. She had no idea of taking a sleeping tablet. She doubted she had any in the house. Yes, she had. When she had come out of hospital at the beginning of last year she hadn't been able to sleep and the doctor had prescribed some for her but telling her not to make a habit of them: 'You're a healthy human being and sleep should come naturally,' he had said. So there must be some somewhere upstairs. They wouldn't be in the medicine cupboard; she didn't keep pills or anything like that in there in case the children got their hands on them. They would be in her toilet drawer in the dressing-table. That's what she would do, she would take a sleeping tablet. She'd blot it out and when she woke in the morning he'd be there.

Yes, he'd be there.

9

'Da, ya didn't come in till late.'

'I know I didn't, but I thought you were asleep.'

'I couldn't get to sleep. They were rowin' next door.'

'They're always rowin' next door, but you sleep through it, usually you do.'

'Aye, I know. But I wasn't really thinkin' about them, but about Mr Bailey.'

'We're all thinkin' about him, lad. Eat yer flakes.'

'I don't feel hungry, Da.'

'*Eat yer flakes.*'

'Why . . . why were you out so late, Da?'

'I went to see a man about a dog.'

'Da, don't be funny. I feel awful inside 'bout Willie's da.'

'You're not the only one that feels awful inside 'bout Willie's da. An' that's why I was out late. You know those two fellas I asked you about? It was some time ago. You remember the car that was stolen?'

'Aye, I do.'

'Well, I asked you if you had seen a tall fella and a one not so tall, thick-set, fatty like. They had been in Kit's bar. And ya said ya had. Would you know their mugs again if you saw 'em?'

'Aye, Da. An' I've seen them a number of times.'

'You have! Then why in hell's blazes didn't you tell me then?'

'I didn't know ya wanted them; the man got the car back, didn't he?'

'Where did you see them?'

'Oh, in the street, an' where they lived.'

'Where they lived?' Davey was now on his hunkers pulling his son round towards him. And the boy said, 'Look out, Da, you've spilt me flakes.'

'Never mind yer bloody flakes! Ya say you know where they live?'

'Well, I did, sometime back. It was behind Gallagher's yard.'

'The scrap-iron place?'

'Aye, Da.'

'There's nothin' behind there, only broken down sheds.'

'There's Gallagher's Mill, the old stone house that's droppin' to bits. They took the machinery away years ago.'

'Gallagher's Mill? How d'you know they're livin' in there?'

'Well, I found a bit o' scrap on the tip. It looked like lead, and I took it to Gallagher's yard and old Mr Gallagher was in the office. But there was a man, clearin' up like, two of 'em, a tall one and a short 'un, and I thought they were the men who I'd seen afore. One of 'em took me scrap an' said it wasn't lead. He gave me fifty p. And when I was goin' away the other one laughed an' said, "That's worth a quid or two," so I knew it was lead. I went out the gate pretendin' I was goin', but I went along by the railin's and I saw them both come behind the office an' go into the mill. They had me bit of lead with 'em. Then I stayed put and I watched 'em. It was on a Saturday so I had plenty of time. An' when they came out they had different jackets on, so I guessed they were livin' there.'

'How long ago was that?'

'Oh, a fortnight ago, Da, or three weeks. P'raps longer. But one thing, they didn't leave by the yard gate they went out the back way an' cut across the fields and onto the road there.'

Davey Love stood up and, looking down on his son, he said,

'It's God's judgement on me for not talkin' to you more. If I had, I'd likely have had those two bastards weeks ago.'

'What have the bastards done, Da?'

'Now enough of that. I've told you. You keep a clean tongue in yer head else it won't be soap I'll wash yer mouth out with but a pan scrub.'

'But ya said it, Da.'

'Never mind what I said. Take no notice of what I say, just do what I tell you. Goin' along to a fancy house like the Bailey's an' pallin' up with a lad like that Willie, then comin' out with words like bastard.'

Sammy looked up at this tall man. He was funny, not laughable funny, well just at times he was laughable funny, but at other times he was funny. He said he hadn't to swear and use bad language, especially four letter words, yet his own mouth was drippin' them all the time. He was a funny man. 'What're ya goin' to do, Da?' he said.

'What I'm goin' to do now, lad, is go to work. But what I'd like to do is go round there an' take those two fellas by the scruff of the neck an' bang their heads together till they were just about insensible. Then I'd half string 'em up until I put the fear of God in 'em with just their toes touchin' the ground. Then I'd punch 'em silly. After that, I'd call the polis an' let 'em deal with what was left. That's what I'd do. But I've got to go to work. But you say nothin' 'bout those two blokes, mind, not a word to anybody. I'll deal with 'em after five o'clock the night. By God! I will. And may He an' His Holy Mother help me. . . . I went to church last night, you know.'

'Did ya, Da?' Sammy's voice came out on a high squeak.

'Aye, I did. And I asked Him to help me find them fellas who had done whatever they had done to the boss. I made a deal with Him. Well, if He carries out His deal I'll carry out mine.'

Sammy's face was one wide smile now and his father, getting into his coat, turned and looked at him, saying, 'That pleased you, me goin' to church, did it?'

'Aye, yes, it did, Da. But Sister Monica told me ya would.'

'Sister Monica told you that I would go to church?'

'Aye, she did an' all.'

'How did that come about?'

'She asked if ya went to Mass, an' when I said no, she said did ya go to Confession and I said, no. Then she said, did ya go to yer Easter duties, and I said, I didn't think so. Well, she said if I lit two candles every week and I said one Our Father and ten Hail Marys every night for a month, ya would go.'

'She did? An' did you?'

'Aye, I have. But the month isn't quite up yet.'

'Well, I'll be buggered. Was that the one I was goin' to skelp if she hit you again across the ears just once more?'

'Oh no, that was Sister Catherine. But as I said, Da, she doesn't hit me 'cross the ears any more, she just shakes the bloody life out of me.'

'Now, now, what did I tell you. Wash your mouth out. You want to go to church every night yerself and ask God to stop you swearin'.'

'Aye, I could. And I could ask Him for both of us, Da, couldn't I?'

There was a grin on Davey's face as he lifted his hand, but it stayed in mid-air and he said, 'You know yer gettin' too big for yer boots; they'll be givin' you corns, but that'll be nothin' to the corns that'll sprout on yer backside if I have any more of that lip of yers. Now I must be off. Do the usual, mind: wash up, make yer bed, and mine; rub the kitchen floor, then lock up. All right?'

'All right, Da. Be seein' ya.'

'Be seein' you.'

When the door had closed on his father and he heard him running down the iron stairs, he sat where he was at the table, not eating now, but thinking. His da was a funny bloke. But he was all right. Oh aye, his da was all right. He was glad he had his da. And he didn't miss his ma now, not like he used to. He knew what he was going to do today, and if his da was to find out he'd skin him alive. Oh aye, he would, because he was one for him stayin' at school, but he was goin' to play the nick. After he'd had his

school dinner he was goin' to slip out. There was something he had to do. His da had said he could go and see Willie the night. But he didn't only want to go and see Willie, he wanted to go and see his mother; there was something about Willie's mother that he liked. And he wanted to take her another present. He had the idea that that teapot could have been part of a set. His ma had a china one on the dresser, an' she'd gone mad when it got broke in a bloody row. People just didn't throw away a teapot like that. If they had a teapot, they wouldn't just have the teapot they would have the sugar basin and the milk jug, wouldn't they? He knew exactly where he had found the teapot, and so if they hadn't tipped any more stuff there and he did some rakin', he'd likely come across either the milk jug or the sugar basin. And then of course he'd have to clean them up, so he needed time. And he couldn't do all that if he stayed at school all afternoon and get to Willie's for teatime. So his day was planned.

He did his chores as he did every morning, locked the door, put the key in his pocket, and went to school.

But Sammy didn't manage to play the nick after school dinner. Sister Catherine, coming into the dining-hall just as they were finishing, called out, 'You, you, you, and you, come with me.'

Sammy was one of the you's, and was about to protest, but he had recent memories of his head wagging at such a rate that he thought it would fly off his body. So he golloped the last of his pudding, joined the other boys who were all bigger than him and followed Sister Catherine's modern skirt along the corridor. He had always thought it unfair that nuns didn't look like nuns any more, but like ordinary human beings, woman human beings.

This one, far from being a human being, marched them into the library and pointed to the shelves saying, 'All these books have to be got down and packed before you leave tonight, before anybody leaves tonight.'

When one of the bigger boys dared to ask, 'Why, Sister? Aren't we goin' to have a library any more?'

'Yes, we're going to have a library some more, Reilly, not

that it would interest you as it's a surprise to me that you even know this is a library because you never use it, do you, except under force, brute force. The fact is, there's all kinds of rot, here, wet rot, dry rot, and all the rest in the walls, and these shelves have to be cleared and the walls behind the racks inspected. Now are you satisfied?'

'Where have the books got to go to, Sister?'

'E block. Sister Monica is over there with her gang. But where they go from there and what's finally going to happen to them will be no concern of yours, Reilly. Now, you see those cardboard boxes there?' The nun pointed to a large stack of flat cardboard in the corner of the room. 'Now you, Baxter, open up those boxes and set them round the shelves. And you, Reilly, get up that ladder and hand books down carefully to Watson, and dear little Samuel Love will take them from you, Watson, and pack them care . . . fully. And I'll see they're done carefully. I'll be back in a minute.' And she stressed this to Sammy by pulling a face at him, and with a nod of the head, so when the door closed on her he did her the courtesy to stick his tongue out as far as it would go. And when Reilly, from the top of the library steps, said, 'I'd like to put a bomb up her bum,' and Watson, who was standing on the bottom step, added, 'Make it a rocket, Reilly, an' she'll fly straight into heaven,' they all laughed until Reilly cried, 'Stop it! You're rockin' the boat. I'll be landin' either on me face or me arse in a minute.' Then looking down on Sammy, he said, 'She's got it in for you, Love, hasn't she? Ever since your da threatened to knock her block off. When I told me ma about that and asked her would my da do the same, she said, no, because he wasn't soft in the head or a bloody fool, 'cos only a bloody fool would tackle a nun.'

'Me da's no bloody fool, Reilly.'

'All right, all right . . . *dear Love*. I was only kiddin'. Don't get your rag out unless you want to blow your nose.'

Sammy glared up at Reilly. He'd often wanted to hit him, especially when he said '*Dear Love*' like that because sometimes the others would take it up and sing songs about his name, like

the one the chorus sang last year in the concert: 'My Love Is Like A Red Red Rose.'

Oh, but why worry about Reilly? He was stuck here for sure this afternoon, and he'd never find what he was lookin' for.

It was at this point that Watson brought up the subject that made it so necessary that he should find something to take to Willie's ma the night. He said to him, 'You're thick with that Protestant, aren't you, whose da's been kidnapped?'

Sammy didn't answer, but glared at the boy who wasn't much bigger than himself and who, he promised himself, he would nobble if he didn't shut his mouth. Then Reilly put his oar in again, saying, 'You know where you go to if you have any truck with Protestants, more than to be civil.'

'Aw, that's all hogwash. Father Cotten said it was. He said that was all in the bad old days; we're all alike now and heading for the same round-up. That's what he said.'

As though backing Sammy up, Watson, with a broad smile on his face, nodded at Sammy, saying, 'Father Cotten's a caution. Me da laughed himself sick when he saw him on telly standin' next to a Hallelujah. He said old Father Whitehead would be kicking the lid off his coffin to get out and at him.'

'Me ma said he only went so he could be seen on telly.' This was from Reilly. 'She says he's an abish . . . abishionist, and God isn't goin' to do away with hell just because he's mixin' with the Protestants.'

'If you ask me, I think your ma and da's up the pole.'

'Watch it, Watson, watch it, 'cos I'll come down there an' stick that pole in one end of ya an' pull it out the other.'

Watson, who wasn't much bigger than Sammy, merely shrugged his shoulders at this dire threat! Reilly, he knew, was all wind and water. As his ma said, the bigger they were the more empty space there was inside them, especially in the head. So he dared to grin up at Reilly, then turn his laughing face towards Sammy while shrugging his shoulders. And when Sammy returned his grin, Reilly purposely missed handing the

books to Baxter and they landed almost between the heads of the two smaller boys.

They had been unaware that the door had opened, but when Sister Catherine's voice boomed over them, 'You do that again, Reilly, and I'll whip the ears off you,' Sammy thought, she's got a thing about ears, that 'un.

It had been a boring, tedious afternoon and when, altogether in the main hall, they sang the last hymn to close the week's work, which was 'Soul Of My Saviour,' Sammy, as usual, half spoke it, for he was no singer, and very half-heartedly he said,

'Soul of my Saviour,
'Sanctify my breast;
'Body of Christ, be
'Thou my saving Guest;
'Blood of my Saviour,
'Bathe me in Thy tide,
'Wash me ye waters
'Gushing from His side.'

He had never understood a word of that hymn except the bit about the water gushing from His side. And then he always imagined a spring like the one he saw up in the hills that Sunday his da took him for a bus trip. It was shortly after his ma had left. He couldn't remember which time it was, the first, or the second, or the third, but he knew he had cried a lot. It was then that his da had stayed with him all day on the Sunday and they'd gone for this ride in the bus, and his da had gone into a weird little pub and he had sat outside and had had ginger beer and a meat pudding. It had been a lovely day, and they had walked and saw this spring which was tumbling out of a rock and rushing down the hillside to the river. He'd always remember that day. . . .

He didn't go home and change his clothes; he hadn't time,

he told himself. Anyway, he'd just have to get into them again if he was going along to Willie's house.

There was great activity on the top of the tip. There seemed to be more lorries than ever the day, and the great big pusher was at it an' all, levelling the muck.

As he made his way around the side to where he could slip down the bank and so reach the old part of the tip, he almost jumped in the air when a voice yelled at him, 'D'you want to land up in the muck?' And there followed a string of words whose meaning he understood but whose use was forbidden to him now. And the man, leaning out of the cab, added to them, saying, 'You should have a revolving light on the top of your head; you could have been under the wheels, you silly little bugger. And keep away from that side; we're emptying sludge.'

He ran some way from the lorry before he turned and saw it really was emptying sludge, and he recalled hearing yesterday someone say the park lake was being drained as it was gettin' silted up near where the stream ran into it.

He ran on again, and didn't stop for breath until he reached the bottom of the tip where it was now sprawling into what had been pasture land. Now the quarry had been filled, they were goin' to fill this little valley up, so it was said. His da said it was a shame, 'cos this was where they used to do rabbit coursin'.

Standing looking back along the sloping bank of the tip, it all looked the same, but he knew where he had found the teapot. And so he scrambled among the debris until he came to the place, not realising he had rounded the curve and was almost where the lorry was tipping the sludge.

He never brought a rake with him, there was always something at hand that he could rake with, and today he was more lucky than usual because he found a piece of iron with a bent end that must have been a proper rake anyway. And so with this he began to pull at the smelling rubbish.

When his rake hit something hard, he grabbed at it, but what he pulled out was just an old brown stone pickle jar. Another time he would have considered it a find because there were no

cracks or chips to be seen in it. It was half full of muck but that would have been easily tipped out, and after the jar had been given a good scrub it would have been handy in the kitchen. But today he threw it aside; he was after bigger bait.

He had been raking for some time when suddenly he cried, 'Aw!' and put his hand into the muck and pulled out the remnants of what had once been a filigree butter dish holder. He didn't know this; he saw only something that was attractive but which seemed to be broken in so many places he could never get it put right to take to her in place of a milk jug or sugar basin; but he placed it to one side 'cos it might be silver and he'd get a copper for it at the scrap-yard.

He had been raking for almost an hour, and he was tired and thirsty, and his clothes and hands and face were dirty, and he was feeling very sad inside when his head was brought up and back by a shout from high up on the bank. A man was standing up there near the back of a waggon. He was yelling something and waving his arms. He saw another waggon come further along the bank and tip its load. It looked like thick treacle running down among all the rubbish. The man was still yelling at him to get out of the way.

He wasn't in anybody's way, but he thought he'd better go 'cos the man would likely scud him if he got hold of him. He had been working some way up the bank, but now he slithered down and as he did so he saw a nice boot; no, it was a shoe, and although it looked mucky the sole was good. It was sticking out of something like a cardboard box. The top part of the box looked just the same as those that had been used for packing the books in this afternoon. He tried to pull the shoe from out of the box, but it wouldn't come. And so he stopped his slithering and put two hands on it to give it a tug, thinking that where there was one there might be the other, and they were men's shoes and might fit his da, at least for work. Then he let out a cry; but it was soundless because it was only in his head. Pulling at the shoe he had seen the trouser leg. And when, gingerly, he

now moved the muck from the sides of the cardboard box he could see the other leg.

Quickly now he said a prayer;

> 'Hail Mary full of grace,
> 'The Lord is with thee;
> 'Blessed art thou among women. . . .'

But that was as far as he got, because the man was shouting at him again. And now he stood and waved and shouted back. But the man simply flung up his arms and turned away. Cautiously now, he slithered further along what his mind wouldn't tell him was there to more cardboard, here ridged like a tent, but almost covered with all descriptions of muck. And when, with the rake, he gingerly pulled this away he exposed the knob of a bedstead.

His hand wavered over the cardboard before he could bring himself to pull it aside. And then he saw the face. It was filthy dirty and covered with dark streaks of blood, and instinctively he stood up and backed away, and in doing so he slid down almost two yards of the bank to where the grass began. And with his instinctive reaction he had cried out, 'Oh Lord Jesus!' for that thing there, that man was Willie's da. He recognised the hair because he had often thought it was nearly like a punk's. Willie had said his da was always brushing it, it only stood up because he was always running his hands through it.

He now put his head back and yelled, 'Mister! Mister!'

But there was no sign of the man at the top of the bank. The two lorries, however, were still there, one was empty and the other full. And then he let out an oath, one that he shouldn't have used, because the lorry was tipping up and the black slime was coming down the bank straight at him. It wouldn't hurt him because he could run, but it would likely cover the man.

He scrambled up the six foot of bank again; then he was tearing the muck and the cardboard away from the prone figure. And now he was yelling at the face, 'Mr Bailey! Mr Bailey! It's me, Sammy. Come on! Come on! They're tippin' the sludge.'

He looked up. It wasn't a broad stream to begin with, just as wide as the lorry, but now it was spreading out. It didn't seem to be sinkin' into the debris but splashin' over it. His mind told him it wouldn't be very thick by the time it reached them, perhaps it would have disappeared, sunk into the muck by then, but he just couldn't be sure; those were big lorries, they held a lot. And it wasn't only sludge that was comin', it seemed to be stones an' all 'cos they were bouncing.

He screamed into the face now, 'Mr Bailey! Mr Bailey! Wake up, man! Come on! Come on! God Almighty! Wake up! Wake up, man, else we'll be covered. It's slimy, all wet.'

When the face made no response he caught at the arm and tugged it; then he let out a high scream for now he and the figure seemed to be embracing and were rolling down the bank. He knew he was screaming in his head as he pushed the body from him, and when he looked up there were the two men again and one was shaking his fist at him and yelling, but he couldn't hear what they were saying.

What they were saying one to the other was, 'That little bugger'll be done for one of these days. If I go down there I'll kick his arse for him.'

'Hold your hand a minute,' said the other one; 'he's waving.'

'Aye, he's waving. He's a cheeky little bugger if ever there was one. He's never off this tip. When he goes missin' they'll blame the likes of us for not chasin' him. There should be a watchman on here. I've said it afore. An' did you notice; it's not this side that needs the sludge, it's yon side. That's burnin' underneath, hot as a volcano in parts.'

'Look, man, the lad's waving us down.'

'Well, he's not gettin' me down there. What does he think he's found? A gold mine?'

'He's found something. Look, he's waving and pointing. Aw, I'd better go.'

'Please yourself. If you took any notice of these kids you'd be doin' overtime till midnight.'

It appeared that the men weren't going to take any notice of

him. So what must he do? What he did was to lift up Bill's head and pat his cheek, saying, 'Aw, Mr Bailey. Come on, man, come on.' Then he asked himself how you knew when people were dead. On the telly they lifted the hand and felt the wrist, the doctors did, or they opened the coat and put their head on the chest. Then they phoned for an ambulance. But he was at the bottom of the tip and everybody had gone. And oh, God! What was he goin' to do?

He raised his eyes upwards and said, 'Please send help. God, please send help.'

And God did send help. A man came round the foot of the tip and yelled at him, 'Come on out of that, you young bugger, come on!'

'Mister! Come here a minute. There's a man here.'

'*God Almighty!*'

The man was looking down onto the dirty blood-stained form, and then he muttered, 'Aw, lad. You've found him.'

'Aye, I did. And I know who it is. It's Willie's da, an' Willie's me pal. He was kidnapped last night. It said on the radio.'

The man now knelt down like they did on the pictures and took hold of Bill's wrist. And he had no need to open his coat because it was open, as was his waistcoat.

He put his ear down to the dirty shirt; then, turning to Sammy, he said, 'I'm not good at this. I can't tell if he's here or not. Look, laddie, just stay with him. I'll be back in a jiffy.'

The jiffy took five minutes but it seemed like five hours to Sammy. All the time he had sat with his legs outstretched, the head on his small lap. Once he thought that the body moved and it made him shout down at the face: 'It's me, Mr Bailey. Wake up! Wake up, man! They've gone for help.' But then they were still on the slope, and he might have slipped slightly.

When the man returned he said, 'They're bringing the ambulance. And I phoned the polis an' all. My God! lad, you've done a good rakin' the night. The morrow would have been too late 'cos we've had orders to fill this part in right down to the field. Whether you've saved his life or not, I don't know, 'cos he looks

a gonna to me; but, in any case, you've found him. Better for his wife to know what's happened to him one way or t'other than to go on in the dark.' . . .

A half-hour ago he had been the only one on this side of the tip. He had previously reasoned this out: very few people were on the tip on a Friday 'cos they seemed to have money then. But now the tip seemed to be swarming.

When the man said, 'I'll have to go and guide them down,' he was once again left with the inert body. And he talked to it, saying, 'When I go to see Willie, I won't have anythin' to take. But me da says you don't have to take presents every day to friends. But still though, I wanted somethin' to take to her, your missis, 'cos she's not for me like you are, not really, and I want her to be. 'Cos as me granny says, men might wear the trousers but women wear the pants and, in most cases, what they say goes. So, I want to get on the right side of her, like.'

It seemed he had talked himself out. They were a long time in comin'. He thought that if he was good he should be prayin'. But, like his da, he knew he was what they called a wooden Catholic: he went to Mass and Confession and Communion 'cos he had to. He wished he was a Methodist, 'cos Methodists always seemed to have money. His da said you never found a Methodist that had to scrape the butter off the bread after he had put it on. He once said that Christ had died to put the Catholics into business and they were still at it an' doing fine. Oh aye, he had said, 'cos they didn't ask you to put a penny on the plate any more but gave you a packet to hold a slab of your wages. His da came out with funny things. He couldn't understand him half the time except when he swore. His voice was different then: you could tell then if he was mad or just bein' funny.

It seemed that suddenly there was a crowd of people round him. He felt he had been dozin' and had just woken up. His legs were cramped. The policeman lifted him up in his arms and took him down onto the grass, all the time smiling at him while saying, 'Stout fella. Stout fella.' And after a while, as if

he couldn't scramble up the bank himself, the policeman again lifted him in his arms and carried him.

In the police car one of the policemen asked, 'Where d'you live, laddie?' And then his mind began to work; it was really as if he had come out of a dream. If he went home his da would likely knock blazes out of him for messin' up his good school clothes even if he had found Mr Bailey. So he told them where he lived but he said, 'I don't want to go back there, I want to go to Willie's house, I mean Mr Bailey's. I want to tell her, Mrs Bailey.'

The policemen looked at each other; then one of them said, 'It's only your due, lad, it's only your due. You want to go to Mr Bailey's house, then go there you shall.'

When the policeman actually lifted him out of the car he endeavoured to shrug him off, saying, 'I can get out meself; I've often been in a car afore;' then again the policeman had to stay him with a hand on his shoulder while talking to the one guarding the gate; and when this policeman said, 'I've had word through from the office. They say, let him go in and break the news,' the other opened the gate, saying, 'Well, it's all yours, big boy.'

He knew they were being funny, so he didn't come out with anything. He walked up the path and knocked on the door; and it was the woman Nell who opened it. She looked at him, from head to foot, then exclaimed, 'My! My goodness! Where've you been? What . . . what d'you want?'

'I want to see Mrs. . . .'

'Oh, Sammy, it's the wrong time; it's. . . .'

''Tisn't. I've got something to tell her.'

Nell lifted her eyes from the boy to the two policemen who had stopped a little way beyond him. And they nodded at her; but although their nodding didn't give her any explanation, she let them all into the house. And when Sammy said, 'Where is she?' Nell, with a slight shake of her head, said, 'She is in the sitting-room.'

She went to stop him, but the policeman's hand stayed her; and by himself, and quietly now, Sammy went to the door.

Fiona was sitting in front of the fire. Katie was on one side

of her, Mamie the other; Mark was in a chair, and Willie was sitting on the mat, his head resting on the edge of the sofa. But they all turned round simultaneously and looked at the dirty apparition standing in the doorway.

The sight of him brought Fiona to her feet. She opened her mouth to speak but closed it as he came towards her. And, his face bright, he looked up at her and said, 'I've found him, your man. He was buried in the tip. I've found him. I was lookin' for a sugar basin or milk jug to go with your teapot, an' I found him.'

'Wh . . . what!' Her lips were trembling so much she stuttered the word out. The children were gathered round her, and Mark stuttered as he said, 'Y . . . y . . . you mean that, Sammy?'

'Aye. Aye. He's been taken by the ambulance to hospital. But it was me what found him. They were emptyin' the sludge down; an' they said the morrow would've been too late, 'cos they're clearin' the lake and it's muck an' sludge an' he would really've been buried. He was buried enough; I only found his boot at first.'

'Oh dear God!' The smell of him was affecting her nostrils; but what she did was to suddenly thrust her arms out and pull him into her embrace; and his head pressed tight against her neck, she said over and over again. *'Oh, Sammy. Sammy. Sammy. Sammy. Thank you.* I must go. I must go to him.'

Katie was crying, Mamie was crying, Mark's face was wet. But Willie stood apart, and he alone seemed to show no emotion.

Fiona now pressed Sammy from her and, looking into his dirty twitching face, she said, 'Sammy, I will love you all my life. But tell me, is . . . is he all right? I must go to the hospital, but is he all right?'

Sammy looked towards Mark and hesitantly said, 'I don't know. I couldn't get him to answer. I kept talkin' to him when I was waitin'. They were a long time comin', I mean with the ambilance an' that. But the polis might know.' He thumbed towards the door.

Fiona hurried towards it, and to the two policemen standing in the hall she cried, 'Is . . . is he all right?'

'He's alive, ma'am. But as far as we can gather, he's in . . .

well, in a pretty bad mess. He's been badly knocked about, but he's alive.'

Fiona now turned to Nell, saying, 'Oh, Nell, Nell. Can you believe it?'

'Yes. Yes, I can Fiona. Where Bill is concerned I can believe it. I told you. . . .' But what she was about to say was checked by a high cry, almost a scream from the sitting-room, and when Fiona turned and rushed back into the room, followed by Nell and the policeman, it was to see Willie beating Mark with his fists, the while crying at him, 'I told you! I told you Sammy was all right. He's my friend. I want him as a friend. He's better than your Roland. I want. . . .'

Fiona picked up her son in an effort to placate him, but, his face awash with tears, he now fought her, too, as he screamed, 'You didn't want him to come to tea. Only Dad, only Dad wanted him. And he saved Dad. And I'm going to be his friend. . . . I am! I am! . . .'

'Yes, of course you are, dear. You were right all the time. You were the only one that was right. Yes, you are. Yes, you are. No more now. No more. Stop crying. And look, I'll tell you what. Take Sammy upstairs and let him have a bath and give him some of your clothes to get into until his own are clean again.' She turned now. 'Would you like that, Sammy? Would you like that?'

'I have a bath on a Friday night, the night, later on. I do it meself. I fill the bowl from the. . . .'

'It would please me, Sammy, if you would use our bath tonight and stay with us until your father comes.'

'Huh!' He jerked his head. 'He'll likely wallop me. He'll be lookin' for me now an' he won't know where I am.'

She turned to the police, saying, 'You'll find Mr Love, won't you, and tell him where Sammy is and tell him to call for him?'

'We'll do that, ma'am, don't worry. And –' he now patted Sammy's dirty hair, saying, 'He won't recognise you when you're cleaned up and got rid of your smell. But he'll be proud of you,

I can tell you that. We're all proud of you. Aren't we constable?' He turned to his companion who said, 'By! yes. You'll be in the papers tomorrow and likely on the telly.'

'Nell, take Willie upstairs.' She went to hand her son over to Nell, but Willie, wriggling in her arms, said, 'I can walk.' And when he was on the floor Sammy looked at him and grinned and said, 'That's what I said to the polis earlier on when he carried me up the tip. And I said I was more used to the tip than he was. He got all mucked up with sludge, didn't he?' He turned to one of the policemen, and he, grinning, said, 'He did an' all, and he didn't like it. He's gone home an' all to change.'

Looking at Mark now, Fiona said, 'See to them, will you?' But before Mark could reply her second son almost barked, 'We can see to ourselves!' and a relieved Nell, smiling broadly, said, 'Back to normal. Oh, back to normal. And thank God. Now get off,' and saying this, she pushed Fiona towards the hall.

A short while later, when she was ready for the road, Fiona turned to Nell and said, 'I meant what I said, Nell. I'll love that boy until the day I die. And I mean to do something for him. Oh, yes, yes. No matter what happens. Yes, Nell, no matter what happens. And to think I couldn't stand the sight of him.'

Nell again pushed her, saying, 'Love at first sight very rarely lasts. Go on now. And if he's conscious at all give him my love too.'

The relief and even the vestige of gaiety that had come back to her being when she knew he had been found slipped away, in fact, was shocked away at her first sight of him.

He was already in the theatre when she had reached hospital. 'They have just taken him down,' the nurse had said; 'he'd needed some cleaning up.' Then she had added, 'Come and sit in the side ward; there's two newspaper hounds already in the waiting-room and you'll have enough of them before you're finished.'

'How . . . how long do you think he'll be?' Even as she had asked it she knew it to be a stupid question, which the nurse

had answered seriously, but just as she should have expected, 'Well, it all depends on the extent of his injuries.' . . .

Twice they had brought her tea and biscuits. She had drunk the tea but left the biscuits. And she had made an effort to smile at the nurse who had come to take the tray away when she said to her, 'If any of my children had been here that would have been an empty plate.'

'Oh, sure,' the nurse had said; 'I have three young brothers so I know.'

It was almost two hours later when there was a commotion outside the ward door and the trolley was brought in; and on it she saw Bill. When she had last looked on him he had been a spruce, good-looking middle-aged man, who, because of his energy, could have lied within ten years about his age. But here they were easing into bed a figure that seemed bandaged from head to foot. His head was bandaged and all down one side of his face. Both arms were bandaged from the wrist to the shoulder. He was dressed in a sort of sleeveless night-shirt. When it fell open as they put him on the bed she saw that his stomach too was bandaged, and one leg was in a sort of splint.

The sister did not ask her to leave the room; she and her nurse and two male nurses were obviously too preoccupied with their patient, so much so that she was thrust back against the wall, and there she stood with one hand pressed tight against her cheek. When the three nurses left the room the sister drew up a chair to the side of the bed and beckoned her forward. And quietly she said, 'You may sit with him for a time; but mind, he won't wake for some hours, so if you'd like to rest there is a visitors' room with a bed in it just along the corridor. You might be able to sleep for a while.'

'How . . . how bad is he?'

'I think the doctor will be able to answer that better than I could. He'll be along in a moment or so. Have you had a cup of tea?'

'Yes, yes, thank you.'

The sister now put her hand on Fiona's shoulder, and what she

said was, 'He's alive,' but her tone could have indicated, 'just'.

She was alone with him now and, bending towards him, she murmured, 'Oh, Bill, Bill, my love.' Then she gently touched the fingers of one hand that was sticking out from the bandages; and the tears running down her face, she cried brokenly, 'How could they do this to you? Whoever it was, I hope I never have to come face to face with them.'

She did not hear the doctor enter the room and so she started when he spoke her name. Hastily, she got to her feet and dried her face, and he, pointing to the chair, said, 'Sit down. Sit down.'

'Tell me' – she was gulping in her throat – 'how . . . how bad is he? He looks' – she spread her hand wide towards him – 'dreadful.'

'Well, first of all I will say to you that he is a very lucky man. I understand a little boy found him on a tip. Another night, in fact a few more hours, and there would have been no hope whatever. How long he's lain smothered in that muck in his condition I don't know. But you've got one thing to be thankful for, he's got a very strong constitution. If he hadn't, well, I'm afraid all this' – he moved his hand from the top to the bottom of the bed – 'would have been in vain.'

'Is . . . are his injuries serious?'

'Well, yes, I can say some of them are. He's had fifteen stitches in the back of his head. There was a big gash there, but fortunately it didn't go deep, nor did the knife that went into his stomach.'

She put her hand tight over her gaping mouth and repeated, 'A knife?'

'Yes; they were out to do a thorough job on him, whoever they were. And I think it must have been more than one because a man of his build would have been able to fight off one. I think it's what they call a gang job, because his arms and legs are lacerated.'

'What damage did the knife do?'

'Oh, it penetrated the gut but fortunately it missed his kidneys and the bladder. But I would say he's gone through enough to

kill an ordinary man. And I think you owe a lot to that little boy. I understand he's only a nipper about eight or so?'

'Yes, yes, I know. He . . . he came to the house to tell me.'

'He did?'

'Yes, yes. I don't know what state my husband was in but the child was filthy and, well, it was as if he too had been buried among the refuse.'

'He deserves a medal whoever he is. They say he's from Bog's End. They don't come tougher than they do from that quarter, children upwards. But there are good 'uns and bad 'uns as in all classes. I would say, though, there's a few more bad 'uns down there than good 'uns.'

He smiled at her. She didn't smile back but she said, 'Thank you. Thank you very much, doctor. You've . . . you've likely saved his life.'

'No, Mrs Bailey, I haven't saved his life, nor Doctor Pinkerton who helped to sew him up; as I said, all your thanks should be due to that little nipper. You don't often hear the police speaking highly of anyone from that quarter. I also understand one of the lorry drivers did his bit too. Slush from the lake, they said they were pouring down on them.' Shaking his head, he turned towards the door as he said, 'The days of miracles are not yet past. I'll be seeing you again shortly, Mrs Bailey.'

She inclined her head towards him, but found it impossible to say anything; he seemed to have said it all: 'The days of miracles are not yet past.'

She resumed her seat by the bedside. She was feeling odd, not faint but just odd, sort of tired. She hadn't taken a sleeping pill last night but had sat on the sitting-room couch and dozed while waiting for the phone ringing. And then today had been the longest day in her life, and the loneliest day in her life, and yet the most surprising, when she came to think of it: her mother had been round twice, and she'd put her arms around her and she had cried and she had even said she was sorry about the things she had said about Bill. But of course, she had thought he was dead. What would she say when she knew he was alive and that he wasn't going

to die? *No! no! He wasn't going to die. He wasn't. He wasn't. . . .*

She must stop her mind from galloping on like this. That's what it was doing all last night and all today. She was talking to people, answering people, yet her mind was away by itself, galloping, galloping.

A nurse came and gently squeezed the bag of blood that was hanging from a hook above the bed-head; then after she had felt Bill's wrist she smiled at her before going out. And she sat on, telling herself she should phone home and tell Nell to tell the children. But she was tired and she didn't want to move. She didn't want to leave him. She never wanted to leave him.

Another nurse came in and, bending over, she said quietly, 'There is a Sir Charles Kingdom and another gentleman. Sister has put them in the visitors' rest room. Do you think you could go and speak to them? The old gentleman seems very anxious.'

'Oh, yes, yes.' She rose from the chair, looked down on Bill, then went out.

On her entry, Sir Charles and his secretary rose quickly, and the old man approached her with hands outstretched, saying, 'I've never been so relieved in all my life. How is he?'

'They think he'll survive.'

'They think?' Sir Charles glanced up at his secretary; then, looking at Fiona again, he said, 'As bad as that?'

'Oh yes. Yes.' Then briefly she gave them a description of what the doctor had told her. And when she finished the old man groped at the chair and sat down again, muttering to himself, 'She wouldn't have meant that. She wouldn't have meant them to go as far as that. Never! Never! I can't believe there's that in her. No. No.'

'Sir.' Rupert bent down towards his employer, saying quietly, 'I think you must face up to the fact that Mrs Brown probably did organise this whole business. She herself mightn't have meant to go as far as murder but she was out to destroy someone. It's right what Lady Kingdom said before we left: you have always seen her through rose-tinted spectacles.'

'Don't you chastise me too, Rupert. I've had enough of it,

and in condemnation from myself too, which is something more bitter and hard than either you or my wife can dole out to me. And I'll show you both that I mean business because I'll bring her to justice over this. Oh yes, I will.'

'She's left the country, sir, and you have no idea where she is. No one seems to have. We've been into all this, sir.'

'If you weren't a distant relation, Rupert, playing at secretary, I would sack you this moment, I would that.'

'It wouldn't be the first time in the last ten years, would it?'

The man now smiled gently at Fiona and he said, 'The last thing you want to witness, Mrs Bailey, is a family quarrel.'

'Oh I don't mind.' There was even a small smile on her lips as she replied, 'It takes my mind off things. But, I will say this, if Mrs Brown is behind attempted murder, and that's what it is, then she must be brought to justice.'

'And she shall be. She shall be.' The old man was nodding his head. 'Once she can be located I will set to work, I promise you. Yes I do, I promise you.'

She put out her hand now and touched the shaking shoulder, saying, 'Please don't distress yourself any further, Sir Charles. You were very fond of this woman, you trusted her. We're often led away by our feelings.' Her mind lifted her back for a moment to her first marriage and how, within a short time, she knew she had made a mistake. Yet, it had given her three beautiful children and so she should be thankful to the man who inveigled her into marriage with soft words, only to tell her within a year that his work would always come first and that one day he would be a famous writer. He never became a famous writer. He never wrote anything good enough to really keep the wolf from the door. But why was she thinking like this? Sir Charles was now standing up and shaking her hand. 'I'll be in tomorrow again. You look very tired, my dear, and that is natural. Can we run you home?'

'No, Sir Charles, thank you very much; I'm staying the night.'

'Yes, well, that's what I would expect. Can I do anything for you? Anything at all?'

'You could call at my house, if you wouldn't mind, and

explain that my husband is as well as can' – she shook her head – 'I think the term is, as well as can be expected. You can say that to my friend, Mrs Ormesby; but tell her to tell the children that he is all right and . . . and will soon be home, and that I too will be home tomorrow sometime.'

'We'll do that. We'll do that.' He was nodding at Rupert now. 'Goodbye then, my dear. Goodbye. I'm a very sad man, yet at the same time a relieved one. You understand?'

Yes, she understood.

It was half-past nine and her head was drooping with sleep when the night sister said, 'I would go and lie down for an hour or so, dear. If there's any change at all, believe me, I'll call you. But I can assure you he won't be conscious for some hours yet.'

But she hadn't the opportunity of going to bed straightaway, for a policeman who was apparently on duty stopped them outside the ward door and said to her. 'There's a man here. He insists on seeing you. He's the father of the boy who found your husband.'

'Oh yes, yes. Oh yes, I'll see him, certainly.'

'Well, if you'll go to the visitors' room, Mrs Bailey, I'll tell him.'

When Davey Love entered the room and stood before her neither of them spoke for a moment. And then he said, 'How is he, ma'am?'

How was he? Could she say all right? She said, 'He's alive.'

'Aye. 'Tis happy I am to hear that. Happy indeed.'

But there was no smile on Davey's face; in fact, now that she looked more closely at him, there was a cut across the bottom right-hand side of his chin, and one eye, although not black, was dark and puffed. And then he said, 'An' my lad saved him. What d'you think of that, eh? 'Twas my own boy that saved him.'

'I think it's wonderful, Mr Love,' she said, 'and I'll never forget him as long as I live.'

'I'm glad to hear yerself say that, ma'am, I am. I am. An' you know, I've thought all this out, ma'am, and I've thought how strange it is.' He did not go on to say what was strange, but seated himself on the edge of the table and said, 'If it's all the same to

you, ma'am, I'll take the weight off me legs, 'cos to tell you the truth you could knock me down with a flannel hammer this minute. And how that's come about I'll tell you shortly. But as I said, there was I thinkin' how strange life is. I haven't got a dirty mouth meself. I swear, oh aye, I know every one in the book an' more; but I'm not gone on the four letter ones, never have been, see no sense in 'em. Yet there was me youngster comin' out with 'em an' levellin' 'em at yer son. Now that was the beginnin' wasn't it? Then yer good man hauls him into the house. An' you don't like that a bit, do you? Now, now, now, it's all right; you needn't bow yer head. In yer place I would 'ave kicked his ar . . . backside out of the door meself. But strangely he takes a shine to you. Oh aye, he does, he takes a shine to you. An' I'll say this for him, if there was nothin' else about him he would be persistent. Oh aye, like me old father, he would be persistent, 'cos himself spent four years in an Irish prison through bein' persistent. Well now, ma'am, what's happened to yer man would have happened in any case, seems to me, 'cos it was a different thing altogether, along different lines, seemingly not connected with me lad or me. Yet, if he hadn't used that language an' he hadn't been allowed to enter yer house an' wanted to give you a present, he would never have gone to the tip now, would he? Well, on the other hand, he would, 'cos he was used to goin' to the tip. But what I mean to say is, after findin' the teapot he would never have gone back there lookin' for the milk jug an' sugar basin or what have you that goes to a set of such. So, as I said to the Chief Constable himself not an hour or so ago, God works in a strange way to clear things up. But mind you, ma'am, I didn't think I'd end up in the clink again just 'cos I went out of me way to help clear this business up.'

'What do you mean, Mr Love? You've been taken to' – she couldn't say clink so she said, 'you've been to jail, I mean put in jail, tonight?'

'Yes, this very night, ma'am. But I didn't go there alone, I can tell you. And it's a good job those bobbies came in time 'cos I lost me head an' there wouldn't have been much left of that fat swine by the time I'd finished with him. But there we were, both

in the clink. And it took me some time to convince the polis that this was one of the two that had tried to do your man in.'

'You've found the man . . . the man who was . . . behind all this?'

'The very one, ma'am. It's a good job there weren't the two together else I doubt if I would have managed 'em. As far as I can gather from what I got out of that bloke an' then the polis after, it was his mate, the big 'un who liked to use the knife and lead piping. You see, it was like this, and I could kick meself black an' blue when I think those two could've been picked up ages gone if I'd listened to the young 'un. But no, I was away washin' the glasses at the Duck and Drake. I feed him an' clothe him, threaten him about school, swear at him about cussin', and all told consider I've done me duty. That's how I have felt, but now I could kick meself, for just this very mornin' he told me where he had seen these two fellas. 'Cos I always said these were the ones that took one of the lads' cars. You remember? I'd seen 'em in the pub that night. They weren't the usual customers an' they looked odd bods, one big an' one small but both hefty. Well, the young 'un had seen 'em at the taggerine yard when he had taken some bits he'd got from the tip. He said they were livin' in the old mill behind the sheds that Gallagher uses for an office an' where he keeps his prize pickin's for the huckster shop dealers or the market stall wallahs to look over. Anyway, there's a field and some scrub behind the old mill an' the ditch that used to carry water long ago. An' so I got in this scrub an' I waited. Then across the field came the smaller one. The lad said they went out the back way, so I thought that's the way they'd come in. The plan in me mind was to see them both in there, then scarper an' ring the polis; it wasn't me intention to tackle 'em together. But when I saw there was just the one, and I made sure there was just one an' nobody else inside before I let go. But I can tell you this, ma'am, I didn't come off scot-free. He could use his feet that 'un, as he admitted later to the polis. It wasn't him that stuck the knife in or battered the boss's head. He said he used his feet an' that was all. But when he used 'em on me he did something to me, ma'am. I almost battered his

brains out. It was Gallagher, hearin' the ructions, who rang the polis. An' that's how we were both hauled in. They wouldn't believe a word I was sayin' until I demanded . . . aye, I did; I threatened the sergeant what would happen to him when the truth came out and to get the Chief Constable down there 'cos there was another murderer at large and he'd be goin' back to that hide-out, and that if Gallagher told him what had happened to his mate the fella would scarper. Well, missis, you never did see such a cafuffle when they finally believed me. There was a young reporter hangin' about as usual, an' the Chief Constable warned him to keep his mouth shut till they got the other one.'

For the moment Fiona felt herself wide awake and she asked, 'Did the man say who had engaged them to do this . . . I mean, who was paying them?'

'Oh, he started to gabble, ma'am, but it was all double Dutch, too airy-fairy, I think. It seems it was the other one that did the business. He went up to London every now an' again an' picked up money from a post office in a letter like with a note tellin' 'em to continue, but it was never signed. He said it was all a funny business.'

'And he didn't know who it was?'

'Well, if he did he wasn't sayin', ma'am. But whoever it was they had their knife in for the boss. By God! they had. And at first they got at him through the lads, the firm like. But him bringin' off that big deal must have been too much for whoever the swine is. I'd like to bet the son of a bitch was one of those big boys that was also after the contract, 'cos who else would be up in London, have their headquarters there like? I've worked it all out in me head, ma'am. It must have been a big boy. Oh, aye. An' they've paid those two to try everythin' in the book, from simple car pinchin' to near murder. If there'd been a woman involved they'd have tried rape.'

Davey Love now chastised himself: That was a damn silly thing to say because she was involved. It could have been her next, or before. Oh aye. It's a wonder they didn't think that one up. But the spite seemed all levelled at the boss. He paused

now, then said, 'You look very tired, ma'am. And you know, as me mother used to say, she took me to be inoculated against whooping-cough but they made a mistake and used a gramophone needle on me. But don't you worry, ma'am, I'll leave you now and you can get some kip . . . sleep. I'll be round first thing in the mornin'. And you know where my lad is the night?'

Fiona didn't answer. She was so tired, so very tired. His voice had almost lulled her to sleep. Yes she just wanted to kip. Yes, she just wanted to kip.

'He's round at yer place. Aye, he is, stayin' the night. Bert's wife fixed him up. Eeh! you know, when I got in from work an' couldn't find him an' there wasn't a sight nor hint nor hair of him, I threatened to murder him, I did honest to God! 'cos he always has the kettle on an' the fryin' pan on the stove an' the table set. An' there it was, the place, as cold as charity. Aw! ma'am, there I go again. Look, I . . . I must be off.' He bent towards her and patted her hand. 'It's because I'm excited inside. I'm so relieved. You know, I made a bargain with the Almighty' – he pointed his finger to the ceiling – 'an' now I've got to keep it. Aye, I did, I made a bargain with Him. Let's find the boss alive, I said, and I'll go to Mass every Sunday for a year. I didn't promise longer 'cos I didn't know whether I would last further than that.'

'Oh, Mr Love, Mr Love.' There was something rising in her, a great burst of laughter. 'Go on,' she said. 'Go on. I don't want to laugh. Go on.'

'Aye, I will, ma'am. Aye, I will. You can laugh the morrow when he comes round. Good-night to you. Good-night.' He backed from her and didn't turn until he reached the door. Then about to say something more, he gave his mouth a whacking clap and went out.

And Fiona, like a mother who had just seen her amusing child leave the room, began to rock herself. The gurgle was mounting, but when it reached her throat it stuck there. And when her mouth opened wide she gasped for air. A current of water seemed to spray from her eyes, nose, throat, and she threw her arms onto the table and buried her face in the crook of her elbow.

10

Fiona opened her eyes but closed them again quickly against the glare of the sunshine. She was dimly aware of a face hanging over her and a strange voice saying, 'I've brought you a cup of tea, Mrs Bailey.'

She had been dreaming she was at home. She muttered, 'What . . . what time is it?'

'Just on eight.'

'What!' She pulled herself up sharply in the bed. 'On eight! I . . . I haven't slept all night?'

'Yes, you have; and you needed it. You'll feel better for it.'

'How . . . how is he? Is he round?'

'Yes. Yes, he's round to some extent, and he's all right. Don't scold yourself; there's plenty of time. Have a wash and make yourself pretty' – she smiled – 'because at the moment you look all eyes and teeth.'

Fiona smiled in return; then, pushing the white quilt from her, she said, 'I've been sleeping in my clothes, I must look a sight.'

'I don't suppose he'll really notice, just your face.' . . .

Five minutes later she entered the side ward. He was lying in the same position, and looked exactly the same as he had

done last night. She stood by the side of the bed and said softly, 'Bill.' And when he slowly lifted his lids and she saw the deep blue of his eyes seeming to sparkle for a moment, she said again, 'Bill. Oh! Bill.'

'Hello . . . love.'

'How . . . how are you feeling? Oh, that's a silly question.'

'Fiona.' He made as if to move his hand towards her, then grimaced, his eyes tight shut and his lips squared from his teeth.

'Oh, my love, don't. Don't. Lie quiet, please.'

A nurse came in and took his temperature and his blood pressure, wrote on a sheet, then went out again.

Another nurse came in and replaced the almost empty blood bag. The surgeon came in accompanied by two young doctors, the sister and a nurse, and after he had indicated she remain seated, he stood looking down on Bill. Then he said, 'There's a lucky man if ever there was one.' And turning to the sister now, he asked, 'What has he had already?' And when she told him, he said, 'Oh well, he should go off again presently.' Then looking across the bed at Fiona, he said, 'You could go home, Mrs Bailey, and give your family the news, because it will be better for him to sleep. Come back this afternoon. And he's likely to be in a similar condition for a few days, you know.'

She rose from the chair now, saying, 'He'll be all right though?'

He raised his eyebrows, then pursed his lips and said, 'Unless there are complications he should do well, but it's going to take time. As I said, he's a very lucky man. . . . Now will you follow my advice and take a short time off, eh?'

'Yes, doctor, if you think he won't be round.'

'I can assure you he won't. And that is the best thing for him you know, sleep. It's the cure now, sleep; all we have to do is just stand by and watch.'

All those present in the room stood aside to let the great man pass. And they did treat him as if he were a great man. She had noticed this before when she was in the hospital: surgeons were

as gods. Nevertheless, she thanked the God she had been praying to for days that there were such men.

She bent over Bill now and gently laid her lips against his blue ones, and she felt sure they moved; but perhaps it was just imagination. She lingered a moment longer before leaving the ward. Then she picked up her coat from the visitors' room, spoke her thanks to the sister and the nurses and said she would be back later, then made her way out and into the bright sunshine. She threaded her way through ambulances and milling cars and was about to walk out of the hospital gates to try to locate a taxi when a voice hailed her from a parked car. And she turned to see Rupert waving to her and Sir Charles's head poking out of the rear window.

Making her way towards them, Sir Charles immediately said, 'How is he?'

'I've left him sleeping peacefully, Sir Charles. The surgeon said he'll be all right, but it'll take time.'

'Where are you going?' Rupert said.

'I was going to find a taxi.'

At this he seemed to jump from his seat, then hurriedly go to the far rear door, which he opened, saying, 'Get in.' And she got in and sat beside the old man who said, 'You want to go home?'

'If you please, Sir Charles.'

'How bad is he really?'

'Well, very bad I should imagine. Apparently he's had a knife into his stomach and a blow to his head, it's split open at the back. Do you know they have caught one of the men?'

She watched his blue-veined hand go to his mouth, and it was some minutes before he spoke, when he said, 'They'll know then about . . . about Eva?'

'No.'

'He hasn't split . . . told?'

'I don't know. I don't think so. Mr Love came to see me last night.' And she told them the gist of what Davey had related to her. And when she finished the old man lay back against the

upholstery of the Rolls. But that was only for a moment, for now, sitting upright again, he turned to her and said, 'But Bailey won't let this pass. He can't, can he? Nor you. Because it's been a near thing, it's touched on murder. And . . . and I'll understand, because in Bailey's place I would feel the same.'

Her voice quiet, she now said, 'It will be up to Bill, Sir Charles.'

'Yes, yes, I understand, my dear.' His voice had been quiet, but now he was leaning forward thumping Rupert on the back as he said, 'And don't say I will try to talk anybody round, because in this case I won't, I'll let justice take its course. I've told you, I'm finished with her.'

'I've never said a word.'

'No, but you've been thinking plenty. I can read you like an open book.'

'Clever . . . fellow.'

'Now watch your tongue.'

'I'm watching the road, Sir Charles, and if you don't stop thumping me in the back there could be an accident at any minute.'

When the old man sat back he turned and nodded to Fiona, saying, 'Some people get too big for their boots.'

And when the voice from the driver said, 'You must finish it, sir: when their toes pinch they find they are walking in their bare feet.'

Fiona wanted to laugh, as she had wanted to laugh last night at Mr Love. But her laughter was still too near to tears to be given a free rein.

'Would you like to come in for a moment?'

'What about it, Rupert, have we time?' The question was quiet and polite.

'Yes, Sir Charles. You've got a good half-hour to spare before you meet her ladyship in Newcastle.'

'Then we'll come in.'

A large car was parked immediately outside the house, and three men were talking to the policeman at the gate. And so

Rupert stopped beyond. The men turned to look enquiringly, and when Fiona emerged on the pavement side, one of them moved forward, saying, 'Good-morning, Mrs Bailey. May I have a word with you?'

'No, you can't! And get yourself to the devil out of it.' And Sir Charles guided Fiona through the gate, still muttering, 'I know this lot, television snoops. And I know him' – pointing back to the man who had spoken to Fiona – 'that's the one with the funny name.'

Rupert and Fiona exchanged glances and smiled. And when Rupert said, 'That one with the funny name did a nice piece on you last year, sir. And, if I recall you pressed drinks on him and practically carried him out of the house.'

'You're asking for trouble, Rupert, aren't you? It's one of those mornings.'

'Most mornings are the same, sir. And look, the time's going on. You have now only twenty-five minutes to spare before you meet her ladyship.'

The old man, walking towards the door with Fiona, nodded at her as he muttered, 'I'll get rid of him. Yes, I will.' But there was a twinkle in his eyes as he said it. And Fiona knew that both of these men, the old man and the young one, enjoyed this daily exchange. There was a similarity between the two of them, like Bill and one of his men. The only difference was in the tone of voice.

'Mam! Mam! We gona be on television.'

'I sat in the front.' Mamie was jumping up and down now.

'And I stood at the back,' Mark mimicked her, as he pretended to bounce. 'And dear Katie there' – Mark now pointed – 'mightn't be on at all. She wasn't on the first lot because she would go upstairs and change her dress. She must look pretty, pretty, pretty.'

'I'll throw something at you, our Mark. Yes I will.'

Only Willie said, 'How did you find Dad, Mam?' And this quiet question brought them all round her, saying, 'Yes, yes, Mam. How is he? How is he?'

She looked over their heads at Nell; then before answering she said, 'Don't you see we've got visitors.'

'Morning, sir. Morning, sir.'

'Hello.' This from Mamie.

'Morning, Sir Charles,' from Mark.

The only one who hadn't spoken was Sammy. He was standing among them yet apart. And he looked at her and she looked at him. And as she addressed her family she continued to look at him as she said, 'You wanted to know how your father is. Well, he's alive, but it's only thanks to Sammy here.'

'You're a brave little fellow.' Sir Charles was now patting Sammy's head. 'And I'd like to shake you by the hand.'

It was noticed that Sammy had to push the sleeve of his coat back before he could take the proffered hand. And when it was grasped by Sir Charles's long thin fingers, Sammy said, 'The sleeves are too long, it's Willie's. Me clothes were all mucky last night.'

'Yes, of course, they would be. That's a very large and dirty refuse heap. Do you often go there?'

'Aye. Ya get some good pickin's. I got Mrs Bailey a nice teapot from it, didn't I?' He turned and looked up at Fiona. And she said, 'Yes, you did, Sammy; and I'll always treasure it. That is one thing I'll never part with.'

Withdrawing his fingers from the tight grip of the old fellow, Sammy said, 'I'll be on television the night an' all. They took me by meself. I wanted to be with them' – he pointed to the children – 'but they said, no, I had to stand by meself. An' they wanted me to smile or laugh and I told 'em I didn't smile or laugh unless I had somethin' to laugh about.'

'You told them that?'

'Aye, I did.'

'You're a man after my own heart, an independent spirit.'

Sir Charles turned now and glanced at Rupert who was standing to the side of him, smiling, and he said, 'Something must be done in that quarter. Make a note of it.'

'Yes, sir.'

'Would you like to come in and have a cup of coffee, sir?' Nell motioned towards the sitting-room. And now Sir Charles, looking at Rupert again, said, 'How's the time going?'

'I don't think there's enough left for coffee, sir.'

'Well, in that case we'd better get along,' he turned to Fiona: 'You'll be going back to the hospital today?' he asked.

'Oh, of course.'

'Well, will you phone me of his progress?'

'Yes, yes, I'll do that.'

'And I'll look in tomorrow and see him myself. Well, goodbye everybody.' Then giving all his attention to Sammy, he said, 'Goodbye, young man. We'll be meeting again, rest assured on that.'

Fiona walked with Sir Charles down the drive, Mark and Nell with Rupert and the children dancing along. From the gate, they watched Rupert help the old man into the car, and Nell said, 'I wouldn't mind having the price of one wheel of that.'

'Oh, it isn't the wheels that cost the money, Nell,' Mark put in, 'it's the engine. I'll go for the engine.'

'One day I'll have a car like that.'

All eyes had been on the disappearing car but now they rested on Sammy, and no one, not even Katie, said, 'Some hope,' because if someone like him could save their father, and had been the means of telling his own father, as it said on the wireless this morning, where the would-be murderers were, at least one of them, then having a Rolls-Royce would be a simple matter.

It was fifteen minutes later when Nell and Fiona had the sitting-room to themselves, and Fiona said, 'How are they next door?'

'Oh, as they used to be. I can't believe it. And the relief they've experienced since Sammy's father caught that man. Well, it's taken years off both of them. As Mam said, there was still a strong suspicion in the police inspector's mind that Dad had done it. But enough of them. How did you really find Bill?'

'Oh Nell.' Fiona sat down on the couch. 'They told me last night there looked as if there was nothing left of him that hadn't

been battered almost to a pulp, his arms, his legs, his head, a knife in his stomach.'

'Oh, those fellows should get life, and whoever's put them up to this. As Bert said, it's been a planned job from the beginning. Have you any idea at all? I mean, did Bill say anything?'

Fiona could look at Nell now and say, 'You mean, who's behind it? No. No, we've no idea. Likely somebody who's jealous of him and his success.'

She said this because she knew that Bill would do nothing to bring further hurt to Sir Charles. And it wasn't because of his strong backing of him to get this great contract, the contract that was going to alter all their lives, a contract that might never have come off but for little Sammy Love.

Her mind kept going back to the child. They had adopted one child because Bill had wanted to do so; they could adopt another because she wanted it. But in this case there was an obstacle, a huge obstacle, the father. He loved the boy and the boy loved him. Still, there were things that could be done for him, and she already had it half planned in her mind; and for the father too. Yes, for the father too. By the time Bill came home she would have it all cut and dried and he would be so pleased, because right from the first meeting with Sammy Love he had associated himself with the boy. In some way they were akin.

11

It was a full six weeks later when Bill came home. He'd had two further operations, but for the past fortnight he had regained fresh strength to such an extent that he had soon been sitting up, then walking about his room.

He had naturally become a favourite with the staff. The first words he spoke to the sister when he had become fully conscious and seen the flower-decked room and the dozens of get-well cards arrayed around it had been, 'I never knew they decorated the morgue like this.' And the day following his second trip to the theatre he said to Fiona, 'I want a divorce because I'm going to marry Nurse Campbell here.' He indicated the plump cheery face of a twenty-four year old girl before adding, 'You see, she knows about places inside me that you've never dreamed of.' And Fiona had answered, 'Oh, that's all right. I'm sure she'll love to take on your whole adopted family.' She had nodded across the bed to nurse Campbell, adding, 'There's only four of them.' Then looking down on Bill again, she had ended, 'I didn't know how to tell you, but this lets me out. I'd been planning to start a new life with Rupert. You know, Sir Charles's secretary.'

The nurse had gone out of the room shaking with laughter,

but Bill had looked up at her and said, 'Look, woman, I'm allowed to make jokes, like that but not you. There's no truth in my line, but with you it's different. There' no smoke without fire, you know. And he's a good looking fella, an' related to the old bloke too.'

'Well, I thought it was about time we both had a change.'

'Fiona.' The look on his face, the sound of his voice brought her face down to his, saying, 'Oh, Bill, Bill. It isn't fair. You can joke like that and I can't.'

'I'm always afraid.'

'Oh, that hurts me,' she had said. 'There's nobody and never will be anybody in my life but you. All I want is for you to get well, really well, and come home. They're all longing for you. The house isn't the same. My bed is cold. I hug your pillow at night.' He had slowly lifted his hand and touched her face, saying, 'I'm a lucky fella;' then had added, 'Talking of Rupert, that leads me to the old fella. He's worried in his mind, isn't he, about what I'm goin' to do? And that inspector keeps poppin' in. Whether the big fella gave him any hint when he was picked up of who was behind this, I don't know. But as Davey said, the little bruiser seemed to think that his partner was in the dark as well as himself. Anyway, if that big lout knows it was her, she's promised to pay him enough to keep his mouth shut.'

'What are you going to do about it then?'

He surprised her when he said, 'I don't really know,' because she had imagined that he wouldn't do anything that would disturb Sir Charles further. And then he had added, 'It narks me to the very core to think that bastard of a woman, because that's what she is, a bastard, will get off with this. And all because I turned down her offer. You can't believe it, can you, dear?'

'Oh, yes, yes, I can believe it. It's a dreadful thing to be spurned.'

'How would you know anything about that? Nell would, but not you.'

'Oh well, perhaps not quite, but I have experienced a cousin

to it, say. *Because*: there were long stretches when I was ignored; I was there only to be used in various ways as a cook, a cleaner, a shopper, a bearer of children, a satisfier of needs . . . without love. I was scarcely eighteen when I married. I knew nothing about men or marriage. Well, if I thought of men I thought they were like my father. I really married to escape from home and my mother. You can understand that. But there were times even during the first year when I longed to be back.'

'Oh, Fiona; I . . . I didn't know. I didn't realise. And the kids have always seemed so . . . so happy and. . . .'

'It's a dreadful thing to say, but they became happy after he died, and so did I. And I swore I'd never marry again.' Her smile widened. 'And just look what I did. Just . . . look . . . what . . . I . . . did. And oh!' Her mouth fell onto his and it was some seconds before she finished, 'How I thank God every day that I did it.'

'I had thought I knew everything about you; but you now somehow appear like a stranger. No, no; not a stranger, someone new, someone who hasn't been touched by anybody but me, and never will. . . . Have you told me all this because you don't want me to take the matter further?'

'Yes and no. I . . . I want her brought to justice, I really do; at the same time the exposure would hurt the old man, because I really think he loved her more than he did his own children . . . his own daughters. And likely his affection was heightened because she'd had a dirty deal in having to marry Brown.'

'Aye, there's that in it. You'd rather that I let it rest then?'

'Well, if you don't there'll be a court case, and she'd go to prison. And I think the old man would rather go himself than see her suffer that. But you've got one satisfaction: those two individuals will, as Mr Love would say, take a long holiday in Durham.'

'Funny, isn't it, how he and his lad have come into our lives? But it seems they had to, else I wouldn't be here now. I'm going to do something for him, you know.'

'Are you?' She widened her eyes and raised her brows.

'Oh yes, definitely. I don't know what yet, but I'll think up something.'

'Well, I'd leave it till you come home, eh?'

He was due to go home on the Saturday, and he guessed there'd be a reception awaiting him. What was worrying him was whether he would feel fit to stand up to it. But on the Friday night, and without preliminary thought, he was forced to face a reception: his room was invaded by eleven men, some awkwardly carrying flowers, some with square boxes which suggested cakes, some with tall boxes that suggested the kind of spirit forbidden in hospitals. And they all stood around his chair. It wasn't the first time they'd been there, but it was the first time they had arrived en masse. And it was Barney McGuire the oldest of them, who, being spokesman, said, 'We would like to have come the morrow, boss, but we knew it would be your family's do. So we decided to come the night and to say we're all looking forward to your gettin' back on the job. Although that's finished, all but tidyin' up.'

'Works better than if you'd been there, boss.' Jos Wright nodded towards him with a solemn face yet with a twinkle in his eye, and Bill answered, 'The same to you, Jos. And may I hope your next lot of leeks are pulled up again.'

There was a burst of laughter, and Tommy Turnbull said, 'Their case comes up next week, boss. We'll likely know who's behind them then, if anybody.'

'I doubt it,' Jack Mowbray said. 'Me cousin Lisa's goin' with a young bobby. He's only just come this way – he was transferred from across the river – but he says it's his opinion that it's been organised from the beginning to sort of break us, you know. Well, break you, boss; first through us, sort of, with the car and the bikes and the lot of them. He thinks they'll likely keep quiet because it's his opinion there's big money behind it. Somebody, you know, with dough, boss, who wanted the contract an' wanted to put you out of business. In any case' – he grinned

now – 'we've got a bet on: thirty quid who's nearest the stretch they'll get.'

'And what d'you think they'll get, Jack?'

'Well' – Jack wagged his head – 'I'd say five years. I hope it's more, for I reckon it could have been murder you see. If the kid hadn't found you it could have been murder.'

'If the kid hadn't found me, Jack, there'd be no case next week because I'd be well down among the dung by this time; that park lake held a lot of silt and slush.'

'Aye. Aye, boss, there's that in it.' And the grim thought of this, caused a few shuffles all round and Bert Ormesby to say, 'I would keep off the subject if you don't mind, boss, because our *mute* and *shy* friend here, Mr David Love, has talked of nothin' else since. He's thinkin' of sendin' the lad to Eton.'

There was a general movement, a spluttering; then quite quietly Davey said, 'Well now, friend Bert, I've kept me tongue quiet for this length of time so's you could all get yer nebs in. But, as they say, there's many a true word spoke in joke an' you'll be surprised if you knew where that lad is headed for.'

'Surprise us then,' said Morris Fenwick.

'Well now, I'll do just that,' said Davey. 'He's headed for a private school, the same as ever the boss's son goes to. Oh aye, 'tis all been arranged. The boss's wife herself saw to it, and I meself went to the headmaster only last week. "Would you like yer son to attend my school, Mr Love?" said he; an' said I, "I would, sir, I would indeed." "We'll be proud to have him, Mr Love," said he.'

A small titter to his side caused Davey to turn and look at Tommy Turnbull. And he said, 'I had afore mentioned the boss's wife, Tommy. If I was after imaginin' things or makin' things up I wouldn't have brought her name into it, now would I? But for two pins I feel like bustin' somebody' mouth, and it's me own, 'cos didn't I promise her that I wouldn't say a word of it till himself' – he pointed to the figure in the chair – 'put in an appearance the morrow. I'm sorry, boss. It's me weakness to open me mouth when I should keep it shut.'

'Well, good for you, Irish,' said Harry Newton. 'I've got three youngsters, and I'd be pleased to send them along there an' all. See what you can do, Davey, will you?'

'Such honours have to be worked for, Harry, and I think my Sammy has worked for his. What d'you say, boss?'

'I say, you're right, Davey. Yes, you're right: Sammy's worked for the honour. And I could tell you all something else that would raise your eyebrows' – he now looked from one to the other – 'but it can wait.'

'You'll have to go to court next week, Davey. Are you expectin' a medal for bustin' that bloke up?'

'No, no,' one of the others put in now; 'he knows what'll happen: the judge will pat him on the shoulder and say, six months for assault and battery. Stand down.'

'You could be right at that, Tommy, you could be right at that. There's queer things happen in this world,' said Davey, laughing now.

As often happens after much laughing, there was silence for a moment in the room; then Bill said, 'You're all ready for the big show?'

'Ready and willin', boss,' came from different quarters, and all their heads nodded.

'You know I'll have to take on a pretty large crew, don't you?'

'Aye, aye.' Barney McGuire was nodding at him again.

'Well now, this is what I've got in mind. Not one of you will be doin' your own job, at least you'll be doin' it but through others. You'll each be in charge of a gang for your own particular work. And you know what I've always wanted from you, so you know what to get out of them. And as I've said afore, you don't find gold nuggets among the workers the day, but pick out the silver and let the dross go down the drain; in other words, get rid of them. There's plenty now needing jobs and there're some good fellas about. And there'll always be shirkers, but you know how to deal with them. When I get home we'll have a meetin' an' we'll discuss your wages. But apart from that you'll have to meet the architects and the overall works manager. I'll have to

have him until I'm fully on me feet. You understand? And there'll be an office staff and a sort of quantity surveyor type of accountant, perhaps two, one to keep the other straight.'

There was laughter at this; then Barney, stepping forward now and shaking Bill's hand, said, 'From me, I say thanks, boss. And I think that goes for all the rest.'

'Aye, aye, I'll say,' was the general chorus.

'And we'll be goin' now because, after havin' seen this lot perhaps they'll keep you in another week, you'll need so much more rest.'

Then came the sound of a gasp from the doorway and a nurse, indignation in her voice, said, 'What on earth do you mean crowding in like this! You know there's only two visitors allowed in at a time. You'd better not let sister see you.'

'We're going, nurse, we're on our way.'

'Good-night, boss.'

'Good-night, boss.'

'Good-night, boss.'

One after the other they shook his hand and filed out laughing; and the last one to leave, by accident or design, was Davey Love, and what he said was, 'I'm never lost for words, but I'll have to find some new ones to express what I'm feelin' inside this minute, boss. Any road, see you the morrow.'

'Aye, see you the morrow, Davey.'

12

When Fiona brought him home there were only the family, Nell and Sammy to greet him. And when he was at last ensconced in the armchair in the sitting-room, Mamie on his knee, Katie in the circle of one arm, Willie in the other, Mark kneeling at one side of the chair, there was Sammy Love at the other.

Sammy was dressed in a pair of well-fitting, long grey trousers. He had on a pale grey shirt and a bright blue tie. And over the shirt he wore a blue pullover. His hair was brushed flat, his nails were clean, and on his feet were the same trainer type shoes as Willie was wearing.

Willie now looked down on his friend's head before he turned to Bill and said, 'Sammy's got something to tell you, Dad.'

'Aw, it can wait till me da comes with the present. He should be here now.' Sammy looked towards the door; but Willie persisted, 'It won't come as such a surprise then 'cos there'll be other things. Go on!' He dug his fist into Sammy's back. 'Tell him, man.'

After a moment's hesitation, Sammy twisted round on the carpet, cast his eyes to where Fiona was sitting smiling at him,

then glanced at Nell, where she too was sitting smiling at him. Then he looked at Bill and said, 'Guess where we live.'

'I know where you live.'

'No; that's where we used to live. Guess where we live now.'

'Aw, Buckingham Palace.'

'Don't be daft.'

There was a giggle from the children, and Bill, looking at Fiona, said, 'That's something to come home to in your own house and be told that you haven't got to be daft. Well, how am I to guess? All the streets and places in this town, and you ask me to guess where you're livin'. Not here?' He pulled a face, and Sammy said, 'No; not here. But not very far away.'

'Oh Lord! don't say we're going to be neighbours.'

Sammy cast a glance in Fiona's direction and she, looking at Bill, said, 'Not quite neighbours, at least to us.'

'I'm intrigued.' Bill nudged Katie. 'That's a good word, isn't it, intrigued?' And she grinned up at him and nestled into his shoulder.

'Primrose Crescent.'

Bill didn't make a sound, he just gaped. His mouth opened, then closed; he looked at Fiona; then at Nell; then around the children; then back to Sammy again. And his voice was a mere whisper for him when he said, 'Primrose Crescent?'

'Aye. Yon end. A bungalow, three bedrooms. And it's got a dinin' room all to itself. And a bathroom, a big bathroom with two basins.' His face was alight now as Bill had never seen it. Then Bill's body began to shake and he said, 'Oh, don't Sammy, don't make me laugh, because there's parts of me that might split open. You shouldn't make me laugh. Primrose Crescent! Do you know who lives in Primrose Crescent?'

'Aye, I do.'

'You do?'

'Aye.'

Bill now looked at Fiona and asked, 'Does she know?'

'Yes, yes, she knows.'

Again he was looking at Sammy. 'Did you know that my mother-in-law lives in Primrose Crescent?'

'Aye, she spoke to me.'

'And you're still alive?'

The children all began to laugh and splutter.

'She seemed all right, O.K. She said she'd seen me on telly an' read about me in the papers.'

'Has she met your father?'

Sammy looked at Fiona, and she, looking at Bill, said, 'I don't think so, not yet.'

'Hallelujah! Hallelujah!'

'Oh, Dad, Dad, don't. But they will meet soon because Gran is coming to tea and she'll meet Mr Love th . . . then.' Mark was giggling.

'And it's all set out in the dining-room and it looks lovely.' This was chirped in by Mamie; and Katie took it up, saying, 'We had to put the two tables together because there'll be fourteen of us.'

'Fourteen!' said Bill. 'Who's the fourteen? I thought I was going to have a quiet home-coming among my family.'

'Well,' said Fiona, 'it will be your family, sort of, with Sammy and Nell and Bert. There are nine of us, Mother is ten. Then there is Mrs Paget –' She did not add that Mr Paget as yet couldn't come and face Bill. But she went on, 'There's Rupert and Sir Charles and Lady Kingdom, and Mr Love. Fourteen, the way I count them.'

'Sir Charles and Lady . . . ? And your . . . mother? An' . . . Mr Love?' His face was screwed up.

'Yes. Sir Charles and Lady . . . and my mother. . . . And Mr Love. Be reasonable, Bill. You've got to put a little salve on the sore, as you yourself would say.'

He looked down on Sammy and he thought, Aye; aye, she's right. A little salve on the sore, and the sore would be Davey Love. It was going to be an interesting tea-party.

When there was a ring at the bell, Nell sprang up and went out of the room, and they all turned to face the door. And when

a voice came to them from the hall Sammy got to his feet, saying, 'That's me da'. And he ran to the door, and there met Davey coming in carrying a large square box done up with fancy paper and a bow.

'Hello, everybody. Hello everybody. Hello there, boss. See you're all settled in.'

'Yes, Davey, all settled in. Come and sit down.'

'Aye, I will in a minute. Here you! Here's what it's all about.' He thrust the parcel into his son's arms and Sammy staggered with it towards the coffee table and just managed to ease it onto the end. Then looking at Fiona, he said, 'Could ya clear it, I mean them things off the end, books and such?'

Both Fiona and Nell grabbed up the books and magazines, the ornamental shell, and the small ebony wood figure of a seated mandarin. And when the table was clear, they looked at Sammy and he, looking at Fiona, tapped the top of the box, saying, 'It's me present for ya. I got some money from the Sir an' some for talkin' to a fella in a magazine, an' me da lent me the rest. So I didn't get it from the tip.' He grinned at her now.

'A present for me in . . . in this big box?'

'Aye. Well, open it.'

She unpinned the bow, then undid the gold cord, and as she had to tear the paper at the top she thought it was a pity because it was such lovely paper and she always kept the Christmas wrappings that weren't stuck up with Sellotape. And when the paper was spread out there was revealed a cardboard box, and that was sealed too.

She looked about her. They were all gathered round the table, and they were all surprised, even amazed, as was Fiona, when at last she pulled the four pieces of cardboard to one side to reveal a number of articles wrapped in tissue paper. Gently picking the first one up, she unwrapped it. It was a silver sugar basin. And looking at Sammy, all she could say was, 'Oh! Sammy.'

His response was: 'Go on! Look at the rest. There's a lot more.'

The next article was a matching milk jug, all of eight inches high with a beautiful handle. She again looked at the boy. Her eyelids were blinking now.

When she next drew out the teapot, she just gasped because it was a beautiful shaped teapot with a small black ebony knob on its lid.

And the reason for this was pointed out to her very quickly by Sammy, who said, 'That's so ya won't burn yer fingers when ya lift up the lid to put more hot water in. That's what the man said. Go on! See the rest.'

The next piece she drew out was a matching hot water jug. She had never seen one like it. It was about twelve inches high and had fluted sides and was shaped in what she could only describe as an exquisite design. Like something one would see, she imagined, in an Egyptian house. Then there was this large thing in the bottom of the box. It had black ebony handles on each side, and when, with some effort, she lifted it out and put it on the table, there was a gasp from everyone in the room except Davey Love and his son, for they were all looking down on a tray over twenty-four inches long, supported on four short curved sturdy legs, and the handles at each end emerging, it seemed, from a deep two inch rim surrounding the tray.

'Oh! *Sammy. Sammy.* Mr Love.' She looked from one to the other. 'This is . . . really, what can I say? It's all so beautiful. But . . . but there was no need for it. And dear me, dear me.'

There was a break in her voice.

'P . . . put them on the tray and see what they look like.'

Slowly she did as Sammy ordered. Then he said, 'There! The man said there were very few like that about, didn't he, Da?'

'He did that, son. He did that. And its the best quality, ma'am. 'Tis, 'tis the best quality. It's what he called Elkington silver. An' look! will you? Just look. 'Tis on the bottom of every piece and on the bottom of the tray an' all. We got it from a real jeweller's. Of course, you know . . . you know, it isn't new. But it's not the modern stuff, 'cos that's femmer. You've only

got to spit on the silver of the modern stuff and it's gone. Oh aye. But this'll last a number of lifetimes. It'll go down to yer children, it will that. An' that's what the man said to me, it'll go down to yer children. And I said, "Sir, it won't go down to *my* children but to that of me son's best friend's mother."'

'Will you excuse me a moment?'

After Fiona had hurried from the room Sammy, looking from his father to Bill, said, 'She doesn't like it?'

'Oh, Sammy, she loves it.' Bill put his hand out and drew the boy into his embrace. 'She loves it. An' so do I. By! yes. It's the most beautiful set I've ever seen in me life. I might be a rich man some day but I would never be able to buy a better. Go on, she'll be in the kitchen. Go and have a word with her.'

When the boy remained still, his father said, 'Did you hear what the boss said? Go on. An' remember, it's not everybody who laughs when they're happy. Go on.'

Sammy went. He crossed the hall slowly and pushed open the kitchen door, and there he saw Fiona sitting at the table, her elbow on it, her head resting on her hand. But she turned and looked at him coming towards her. And when he was near her knee, he said, 'Ya did like it, didn't ya.'

She had difficulty in speaking at first, then she said, 'Like it? It's a beautiful set, really beautiful. I love it, but not half as much as I love you.'

Who put their arms around the other first they didn't know, but she bent over him and held him close and he reached up and, his arms around her neck, he pressed his face against hers. And after a moment they were standing apart, both sniffling. And then she touched his face gently as she said, 'No matter where you live I want you always to consider this your second home. And you'll always be loved, not only by Willie, but by all of us.'

'Ya mean you an' all?'

'Oh yes, me an' all, me first.'

'Me da had a letter this mornin'. Me ma wants a divorce, an' me da says that suits him 'cos she would never fit into Primrose Crescent.'

Here was a place for laughter: the child's mother couldn't fit into Primrose Crescent but his father considered he could. And who knew, who knew but that he would. But oh, what her mother's reaction would be when she saw who her neighbour was. She didn't know how far along the crescent Davey Love's house was, but that it was in the actual vicinity was a sign for foreboding.

He half turned from her now, saying, 'There's the bell. I wonder which one it is?'

She rose to her feet and he, looking up at her now, said, 'Your hair's all fluffed an' ya want to dab yer eyes with cold water else ya'll look a sight.'

'Oh, Sammy, Sammy.'

He laughed now. 'I'll have to stop sayin' what I think, won't I?'

Again she put her arms around him, and again he clung to her. And what did she hear him say? It seemed like a whisper, like a repeat of his own name, but it had sounded like, 'I love ya.' Then he was running from her; and she hurried to the kitchen mirror, straightened her hair, wet the side of her forefinger and rubbed it in turn under her eyelashes, giving them a sweep.

Her eyes looked bright, sparkling. Her face looked good in spite of the tears, and she wanted to keep it good always, for Bill. She swung round from the mirror as she heard her mother's voice, and muttering to herself now, 'Oh dear. Oh dear,' for she couldn't imagine her mother stomaching Davey Love. The boy, yes, for as long as he didn't come out with warm language he could appear funny, amusing. But Mr Love's form of amusement could be uproarious, and her mother had never cared for uproarious people or occasions.

Mrs Vidler was already in the sitting-room and Bill was saying, 'You know everybody except Mr Love. This is Sammy's father.'

'How do you do, Mr Love? I've . . . I've heard quite a bit about you.'

'How do you yerself, ma'am? I've yet to hear anythin' about you, but I'm sure it could be nothin' but good. No, nothin' but good.'

'You are very gallant, Mr Love.'

'Who could not be gallant to a beautiful lady, ma'am?'

Never. Never. Never. She couldn't believe it. Fiona, thinking she had better break it up before the illusion was shattered, said, 'Mother, look what Sammy has bought me.'

Mrs Vidler moved towards the table at the other end of the room and she looked down on what she recognised immediately as a beautiful Victorian tea-service. And she turned to Fiona and said, 'You mean, Mr Love?'

'No, no. Sammy. The boy, the child.'

'*He bought you that?*'

'Yes, Mother, he bought me that.'

'Oh, Fiona!' She turned her head away in disbelief. But when a voice said, 'I did; and it was me own money from the newspaper an' the old fella, Sir Charles. I hadn't it all but me da subbed me some and I bought it. Me da went with me.'

She turned and looked at Davey, and Davey, looking at Mrs Vidler, said, 'Aye, he's right, ma'am. The boy bought it for your daughter, a beautiful woman who undoubtedly takes after her mother.' And without pause he went on, 'And he picked it himself, ma'am. He'd seen it in a jeweller's shop. We travelled the city, we did, footsore I was, but a tea-set he wanted for the boss's missis. But nothin' would suit him till he saw that one. And it is as I said already in this room, it is Elkington silver. And you will know, ma'am, that you cannot get much better than that unless you have the real Mackay.'

There came a diversion with the bell ringing, and when a moment later Nell ushered into the room Sir Charles and Lady Kingdom, accompanied by Rupert, Mrs Vidler became her most charming. And as Fiona watched and heard her, she thought:

her coffee morning manner and her ladies' bridge evening rolled into one.

Lady Kingdom caught sight of the tea-service and the cardboard box near it and, realising it was a present, she exclaimed, 'Oh, what a beautiful service! Where did this come from? You've been given this as a present, Mrs Bailey?'

'Yes, ma'am.'

And again the pattern was repeated. But it was under Willie's oration now. He described to the admiring old couple how his friend had bought this for his mother and how he had come by the money. And he finished up by looking at Sir Charles and saying, 'You gave him the most, else he wouldn't have done it.'

'*Willie!*'

'Yes, Mam?'

Sir Charles, laughing now, said, 'Glad I've been of help.'

'An' not only to the boy, sir, not only to the boy. Meself, I've never had the chance of thankin' you for the house.' Once again Davey had the attention of all those present. 'Now who would have thought in this wide world that you'd go an' give me one of your houses?'

'Oh, now, now, now, Love . . . Mr . . . er. Get things absolutely straight: I have not given you a house, I have allowed you to rent it.'

'Aw, you know what I'm after meanin', sir. And I know a hundred or two in Bog's End who'd give their eye teeth, or their false sets, to get the chance of rentin' a house like the one you offered to me. For offer it you did, sir, didn't you? Never in me wildest dreams would I have had the nerve to come and ask you for such a place, even if I'd known you owned the whole crescent. Now what's the difference atween a street and a crescent?' He looked around everyone now. And it was Mark who said, 'It's the shape.'

'Oh, aye, yes, lad, yer right, it's the shape. I'm as dull as an Irish bog an' as ignorant as the runt of a sow's litter.'

Fiona turned away from Bill's straining face, then closed her eyes for the moment; but only to open them wide as a deep bass

laugh came from Rupert and an accompanying chuckle from Sir Charles, with Lady Kingdom exchanging an amused glance with Fiona, before moving towards her, saying, 'How are you now, my dear? I haven't had the chance to say a word.'

'Very well, Lady Kingdom, since I know everything is going to be all right with my husband's health.'

'Naturally. Naturally.'

There was another diversion when Nell brought her mother-in-law in, with Bert following them. There were more introductions, and almost before these were finished, Nell gave the signal to Fiona that all was ready in the dining-room. And so the children, following instructions, allowed the elders to go before them.

It wasn't until all were seated that Fiona realised with dismay that her mother was placed next to Davey Love, and she almost groaned to herself, 'Oh dear me! Something will happen.' And eventually it did.

As usual, Bill was at the head of the table and she herself at the foot; Lady Kingdom was on Bill's right, and Mrs Vidler on his left. Next to her was Davey Love. Sir Charles was seated on Fiona's right with Rupert next to him. The children were arranged between Davey and Rupert at the one side, and Nell and Bert at the other. Fiona had seated Sammy to her left, thinking she would be more able from this position to control any ribald remark he might make. Unfortunately, though, there would be no one to so control his father. Still, what did it matter? She was feeling happy, even elated. Yet as she looked round the table she thought, What a mixture of characters.

Sir Charles was saying, 'I've never been at a party for years.'

'Don't be silly, dear,' His wife nodded down the table towards him. 'We have two parties at Christmas and one in the New Year.'

'Yes, but that's family, people you see every day in the week. And anyway, you know I escape if I can up to my snug.' He bent forward in front of Fiona and, addressing Sammy, he said, 'I've got a hidey-hole in the roof; I'll show it to you when you

come to my place. And some day when you're grown up and married you'll remember it and make one for yourself because you'll want to escape.'

Sammy did not quite understand this old fella, except the married bit, and he said, 'I'm not gona get married, never.'

He had the attention of the table now, and Sir Charles, bending forward again, said, 'Why are you so dead against marriage already?'

''Cos ya've only got to get divorced . . . me da's gettin' divorced.'

As at a tennis match all heads now were turned towards Davey as he cried down the table, 'Nobody wants to know about me business, and when I get you home I'll put me foot in . . . what I'll do is to give you a lesson in tea . . . tea-table conversation.'

'That a fact? You getting divorced?'

Davey looked down the table at Sir Charles and, simply as one adult to another now, said, 'Aye, well, you might as well know, them that he hasn't already opened his mouth to, this morning I got a letter from me wife sayin' she wants a divorce.'

'I'm very sorry,' said Sir Charles; but then before Davey had a chance to reply, his son leant forward in front of Fiona and answered for him, 'Oh, ya needn't worry, ya needn't be sorry.'

'No?'

'No; 'cos as me da says, me ma would never have fitted into the crescent. She wasn't the type. He says he'll look out for a body a bit more refined like.'

The laughter around the table was like a smothered rustle as Davey now cried at his son, 'You remember Sister Catherine an' what she did to yer ears?' It was as if the two of them were quite alone now. 'Well, begod! I'm tellin' you there won't be a part of you that I'll miss the night when I get you home.'

'Why? He's only speaking the truth. And what's more, I think it's very commendable of you that you should look for someone refined. I do indeed. What do you say, Mrs Vidler?'

'Oh. . . . Oh, Sir Charles, I . . . I agree with you. I think every man should marry, especially if there's a child in the case,

and he's aiming, as he says, for more refinement in his life.' And when she turned and bestowed on Davey a beautiful smile, Fiona looked up the table at Bill and he looked down at her, and they yelled from the one to the other: No! No! *No*. She's surely having him on. But no; Fiona could read her mother only too well: Davey Love's reformation would be a crusade. And under the patronage of Sir Charles! Well, what was good enough for the gentry would indeed be good enough for her.

She could see Bill was beginning to laugh: his body was shaking; she knew the symptoms, soon it would explode into a bellow. And in this, he was helped when Sir Charles, once again leaning forward and his mouth full of cake and grinning mischievously, said to Sammy, 'What will your father really do to you when you get home tonight?' And Sammy replied with an equally mischievous grin and in no small voice, 'Threaten to knock bloody hell out of me. But I don't give a tinker's cuss 'cos it's just his mouth workin'.'

A table-cloth had been stained with tea at Willie's birthday party, but now Fiona looked at the chaos that was breaking out up and down the table, then at Rupert who, thumping his employer on the back, called to her, 'How long has he been at that private school?' And Sammy, as though just becoming aware that he was an actor and could make people spill their tea, laughed himself as he shouted, 'Three weeks!'

EPILOGUE

The party was over. The visitors had taken their leave. The children were in bed. Nell and Bert were doing the last tidying up in the kitchen, and Bill and Fiona were really alone for the first time since his return home.

They were sitting on the couch, his arm about her, and neither had spoken for some minutes when she said, 'Tired?'

'Yes; I suppose I am; it's been a day and a half. As long as I live I'll never forget that tea. I've never seen so much havoc at a table.'

Fiona did not enlarge on this but said, 'You've had presents from everyone but me. Do you know that?'

'No, Mrs B. Anyway, I've never given it a thought. You're my present. By! aye.'

When he kissed her, she gently pressed him away and, looking into his face, she said, 'I've got a present for you.'

'You have? Well then, let's have it.'

She took his hand and brought it to her stomach, saying, 'It's in there.'

His ruddy colour had somewhat dimmed during the weeks in hospital; even so, his complexion was still somewhat high; but now, to her consternation, she saw the colour disappear from around his mouth when twice he opened it without emitting a sound.

'Bill, aren't you pleased? . . . *Bill!*'

'When? . . . How long?'

'Oh.' She wagged her head. 'Two and a half months, a bit over. I didn't tell you in hospital because I thought it best not to excite you. But I needn't have troubled myself.'

'*Oh Fiona!*' He closed his eyes.

'What is it, Bill? What is it? Tell me.'

She was asking him to tell her. Tell her what was happening